A PLANET
EVERYTHING SEEMED
PERFECT

The travelers from the stars had come to the planet Gwydion on a diplomatic mission. They consisted of spacemen, diplomats, and soldiers. What they sought was permission to build an interplanetary spaceport. However, what they found was a planet of true wonder, a world of sheer physical beauty graced with lofty peaks, sparkling streams, and lush valleys. Its inhabitants were like no other race of humanoids in the galaxy, seemingly devoid of all vice, with no overt thoughts of selfishness, lust, crime, or killing. It all seemed a little too perfect.

But the Gwydionians were a devoutly religious people, and with the coming of Bale time—the time of religious rejoicing and ecstasy, the visitors from space discovered just how unique the people of Gwydion really were…

FOR A COMPLETE SECOND NOVEL, TURN TO PAGE 81

CAST OF
CHARACTERS

RAVEN
As Commandant to the mission's security force, his pragmatic nature told him something was amiss on the planet Gwydion.

ELFAVY
With a twinkle in her eyes and golden sunlight in her hair, she seemed like the ideal woman…perhaps a little too ideal.

TOLTECA
Whatever the mystery was on Gwydion, this inquisitive diplomat from Nuevamerica was determined to get to the bottom of it.

DAWYD
This physician seemed to be a man of some importance on Gwydion—a fact he seemed totally blasé about.

KORS
Being brought up on a warrior planet like Lochlann made him perfect for the role of the Commandant's strong-armed sideman.

BYORD
He was was just a kid—happy, playful; but he'd reached the age of participation for Bale time—a time that spelled childhood's end.

CAPTAIN UTIEL
Just an old spacedog who didn't want to get in the way of diplomats and security men.

A TWELVEMONTH AND A DAY

By
POUL ANDERSON

Illustration by Virgil Finlay

ARMCHAIR FICTION
PO Box 4369, Medford, Oregon 97504

For more information about Armchair Books and products, visit our website at…

www.armchairfiction.com

Or email us at…

armchairfiction@yahoo.com

CHAPTER ONE

AFTER the boat, which went ahead to make arrangements, had radioed all clear, the *Quetzal* departed orbit and swung toward the planet. Her approach was cautious, as befitted a craft in regions hardly known, and Miguel Tolteca expected a couple of hours free to watch.

He was not exactly a sybarite, but he liked to do things in style. First he dialed *Privacy* on his door, lest some friendly soul barge in to pass the time of day. Then he put Castillo's Symphony No.2 in D Minor with Subsonics on the tapester, mixed himself a rum and conchoru, converted the bunk to a lounger, and sat down with his free hand on the controls of the outside scanner. Its screen grew black and full of wintry unwinking stars. He searched in a clockwise direction until Gwydion swam into view, a tiny disc upon darkness, the clearest blue he had ever seen.

A fist struck the door. "Oa," called Tolteca, irritated, "can you not read?"

"My mistake," said the voice of Raven. "I thought you were the chief."

Tolteca swore, folded the lounger into a stool, and stepped across the tiny cabin. A momentary change in weight informed him that the *Quetzal* had put on a spurt of extra acceleration. Doubtless to dodge some meteor swarm, the engineer part of him thought. They'd be more common here than around Nuevamerica, this being a newer system... Otherwise the pseudogee held firm. The spaceship was a precision instrument.

He opened the door. "Very well, Commandant." He pronounced the hereditary title with a curtness that approached insult. "What is so urgent?"

Raven stood a moment watching him. Tolteca was a young man, middling tall, with wide stiffly held shoulders. His face

5

was thin and sharp, under brown hair drawn back into the short queue customary on his planet, and the eyes were levelly aimed. However much the United Republics of Nuevamerica made of their shiny new democracy, it meant something to stem from one of their old professional families. He wore the uniform of the Argo Astrographical Company, but that was only a simple, pleasing version of everyday garb, blue tunic, gray culottes, white stockings, and no insignia.

Raven closed the door. "By chance," he said, his tone mild again, "one of my men overheard some of yours dicing to settle who should debark first after you and the ship's captain."

"Well, that sounds harmless enough," said Tolteca sarcastically. "Do you expect us to observe any official pecking order?"

"No. What, um, puzzled me was, nobody mentioned my own detachment."

Tolteca raised brows. "You wanted your men to sit in on the dice game?"

"According to what my soldier reported to me, there appears to be no doctrine for planetfall and afterward."

"Well," said Tolteca, "as a simple courtesy to our hosts, Captain Utiel and f—and you, if you wish—will go out first to greet them. There's to be quite a welcoming committee, you know. But beyond that, good ylem, Commandant, what difference does it make who comes down the gangway in what order?"

Raven stood quite still. It was the common habit of Lochlanna aristocrats. They didn't stiffen; their manners never showed any rigidity, least of all at moments of importance; but their muscles seemed to go loose and their eyes glazed over with calculation. Tolteca sometimes thought that that alone made them so alien that the Namerican Revolution had always been inevitable.

Finally—thirty seconds later, but it seemed longer—Raven said, "I can see how this misunderstanding occurred, Sir Engineer. Your people have developed several unique institutions in the fifty years since gaining independence, and have forgotten some of our customs. Certainly the concept of exploration, even treaty making, as a strictly individual, commercial, enterprise, is not Lochlann. We have been making unconscious assumptions about each other. The fact that our two groups have kept so much apart on this voyage has helped maintain those errors. I offer apology."

It was not relevant, but Tolteca was driven to snap. "Why should you apologize to me? I'm doubtless also to blame."

Raven smiled. "But I am a Commandant of the Oakenshaw Ethnos."

As if that bland purr had attracted him, a cat stuck his head out of the Lochlanna's flowing surcoat sleeve. Zio was a Siamese tom, big, powerful, and possessed of a temper like mercury fulminate. His eyes were cold blue in the brown mask. "Mneowrr," he said remindingly. Raven scratched him under the chin. Zio tilted back his head and rumbled his motor.

Tolteca gulped down an angry retort. Let the Fellow have his superiority complex. He struck a cigarette and smoked in short hard puffs. "Never mind all that," he said. "What's the immediate problem?"

"You must correct the wrong impression among your men. My troop goes out first."

"What? If you think—"

"In combat order. The spacemen stand by to lift ship if anything should go awry. When I signal all clear, then you and Captain Utiel may emerge and make your speeches. But not before."

For an instant, Tolteca could find no words. He could only stare.

Raven waited, impassive. He had the Lochlanna build, the result of many generations of a planet with one-fourth again the standard surface gravity, though tall for one of his own race he was barely of average Namerican height. Thick-boned and thick-muscled, he moved like his own cat, a gait that had always impressed Tolteca's people as slippery and sneaking. His head was typically long, with the expected dysharmonically broad face, high cheekbones, hooknose, sallow skin that looked youthful because genetic drift had eliminated the beard. His hair, close cropped, was a cap of midnight, and his brows met above the narrow green eyes. His clothes were not precisely gaudy, but the republican simplicity of Nuevamerica found them barbaric—high-collared blouse, baggy blue trousers tucked into half boots, surcoat embroidered with twined snakes and flowers, a silver dragon brooch. Even aboard ship, Raven wore dagger and machine pistol.

"By all creation," whispered Tolteca at last. "Do you think we're on one of your stinking campaigns of conquest?"

"Routine precautions," said Raven.

"But—the first expedition here was…was welcomed like… Our own advance boat, the pilot, he was feted till he could hardly stagger!"

Raven shrugged, earning an indignant look from Zio. "They've had almost one standard year to think over what the first expedition told them. We're a long way from home in space, and even longer in time. Twelve hundred years since the breakup of the Commonwealth isolated them. The whole Empire rose and fell while they were alone on that one planet. Genetic and cultural evolution have done strange work in less time."

Tolteca dragged on his cigarette and said roughly, "Judging by all the data, those people think more like Namericans than you do."

"Indeed?"

"They have no armed forces. No police, even in the usual sense; public service monitors is the best translation of their word. No—well, one thing we have to find out is the extent to which they do have a government. The first expedition had too much else to learn to establish that clearly. But beyond doubt, they haven't got much."

"Is this good?"

"By my standards, yes. Read our Constitution."

"I have done so. A noble document, for your planet." Raven paused, scowling. "If this Gwydion were remotely like any other lost colony I've ever heard of, there would be small reason for worry. Common sense alone, the knowledge that overwhelming power exists to avenge any treachery toward us, would stay them. But don't you see, when there is no evidence of internecine strife, even of crime...and yet they are obviously not simple children of nature...I can't guess what *their* common sense is like."

"I can," clipped Tolteca, "and if your bully boys swagger down the gangway first, aiming guns at people with flowers in their hands, I know what that common sense will think of us."

Raven's smile was oddly charming on that gash of a mouth. "Credit me with some tact. We will make a ceremony of it."

"Looking ridiculous at best—they don't wear uniforms on Gwydion—and transparent at worst—for they're no fools. Your suggestion is declined."

"But I assure you—"

"No, I said. Your men will debark, individually, and unarmed."

Raven sighed. "As long as we are exchanging reading lists, Sir Engineer, may I recommend the articles of the expedition to you?"

"What are you slinking toward now?"

"The *Quetzal,*" said Raven patiently, "is bound for Gwydion to investigate certain possibilities and, if they look hopeful, to open negotiations with the folk. Admittedly you are in charge of that. But for obvious reasons of safety, Captain Utiel has the last word while we are in space. What you seem to have forgotten is that once we have made planetfall, a similar power becomes mine."

"Oa! If you think you can sabotage—"

"Not at all. Like Captain Utiel, I must answer for my actions at home, if you should make complaint. However, no Lochlanna officer would assume my responsibility if he were not given corresponding authority."

Tolteca nodded, sickly. He remembered now. It hadn't seemed important. The Company's operations took men and valuable ships ever deeper into this galactic sector, places where humans had never been even at the height of the Empire. The hazards were unpredictable, and an armed guard on every vessel was in itself a good idea. Then a few old women in culottes, on the Policy Board, decided that plain Namericans weren't good enough. It had to be soldiers born and bred. In these days of spreading peace, more and more Lochlanna units found themselves at loose ends and hired out. They kept pretty much aloof, on ship and in camp, and so far it hadn't worked out badly. But the *Quetzal*—

"If nothing else," said Raven, "I have my own men to think of, and their families at home."

"But not the future of interstellar relations?"

"If those can be jeopardized so easily, they don't seem worth caring about. My orders stand. Please instruct your men accordingly."

Raven bowed. The cat slid from his nesting place, dug claws in the coat, and sprang up on the man's shoulder. Tolteca could have sworn that the animal sneered. The door closed behind them.

A while Tolteca stood motionless. The music reached a crescendo, reminding him that he had wanted to enjoy approach. He glanced back at the screen. The ship's curving path had brought the sun Ynis into scanner view. Its radiance stopped down by the compensator circuits, it spread corona and great wings of zodiacal light like nacre across the stars. The prominences must be spectacular, too, for it was an F8 with a mass of about two Sols and a corresponding luminosity of almost fourteen. (Being middle Population One, it was still young enough to be in the main sequence.) But at its distance, 3.7 Astronomical Units, only the disc could be seen, covering a bare ten minutes of arc. All in all, a most ordinary star. Tolteca twisted dials until he found Gwydion again.

The planet had gained apparent size, though he could still only see it as a chipped turquoise coin. Later the cloud bands and aurora should become visible, but no continents. While the first expedition had reported Gwydion to be Earthlike in astonishing detail, it was about 10% smaller and denser—to be expected of a younger world, formed when there were more heavy elements in the universe—and thus possessed less total land area, all divided into islands and archipelagos, great shallow oceans making the climate mild from pole to pole. Here came its moon, 1600 kilometers in diameter, 96,300 kilomets in orbital radius, swinging from behind the disc like a tiny hurried firefly.

Tolteca considered the backdrop with a sense of eeriness. This close, the Nebula's immense cloud of dust and gas showed us little more than a region where stars were fewer and paler. Even nearby Rho Ophiuchi was blurred. Sol, of course, was hidden even from telescopes, an insignificant yellow dwarf 200 parsecs beyond that veil, which its light would never pierce. *I wonder what's happening there,* thought Tolteca. *It's long since anyone went to Earth.*

He recollected what Raven had ordered, and cursed Raven.

CHAPTER TWO

The pasture where the *Quetzal* had been asked to settle its giant cylinder was about five kilometers south of Instar. From the gangway Tolteca had looked widely across rolling fields, divided by hedges into meadows of intense blossom-starred green; plowland where the first delicate shoots of grain went like a breath across brown furrows; orchards and copses and scattered homes made tiny by distance. The River Camlot gleamed between trees that might almost have been poplars; Instar was red tile roofs above enclosed flower gardens. All roads across the landscape were paved, but narrow and leisurely winding. Sometimes, Tolteca felt sure, a detour had been made to preserve an ancient tree or the lovely upswelling of a hill. Eastward the land flattened, sloping down to dikes that cut off view of the sea; westward it climbed, until forested hills rose abruptly on that horizon with a few dim mountain peaks beyond, some of which looked volcanic. The sun hung just above them; you didn't notice how small it was, for it radiated too brightly and the total illumination was almost exactly one standard sol. Cumulus clouds loomed to the southwest, and a low cool wind ruffled the puddles left by a recent shower.

"It is even more peaceful and beautiful than the finest places on my own planet," said Tolteca to Dawyd. "And Nuevamerica is considered extremely Earthlike."

"Thank you," replied the Gwydiona. "Though we can take little credit. The world was here, with its own intrinsic conditions, its native biochemistry and ecology, all eminently suited to human life. I understand that God wears a different face in most of the known cosmos."

"Uh—" Tolteca hesitated. The local language, as recorded by the first expedition and learned by the second before starting out, was not altogether easy for him. Like Lochlanna, it derived from Anglic, whereas the Namericans had always spoken Ispanyo. Had he quite understood that business with "God?" Somehow, it didn't sound conventionally religious. But then, the secular orientation of his own society made him liable to misinterpret any theological reference.

"Yes," he said after a moment. "The variations in so-called terrestroid planets are not great from a percentage standpoint, but to human beings they make all the difference. On one continent of my own world, for example, settlement was impossible until a certain common genus of plant had been eradicated. It was harmless most of the year, but the pollen it broadcast in spring happened to contain a substance identical with botulinus toxin."

Dawyd gave him a startled look. Tolteca wondered what he had said wrong. Had he misused some local word? Of course he'd had to use his own name for the poison... "Eradicate?" murmured Dawyd. "Do you mean destroyed? Entirely?" Catching himself, slipping back into the normal serene manner with what looked like practiced ease: "Well, let us not discuss technicalities right away. It was doubtless one of the Night Faces." He took his hand from the steering rod long enough to trace a sign in the air.

Tolteca leaned back, a trifle puzzled. The first expedition had emphasized in its reports that the Gwydiona were not superstitious, though they employed a vast amount of ceremony and symbolism. To be sure, the first expedition had landed on a different island; but it had found an identical culture wherever men dwelt. (And failed to understand why men occupied only the region between latitudes 25° and 70° N., although many other spots looked equally pleasant. There had been so much else to learn.) When the *Quetzal's* advance boat arrived, Instar had been suggested as the best place for the spaceship merely because it was one of the larger towns and possessed a college with an excellent reference library.

The ceremonies of arrival weren't overwhelming, either. All Instar had turned out: men, women, and children with garlands, pipes, and lyres; and visitors had come from afar. After the formal speeches, music was played and a ballet presented—a thing with masks and thin costumes whose meaning escaped the outworlders but which made a stunning spectacle. That was all. It broke up in general cordiality; not the milling, backslapping, handshaking kind of welcome that Namericans would have given, but neither the elaborate and guarded courtesy of Lochlann. Individuals had talked in a friendly way to individuals, given invitations to stay at private homes, asked eager questions about the outside universe. And at last most of the people walked back again; but each newcomer got a ride in a small, exquisite electric automobile.

Only a nominal guard of crewmen, and a larger detachment of Lochlanna, remained with the ship. No offense had been taken at Raven's wariness, but Tolteca still smoldered.

"You will indeed abide at my house?" asked Dawyd.

Tolteca bowed in his seat. "It would be an honor, Sir—" He paused. "Forgive me, but I am not sure what your title is."

"I belong to the Simnon family."

"No. I knew that. I mean, your…not your name, but what you do."

"I am a physician, of that rite which heals by songs as well as medicines." (Tolteca wondered just how much he was misunderstanding.) "I also have charge of a dike patrol and instruct youth at the college."

"Oh." Tolteca was disappointed. "I thought— You are not in the government, then?"

"Why, yes. I said I am in the dike patrol. What else had you in mind? Instar employs no Year-King or— No, that cannot be what you meant." Dawyd frowned with thought.

Tolteca watched him, as if to read what could not be said. The Gwydiona all had that basic similarity that results from a very small original group and no later immigration. The first expedition had reported a legend that their ancestors were no more than a man and two women, one dark and one blonde, survivors of an atomic blast lobbed at the colony by one of those fleets that went a-murdering during the Breakup; but records were admittedly vague. Be that as it may, this case was untypical in that there had been no degeneracy; rather, a refinement. The first generations had followed a careful program of outbreeding. To this day, the bearers of observable hereditary defects, including low intelligence and nervous instability, were sterilized, though not otherwise discriminated against.

Dawyd was a pure Caucasoid, which alone proved how old his nation must be. He was tall, slender, still supple in middle age. His yellow hair, worn shoulder length, was grizzled, but the blue eyes required no contact lenses and the suntanned skin was firm. The face, clean-shaven, high of brow, and strong of chin, bore a straight nose and gentle mouth. His clothes were a green tunic and white cloak, golden fillet, leather sandals, a locket about his neck that was gold on one side and black on the other. A triskele was tattooed on his forehead, but gave no effect of savagery.

His language had not changed much from Anglic; the Lochlanna had learned it without difficulty. Doubtless, as usual, printed books and sound recordings had tended to stabilize it. But whereas Lochlann barked, grunted, and snarled, thought Tolteca, Gwydion trilled and sang. He had never heard such voices before.

"Ah, yes," said Dawyd. "I think I grasp your concept. Yes, my advice is often asked, even on worldwide questions. That is my pride and my humility."

"Excellent. Well, Sir Councillor, I—"

"But councillor is no...no calling. I said I was a physician."

"Wait a minute, please. You were not formally chosen in any way to...guide, advise, control—?"

"No. Why should I be? A man's reputation, good or ill, spreads. Finally others may come from halfway around the world, to ask his opinion of certain proposals." Dawyd added shrewdly, "Bear in mind, far-friend, that our whole population numbers a mere ten million, and that we have both radio and aircraft, and travel a great deal between our islands."

"But who, then, is in charge of public affairs?"

"Oh, some communities employ a Year-King, or elect presidents to manage their local meetings, or appoint an engineer to handle routine. It depends on regional tradition. Here in Instar, we lack such customs, save that we crown a Dancer each solstice to bless the year."

"That isn't what I mean, Sir Physician. Suppose a...oh...a project, like building a new road; or a policy like, well, deciding whether to have regular relations with other planets...suppose this vague group of wise men you speak of—men who depend simply on a reputation for wisdom—suppose they decide such a question, one way or another. What happens next?"

"Then, normally, it is done as they have decided. Of course, all hear about it beforehand. If the issue is at all important, there will be much public discussion. But naturally, men will lay more weight on the suggestions of those known to be wise."

"So everyone agrees with the final decision?"

"Why not? The matter has been threshed out and the most logical answer arrived at. To be sure, a few are always unconvinced or dissatisfied. But being human, and therefore rational, they accommodate themselves to the general will."

"And—uh—funding such an enterprise?"

"That depends on its nature. A purely local enterprise, like building a new road, is carried out by the people of the community involved, with feasting and merriment each night. For larger and more specialized projects, coin may be needed, and then its collection depends on local custom. We of Instar let the Dancer go about with a sack, and all contribute as much as is reasonable."

Tolteca gave up for the time being. He was no further along than the anthropologists of the first expedition. Except maybe that he was mentally prepared for some such answer as he'd received, and could accept it. If you had a society with a simple economic structure (automation helped marvelously in that respect, provided that the material desires of the people remained modest) and if you had a homogeneous population of high average intelligence, and low average nastiness, well, then perhaps the ideal anarchic state was possible.

And it must be remembered that anarchy, in this case, did not mean amorphousness. The total culture of Gwydion was as intricate as any that men had ever evolved. Which in turn was paradoxical, since advanced science and technology usually dissolved traditions and simplified interhuman relationships. However—

Tolteca asked cautiously, "What effect do you believe contact with other planets would have on your people? Planets where things are done in radically different ways?"

"I don't know," replied Dawyd, thoughtful. "We would need more data, and a great deal more discussion, before even attempting to foresee the consequences. I do wonder if a gradual introduction of new modes may not prove best for you."

"For us?" Tolteca was startled.

"Remember, we have lived here a long time. We know the Aspects of God or Gwydion better than you, even as *we* should be most careful before venturing to *your* home."

Tolteca could not help saying, "It's strange that you never built spaceships. I gather that your people preserved, or reconstructed, all the basic scientific knowledge of their ancestors. As soon as you had a large enough population, enough surplus wealth, you could have coupled a thermonuclear power plant to a gravity beamer and a secondary-drive pulse generator, built a hull around the ensemble, and—"

"No!"

It was almost a shout. Tolteca jerked his head around to look at Dawyd. The Gwydiona had gone quite pale.

Color flowed back after a moment. He relaxed his grip on the steering rod. But his eyes were still rigidly focused ahead of him as he answered, "We do not use atomic energy. Sunpower, waterpower, and windpower, stored in electric accumulators, are sufficient. No vehicle need be much larger or much more powerful than this car, and no community needs many vehicles."

Then they were in the town. Dawyd guided the automobile through wide straight avenues, which seemed almost to contradict the vine-covered houses and peaked red roofs, the parks and splashing fountains. Tolteca noticed only one large building, a massive structure of fused stone, tearing above all chimneys with an incongruous grimness. Dawyd stopped just beyond a bridge, which spanned the river in a graceful serpent shape. He had calmed down, and smiled at his guest. "My abode. Will you enter?"

As they stepped from the bubble, a tiny scarlet bird flew from the eaves, settled on Dawyd's finger, and warbled joy. He murmured to it, grinned half awkwardly at Tolteca, and led the way to his front door, which was screened from the street by a tall bush with star-shaped leaves new for the spring season. The door's lock was sturdy but unused; Tolteca recalled again that Gwydion was apparently without crime, that its people had been hard put to understand the concept when the outworlders interviewed them. Having opened the door, Dawyd turned about and bowed very low.

"O guest of the house, who may be God, most welcome and beloved, enter. In the name of joy, and health, and understanding; beneath Ynis and She and all the stars; fire, food, fleet, and light be yours." He crossed himself, and reaching up he drew a cross on Tolteca's brow with his finger. The ritual was obviously timeworn, and yet he did not gabble it, but spoke with vast seriousness.

Entering, Tolteca noticed that the door was only faced with wood. Basically, it was a slab of steel, set in walls that were—under the stucco—two meters thick and of reinforced concrete. The windows were broad, sunlight streaming through them to glow on polished wood flooring; but each window had steel shutters. He wondered why, then forgot the matter as he watched Dawyd kneel down to light a candle before a niche. The shrine held a metal disc, half-gold and half-black with a bridge between, the Yin and Yang of immemorial antiquity. And still it was flanked by books, full-size and micro, with titles like *Diagnostic Application of Bioelectric Potentials.*

Dawyd got up. "Please be seated, friend of the house. My wife went into the Night—" he hesitated— "She died, several years ago, and only one of my daughters is unwedded. She danced for you this day, and thus is late. When she comes, we will take food."

Tolteca looked at the indicated chair. It was designed as rationally as any Namerican lounger, but made of bronze and tooled leather. He touched a fylfot recurring in the design. "I understand that all your ornamentation is symbolic. Would you explain this to me, as an example?"

"That is the Burning Wheel," answered Dawyd, "which is to say the Sun, Ynis, and all suns in the universe. The Wheel also represents Time. Thermodynamic irreversibility, if you are a psysicist," he added with a chuckle. "The interwoven vines are crisflowers, which bloom in the first hay gathering season of our year and are therefore sacred to that Aspect of God called the Green Boy. Thus together they mean Time: the Destroyer and Regenerator. The leather is from the wild areas, which belongs to the autumnal Huntress Aspect, and when she is linked with the Boy symbol it reminds us of the Night Faces and, at the same time, that the Day Faces are their other side. Bronze, being an alloy, manmade, says by forming the framework that Man embodies the meaning and structure of the world. However, since bronze turns green on corrosion, it also signifies that all structure vanishes at last, but into new life—"

He stopped and laughed. "You don't want a sermon!" he exclaimed. "Look here, do sit down. Go ahead and smoke. We already know about that custom. We can't do it ourselves—a bit of genetic drift, nicotine is too violent a poison for us—but it doesn't bother me in the least if you. Coffee grows well on this planet, would you like a cup, or would you rather try our beer or wine? Now that we are alone for awhile, I have about ten to the fiftieth questions to ask!"

CHAPTER THREE

That evening Raven left Instar, where he had prowled around looking, and wandered along the river road to the sea dikes. A couple of his men followed, in the byrnies and conical helmets of full battle gear; rifles were slung on their shoulders. Behind them the western hills lifted black against a sky that blazed and smoldered with gold; the river was like running metal, the light seemed to fill the air and touch every separate grass blade. Ahead, beyond trees, the eastern sky had become imperially blue and the first stars trembled.

Raven moved unhurriedly, without fear of being caught in the dark. Not on a planet with an 83-hour rotation period. He stopped for a moment at a long wooden dock where double-ended fishing craft lay tied. The sheds nearby were as solidly built as every house in town, and as gracious.

"Ketch rigged," he pointed out. "Small auxiliary engines, but I dare say those are used only when it is absolutely necessary."

"And otherwise sail?" Kors, long and gaunt, spat between his front teeth. "Now why do such a fool thing, Commandant?"

"It's more esthetically pleasing," said Raven.

"More work, though, sir," offered young Wildenvey. "I sailed a bit myself, during the Ans campaign. Just keeping all those damn ropes untangled—"

Raven grinned. "Oh, I agree. Quite. But you see, as far as I can gather, the Gwydiona don't think that way. Not like any of us visitors. A Namerican is concerned only with getting his work done, regardless of whether it really should be accomplished, and then with getting his recreation done—both with maximum bustle. A Lochlanna tries to make his work and his games approach some abstract ideal; and when he fails…he's apt to give up completely and jump over into brutishness. But they don't seem to make such distinctions here. They say, 'Man goes where God is,' and it seems to mean that work and play and art and everything else aren't divided up, no distinction is made, it's all part of one harmonious whole. So they'll fish from sailboats with elaborately carved figureheads, each element in the pattern having a dozen different symbolic overtones; and doubtless they'll take musicians along; and they'll claim that the total effect, food-gathering plus pleasure plus artistic accomplishment plus I don't know what, is more efficiently achieved than if all those things were in neat little compartments."

He shrugged and resumed his walk. "They might be right," he finished.

"I don't know why you're worried, sir," said Kors. "They're as harmless a pack of loonies as I ever met. I swear they haven't any machine more powerful than a light tractor, no weapon more dangerous than a bow."

"The first expedition reported that they don't even go hunting, except when they must for food or to protect their crops." Raven continued for a while, unspeaking. Only the scuff of boots, chuckling river and murmur in the leaves and slowly rising thunders beyond the dike, stirred that silence. The young five-pointed leaves of a bush that grew everywhere around gave a faint green fragrance to the air. Then, far off and winding down the hills, a bronze horn blew, calling antlered cattle home.

"That's what makes me afraid," said Raven.

Thereafter the men did not venture to break his wordlessness. Once or twice they passed a Gwydiona, who hailed them gravely, but they didn't stop. When they reached the dike, Raven led the way up a staircase. The wall stretched for kilometers, set at intervals with slim towers. It was high and massive, but the long curve of it and the stone facing made it graceful. The river poured through a gap, past a beach, into a dredged channel and a crescent-shaped bay whose waters tumbled and roared, molten in the sunset light. Raven drew his surcoat close about him; a wind blew here, chill and wet and smelling of salt. There were many gray sea birds in the sky.

"Why did they build this?" wondered Kors.

"Close moon. Big tides," said Wildenvey.

"They could have moved further up in the hills. They've room enough, for hellfire's sake. Ten million on an entire planet!"

Raven gestured at the towers. "I inquired," he said. "Tidepower generators in those. Furnish most of the local electricity. Shut up."

He stood staring out to a night horizon. The waves ramped and the sea birds mewed. His eyes were bleak with thought. Finally he sat down, took a wooden flute from his sleeve, and began to play, absent-mindedly, as something to do with his hands. The music grieved a minor key beneath the wind.

Kors' bark recalled him to the world. "Halt!"

"Be still, you oaf," said Raven. "It's her planet, not yours." But his palm rested casually on the butt of his pistol as he rose.

The girl came walking along the diketop, which was planted with a velvetlike pseudomoss. She was perhaps twenty-three standard years old, slim, dressed in a white tunic and wildly fluttering blue cloak. Her hair was looped in thick yellow braids, pulled back from her forehead to show a conventionalized bird tattoo. Beneath dark brows, her eyes were violet, set far apart; the mouth and the heart-shaped face were grave, but the nose tiptilted and faintly dusted with freckles. She led a boy, perhaps four, by the hand: a little male version of herself, who had been skipping but sobered when he spied the Lochlanna. Both were barefoot.

"At the crossroads of the elements, greeting," she said. Her husky voice sang the language, like all Gwydiona voices.

"Salute, peacemaker." Raven found it simplest to translate his home phrases.

"I came up here to dance for the sea," she told him, "but heard a music that called."

"Are you a shooting man?" asked the boy.

"Byord, hush!" The girl colored with embarrassment.

"Yes," laughed Raven, "you might call me a shooting man."

"But what do you shoot?" asked Byord. "Gol! Targets? Can I shoot a target?"

"Perhaps later," said Raven. "We have no targets with us at the moment."

"Mother, he says I can shoot a target! Pow! Pow! Pow!"

Raven lifted one brow. "I thought chemical weapons were unknown on Gwydion, milady," he said, as offhand as possible.

She answered with faint distress, "That other ship, which came in winter…the men aboard it also had, what did they call them…guns. They explained and demonstrated. Since then, probably every small boy on the planet has imagined— Well, no harm done, I am sure." She ruffled Byord's hair, smiling.

"Ah…I am Raven, a Commandant of the Oakenshaw Ethnos, Windhome Mountains, Lochlann."

"And your other souls?" asked the girl.

Raven waved them back. "Followers. Sons of yeomen on my father's estate."

She was puzzled that he excluded them, but accepted it as an alien custom. "I am Elfavy," she said, accenting the first syllable. She flashed a grin. "My son Byord you already know! His surname is Varstan, mine is Simnon."

"What? Oh, yes, I remember. Gwydiona wives retain their family name; sons take the father's, and daughters the mother's. Am I correct? Your husband—"

She looked outward. "He drowned there, one storm last fall," she answered quietly.

Raven did not say he was sorry, for his culture had its own attitudes toward death. He couldn't help wondering aloud, tactless: "But you said you danced for the sea."

"He is of the sea now, is he not?" She continued regarding the waves where they swirled and shook foam loose from their crests. "How beautiful it is tonight."

Then, swinging back to him, altogether at ease: "I have just had a long talk with one of your party, a Miguel Tolteca. He is staying at my father's house, where Byord and I now live."

"Not precisely one of mine," said Raven, suppressing offendedness.

"Oh? Wait…yes, he did mention having some men along from a different planet."

"Lochlann," said Raven. "Our sun lies near theirs, both about 50 light-years hence in that direction." He pointed past the evening star to the Hercules region.

"Is your home like his Nuevamerica?"

"Hardly," for a moment Raven wanted to speak of mountains that rose sheer into a red-sun sky, trees dwarfed and gnarled by wind, moorland, ice plains, oceans too dense and bitter with salt for a man to sink. He remembered a peasant's house, its roof held down by ropes lest a gale blow it away, and he remembered his father's castle, gaunt above a glacier, and hoofs ringing in the courtyard, and he remembered bandits and burned villages and dead men gaping around a smashed cannon.

But she would not understand. Would she?

"Why do you have all the shooting things?" exploded from Byord. "Are there bad animals around your farms?"

"No," said Raven. "Not many wild animals at all. The land is too poor for them."

"I have heard…that first expedition—" Elfavy grew troubled again. "They said something about men fighting other men."

"My profession," said Raven. She looked blankly at him. Wrong word, then. "My calling," he said, though that wasn't quite right either.

"But killing *men!*" she cried.

"Bad men?" asked Byord, round-eyed.

"Hush," said his mother. " 'Bad' means when something goes wrong, like the cynwyr swarming down and eating the grain. How can men go wrong?"

"They get sick," Byord said.

"Yes, and then your grandfather heals them."

"Imagine a situation where men often get so sick they want to hurt their own kind," said Raven.

"But horrible!" Elfavy traced a cross in the air. "What germ causes that?"

Raven sighed. If she couldn't even visualize homicidal mania, how explain to her that sane, honorable men found sane, honorable reasons for hunting each other?

He heard Kors mutter to Wildenvey, "What I said, guts of sugar candy."

If that were only so, thought Raven, he could forget his own unease. But they were no weaklings on Gwydion. Not when they took open sailboats onto oceans whose weakest tides rose fifteen meters. Not when this girl could visibly push away her own shock, face him, and ask with friendly curiosity—as if he, Raven, should address questions to the sudden apparition of a saber-toothed weaselcat:

"Is that the reason why your people and the Namericans seem to talk so little to each other? I thought I noticed it in the town, but didn't realize who came from which group."

"Oh, they've done their share of fighting on Nuevamerica," said Raven dryly. "As when they expelled us; we had divided their planet into fiefs, a century ago. They were aided by the fact that Lochlann was simultaneously fighting the Grand Alliance—but still, it was well done of them."

"I don't see why—well, no matter. We will have time enough to discuss all this. You are going in to the hills with us, are you not?"

"Why, yes, if... What did you say? You too?"

Elfavy nodded. Her mouth quirked upward. "Don't be so horrified, far-friend. I will leave Byord with his aunt and uncle, even if they do spoil him terribly." She gave the boy a brief hug. "But the group does need a dancer, which is my calling."

"Dancer?" choked Kors.

"Not *the* Dancer. He is always a man."

"But—" Raven relaxed. He even smiled. "In what way does an expedition into the wilderness require a dancer?"

"To dance for it," said Elfavy. "What else?"

"Oh...nothing. Do you know precisely what this journey is for?"

"You have not heard? I listened while my father and Miguel talked it over. You see, planets where men can live without special equipment are rare and far between. The explorers from Nuevamerica would like a base on Gwydion, to refuel their ships, make needful repairs, rest in greenwoods." Elfavy gave Kors and Wildenvey a surprised look, not knowing why they both laughed aloud. Raven himself would not have interrupted her naive recital for money.

She brushed the blown yellow hair off her brow and resumed. "Well, of course all our people must decide the matter. But it can do no harm meanwhile to look at possible sites for such a base, can it? Father proposed an uninhabited valley some days' march inland, beyond Mount Granis. The journey afoot would be pleasant, much could be shown to you and discussed en route, and we would return well before Bale time."

She frowned the faintest bit. "I am not certain it is wise to have a foreign base so near the Holy City. But that can always be argued later." Her laughter trilled forth. "Oh, dear, I do ramble, don't I?" She caught Raven's arm, impulsively, and tucked her own under it. "But you have seen so many worlds, you can't imagine how we here have all looked forward to meeting you. The wonder of it! The stories you can tell us, the songs you can sing us!"

She dropped her free hand to Byord's shoulder. "Wait till this little chatterbird gets over his shyness with you, far-friend. If we could only harness his questions to a generator, we could illuminate all Instar!"

"Awww," said the boy, wriggling free.

They began to walk along the diketop, almost aimlessly. The two soldiers followed. The rifles on their backs stood black against a cloud like roses. Elfavy's fingers slipped down from Raven's awkwardly held arm—men and women did not go together thus on Lochlann—and closed on the flute in his sleeve. "What is this?" she asked.

He drew it forth. It was a long piece of darvawood, carved and polished to bring out the grain. "I am not very good with this," he said. "A man of rank is expected to have some artistic skills. But I am only a younger son, which is why I wander about seeking work for my guns, and I have not had much musical instruction."

"The sounds I heard were—" Elfavy searched after a word. "They spoke to me," she said finally, "but not in a language I knew. Will you play that melody again?"

He set the flute to his lips and piped the notes, which were cold and sad. Elfavy shivered, catching her mantle to her and touching the gold-and-black locket at her throat. "There is more than music here," she said. "That song comes from the Night Faces. It *is* a song, is it not?"

"Yes. Very old. From Earth, they say, centuries before men had even left the Home. We still sing it on Lochlann."

"Can you put it into Gwydiona for me?"

"Perhaps. Let me think." He walked for a while more, turning phrases in his head. A military officer must also be adept in the use of words, and the two languages were close kin. Finally he sounded a few bars, lowered the flute, and began:

> " *The wind doth blow today, my love,*
> *And a few small drops of rain.*
> *I never had but one true love,*
> *And she in her grave was lain.*
>
> *I'll do as much for my true love*
> *As any young man may;*
> *I'll sit and mourn all at her grave*
> *For a twelvemonth and a day:*
>
> *The twelvemonth and a day being up,*
> *The dead began to speak:*
> *'Oh, who sits weeping on my grave*
> *And will not let me sleep?' —*"

He felt her grow stiff, and halted his voice. She said, through an unsteady mouth, so low he could scarce hear: "No. Please."

"Forgive me," he said in puzzlement, "if I have— What?"

"You couldn't know. I couldn't." She glanced after Byord. The boy had frisked back to the soldiers. "He was out of earshot. It doesn't matter, then, much."

"Can you tell me what is wrong?" he asked, hopeful of a clue to the source of his own doubts.

"No." She shook her head. "I don't know what. It just frightens me somehow. Horribly. How can you live with such a song?"

"On Lochlann we think it quite a beautiful little thing."

"But the dead don't speak. They are *dead!*"

"Of course. It was only a fantasy. Don't you have myths?"

"Not like that. The dead go into the Night, and the Night becomes the Day, is the Day. Like Regan, who was caught in the Burning Wheel, and rose to heaven and was cast down again, and was wept over by the Mother—those are Aspects of God, they mean the rainy season that brings dry earth to life and they also mean dreams and the waking from dreams, and loss-remembrance-recreation, and the transformations of physical energy, and— Oh, don't you see, it's all one! It isn't two people separate, become nothing, desiring to be nothing, even. It mustn't be!"

Raven put away his flute. They walked on until Elfavy broke from him, danced a few steps, a slow and stately dance, which suddenly became a leap. She ran back smiling and took his arm again.

"I'll forget it," she said. "Your home is very distant. This is Gwydion, and too near Bale time to be unhappy."

"What is this Bale time?"

"When we go to the Holy City," she said. "Once each year. Each Gwydiona year, that is, which I believe makes about five of Old Earth's. Everybody, all over the planet, goes to the Holy City maintained by his own town. It may be a dull wait for you people, unless you can join us... Perhaps you can!" she cried, eagerness washing out the last terror.

"What happens?"

"God comes to us."

"Oh." He thought of dionysiac rites on certain backward planets and asked with great care, "Do you see God, or feel Vwi?" The last word was a pronoun; Gwydiona employed an extra gender, the universal.

"Oh, no," said Elfavy. "We are God."

CHAPTER FOUR

The dance ended in a final exultant jump, wings fluttering iridescent and the bird head turned skyward. The pipe and drum tape fell silent. The dancer's plumage swept the grass as she bowed. She vanished into a canebrake. The audience, seated cross-legged, closed eyes for an unspeaking minute, which Tolteca thought was a more graceful tribute than applause.

He looked around again as the ceremony broke up. It didn't seem quite real to him, yet, that camp should be pitched, supper eaten, and the time come for rest and sleep, while the sun had not reached noon. The long day, of course: Gwydion was just past vernal equinox; but even at its mild and rainy midwinter, daylight lasted a couple of sleeps.

The effect hadn't been so noticeable at Instar. The town employed an auroral generator to give soft outdoor illumination, and went about its business. Organized during that period, the survey expedition had marched into the hills at dawn. Already one day had passed on the trail, with two campings—and one night, where the moon needed little help from the travelers' flashbeams, and now another forenoon. Sometime tomorrow they ought to reach the upland site that Dawyd had suggested might make a spaceport.

Tolteca could feel the tiredness due rough kilometers in his muscles, but he wasn't sleepy yet. He stood up, glancing over the camp. Dawyd had selected a good spot, a meadow in the forest. The half-dozen Gwydiona who accompanied him chattered gaily as they banked the fire and spread out sleeping bags. One man, standing watch against possible carnivores, carried a longbow. Tolteca had seen what that weapon could do, when a hunter had brought in a carcass for meat.

Nonetheless, he wondered why everyone had courteously refused those firearms the *Quetzal* brought as gifts.

The ten Namerican scientists and engineers who had come along were in more of a hurry to bed down. Tolteca chuckled, recalling their dismay when he announced that this trip would be on shank's mare. But Dawyd was right, there was no better way to learn an area. Raven had also joined the group, with two of his men. The Lochlanna seemed incapable of weariness, and their damned slithering politeness never failed them, but they were always a little apart from the rest.

Tolteca sauntered past the canebrake, along a side path. Though no one lived in these hills, the Gwydiona often went up here for recreation, and small solar-powered robots maintained the trails. He had not quite dared hope he would meet Elfavy. But when she came around a flowering tree, the heart leaped in him.

"Aren't you tired?" he asked, lame-tongued, after she stopped and gave greeting.

"Not much," she answered. "I wanted to stroll a while before sleep. Like you."

"Well, let's go into partnership."

She laughed. "An interesting concept. You have so many commercial enterprises on your planet, is this another one? Hiring out to take walks for people who would rather sit at home?"

Tolteca bowed. "If you'll join me, I'll make a career of that."

She flushed and said quickly, "Come this way. If I remember this neighborhood since the last time I was here, it has a beautiful view not far off."

She had changed her costume for a plain tunic. Sunlight came through leaves to touch her lithe dancer's body; the hair, loosened, fell in waves down her back. Tolteca could not find the words he really wanted, nor could he share her easy silence.

"We don't do everything for money on Nuevamerica," he said, afraid of what she might think. "It's only, well, our particular way of organizing our economy."

"I know," she said. "To me it seems so…impersonal, lonely, each man fending for himself—but that may just be because I am not used to the idea."

"Our feeling is that the state should do as little as possible," he said, earnest with the ideals of his people. "Otherwise it will get too much power, and that's the end of freedom. But then private enterprise must take over; and it must be kept competitive, or it will in turn develop into a tyranny." Perforce he used several words that Gwydiona lacked, such as the last. He had introduced them to her before, during long discussions at Dawyd's house, when they had tried to understand each other's viewpoints.

"But why should the society, or the state as you call it, be opposed to the individual?" she asked. "I still don't grasp what the problem is, Miguel. We seem to do much as we please, all the time, here on Gwydion; and yet it all works out for mutual benefit. Money is only an economic convenience and its possession does not give a man power over his fellows."

"You are all reasonable people," said Tolteca. "Nor have you any need to curb violence. You hardly know what anger is. And hate…another word that isn't in your language. Hate is to be *always* angry with someone else." He saw shock on her face, and hurried to add, "Then we must contend with the lazy, the greedy, the unscrupulous— Do you know, I begin to wonder if we should carry out this project. It may be best that your planet have nothing to do with any others. You are too good; you could be too badly hurt."

She shook her head. "No, don't think that. Obviously, we are different from you. Perhaps genetic drift has caused us to lose a trait or two otherwise common to mankind. But the difference isn't that great, and it doesn't make us superior. After all, you came to *us*. We never managed to build spaceships."

"Never chose to," he corrected her.

He remembered a remark of Raven's one time in Instar: "It isn't natural for humans to be gentle and rational all the time. They've done great things here; they don't lack energy. But where does the excess energy go?" At the time, Tolteca had bristled. Only a professional killer would be frightened by total sanity, he thought. Now he began, unwilling, to see that Raven had asked a legitimate scientific question.

"We never chose to do many things," said Elfavy with a hint of wistfulness.

"I admit wondering why you don't at least colonize the uninhabited parts of Gwydion."

"We stabilized the population by general agreement, several centuries ago. More people would only destroy nature."

They emerged from the woods again. Another meadow sloped upward to a cliff edge. The grass was strewn with white flowers; here and there a tree stood, slender, full of gold blossoms; the common bush of star-shaped leaves grew everywhere about, its buds swelling, the air heady from their odor. Beyond this spine of the hills lay a deep valley and then the mountains rose, clear and powerful against the sky.

Elfavy swept an arm in an arc. "Should we crowd out this?" she asked.

Tolteca thought of his own brawling unrestful folk, the forests they had already raped, and made no answer.

The girl stood a moment, frowning, on the cliff top. A west wind blew strongly up here, straining the tunic against her and tossing sunlit locks of hair. Tolteca caught himself staring so rudely that he forced his eyes away, across kilometers toward that gray volcanic cone named Mount Granis.

"No," said Elfavy, her tone stubborn. "I must not be smug. People did live here once. Just a few farmers and woodcutters, but they did maintain isolated homes. However, that is long past. Nowadays I don't believe we would occupy these regions even if it were safe. It would be wrong. All life has a right to existence, has it not? Men shouldn't wear more of a Night Face than they must."

Tolteca concentrated on the meaning with some difficulty, because the sound was so pleasant. Night Face—oh, yes, part of the Gwydiona religion. (If "religion" was the right word.

"Philosophy" might be better. "Way of life" might be still more accurate.) Since they believed everything to be a facet of that eternal and infinite Oneness which they called God, it followed that God was also death, ruin, sorrow. Though they didn't say much, or seem to think much, about that side of reality. He remembered that their arts and literature, like their daily lives, were sunny, cheerful, completely logical once you had mastered the complex symbolisms. Even the pain and loss of one much beloved was mourned in a controlled manner, which Raven admired but Tolteca had had trouble understanding.

"I don't believe your folk could harm nature," he said. "You work with it, make yourselves part of it."

"That's the ideal," laughed Elfavy, "but I'm afraid practice has no more statistical correlation with preaching on Gwydion than anywhere else in the universe," She knelt and began to pluck the small white flowers. "I shall make a garland of jule for you," she said. "A sign of friendship, since the jule blooms when the year is being reborn. Now that's a nice harmonious thing for me to do, isn't it? And yet if you asked the plant, it might not agree!"

"Thank you," he said, overwhelmed.

"The Bird Maiden had a chaplet of jule," she said. By now he realized that the retelling of symbolic myths was a standard conversational gambit here, like a Lochlanna's inquiry after the health of your father. "That is why I wore bird costume this time. It is her season, and today is the Day of the River Child. When the Bird Maiden met the River Child, he was lost and crying. She carried him home and gave him her crown." She glanced up. "It is a seasonal myth," she explained. "The end of the rainy season, lowland floods, then sunlight and the blooming jule. Plus all those moral lessons the elders are always quacking about, plus about a hundred other possible interpretations. The entire story is too complicated to tell on a warm day, even if the episode of the Riddling Tree is one of our best poems. But I always like to dance the story."

She fell silent, her hands busy in the grass. For lack of anything else, he pointed to one of the budding bushes. "What's this called?" he asked.

"With the five-pointed leaves? Oh, bale flower. It grows everywhere."

"So I've noticed. It must have quite a lot of mythology, then."

Elfavy stopped. She looked up at him. The violet eyes seemed, for an instant, almost blind. "No," she said.

"What? But I thought... I thought everything means something on Gwydion, as well as being something. Usually it has many different meanings—"

"This is only baleflower..." Her voice grew thin, "...nothing else."

Tolteca pulled himself up short. Some taboo—no, surely not that, the Gwydiona were even freer from arbitrary prohibitions than his own people. He resolved to have the plant studied, botanically and chemically, when he got back to the ship. But don't tell anyone...

The girl finished her work, jumped to her feet, and flung a wreath about his neck. "There!" she laughed. "No, hold still, it's caught on one ear— Ah, good."

He gestured to the one in her hand. "Aren't you going to put that on yourself?"

"Oh, no. A jule garland is always for someone else. This is for Raven."

"What?" Tolteca stiffened.

Again she flushed and looked past him toward the mountains. "I got to know him a little in Instar. I drove him around, showing him the sights. Or we walked."

Tolteca thought of all the times in that long moonlit night when she had not been at home. He said, "I don't believe Raven is your sort," and heard his voice go rough.

"I don't understand him," she whispered. "And yet in a way I do. Maybe. As I might understand a storm."

She started back toward camp. Tolteca said bitterly, "I should think you, of everyone alive, would be immune to such cheap glamour. Soldier! Hereditary aristocrat!"

"Those things I don't comprehend," she said, her eyes still averted. "To kill people, or make them do your bidding, as if they were machines— But it isn't that way with him. Not really."

They went down the trail in stillness, boots thudding next to sandals. At last she murmured, "He lives with the Night Faces. All the time. I can't even bear to think of that, and yet he endures it."

Enjoys it. Tolteca wanted to growl. But he realized he had been backbiting, and held his peace.

They returned to find most of the party asleep, eyelids padded against daylight. The sentry saluted them with a raised arrow. Elfavy continued to the edge of camp, where the three Lochlanna had spread their bedrolls. Kors snored, a gun in his hand; Wildenvey looked too young and helpless for his gory shipboard brags. Raven was still awake. He squatted on his haunches and frowned at a sheaf of photographs.

As Elfavy approached, his grin sprang forth, he seemed quite honestly pleased. "Well, this is a happy chance," he called. "Will you join me? I have a pot of tea on the grill over the fire."

"No, thank you. I like that tea stuff of yours, but it would keep me from sleeping." Elfavy stood before him, looking down at the ground. The wreath dangled in her hand. "I only—"

"Never come between an Oakenshaw and his tea," said Raven. "Ah, there, Sir Engineer."

Elfavy's face burned. "I only wanted to see you a moment," she faltered.

"And I you. Someone mentioned former habitation in this area, and I noticed traces on a ridge near here. I went up there with a camera." Raven flowed erect and fanned out his self-developing films. "It was a thorp once, several houses and out-buildings. Not much left now."

"No. Long abandoned." The girl lifted her wreath and lowered it again.

Raven gave her a steady look. "Destroyed," he told her.

"Oh? Oh, yes. I have heard this region was dangerous. The volcano—"

"No natural catastrophe," said Raven. "I know the signs. My men and I cleared away the brush with a flash pistol and dug in the ground. Those buildings had wooden roofs and rafters—which burned. We found two human skeletons, more or less complete. One had a skull split open, the other a corroded iron object between its ribs." He raised the pictures toward her eyes. "Do you see?"

"Oh…" She stepped back. One hand crept to her mouth. "What—"

"Everyone tells me there is no record of men killing men on Gwydion," said Raven. "It's not merely rare, it's unknown. And yet that thorp was attacked and burned once."

Elfavy gulped. Anger rushed into Tolteca, thick and hot. "Look here, Raven," he snapped, "you may be free to bully some poor Lochlanna peasant, but—"

"No," said Elfavy. "Please…"

"Did all the other homes up here suffer a like fate?" Raven flung the questions at her, not loudly but nonetheless like bullets. "Were the hills deserted because it was too hazardous to live in such isolation?"

"I don't know." Elfavy's voice lifted with a raggedness it had not borne until now. "I…have seen ruins, here and there…nobody knows what happened." Her voice raised suddenly in a near yell: "Everything isn't recorded in history, you know! Do you know every answer to every question about your own planet?"

"Of course not," said Raven. "But if this were my world, I'd at least know why all the buildings are constructed like fortresses."

"Like what?"

"You know what I mean."

"Why…you asked me that once before…I told you," she stammered. "The strength of the house, the family—a symbol—"

"I heard the myth," said Raven. "I was also assured that no one has ever believed those myths to be literal truth, only poetic expressions. Your charming tale about Anren who made the stars has not prevented you from having an excellent grasp of astrophysics. So what are you guarding against? What are you afraid of?"

Elfavy crouched back. "Nothing." The words rattled from her. "If, if, if there was anything…wouldn't we have better weapons against it…than bows and arrows? People get hurt in accidents, by sickness and old age—they die, the Night has them— But nothing else! There can't be!"

She whirled about and fled.

Tolteca stepped toward Raven, who stood squinting after the girl. "Turn around," he said. "I'm going to beat the guts out of you."

Raven laughed, a metallic noise. "How much combat karate do you know, trader's clerk?"

Tolteca dropped a hand to his gun. "We're in another culture," he said between his teeth. "A generation of scientific study won't be enough to map all its thought processes. If you think you can go trampling freely on these people's feelings, no more aware of what you're doing than a bulldozer with a broken autopilot—"

They both felt the ground shiver. An instant afterward the sound reached them, booming down the sky.

CHAPTER FIVE

The three Lochlanna were on their feet in a ring, weapons aimed outward, without seeming to have moved. Elsewhere the camp stumbled awake, men calling to each other through thunders.

Tolteca ran after Elfavy. The sun seemed remote and heatless, the explosions rattled his teeth together; he felt the ground vibrations in his bones.

The noise died away, but echoes flew about for seconds longer. Dawyd joined Elfavy and threw his arms around her. A flock of birds soared up, screaming.

The physician's gaze turned westward. Black smoke boiled above the treetops. As Tolteca reached the Simnons, he saw Dawyd trace the sign against misfortune.

"What is it?" cried the Namerican. "What happened?"

Dawyd looked his way. For a moment the old eyes were without recognition. Then he answered curtly, "Mount Granis."

"Oh." Tolteca slapped his forehead. The relief was such that he wanted to howl his laughter. Of course! A volcano cleared its throat, after a century or two of quiet. Why in the galaxy were the Gwydiona breaking camp?

"I never expected this," said Dawyd. "Though I daresay our seismology is less developed than yours."

"Our man made some checks, and didn't think we would have any serious trouble if we built a spaceport here," said Tolteca. "That wasn't a real eruption, you know. Just a bit of lava and a great deal of smoke."

"And a west wind," said Dawyd. "Straight from Granis to us."

He paused before adding, almost absent-mindedly: "The site I had in mind for your spaceport is protected from trouble of this kind. I checked the airflow patterns with the central meteorological computer at Bettwis. It is a mere unlucky happenstance that we should be at this exact spot, this very moment. Now we must run, and may fear give speed to us."

"From a little smoke?" asked Tolteca incredulously.

Dawyd held his daughter close. "This is a planet of middle Population One," he said. "Rich in heavy metals. That smoke and dust, when it gets here, will include enough such material to kill us."

By the time they got in motion, jogging southward along a sparsely wooded ridge, the cloud had overshadowed them. Kors looked up past a dim red ball of sun, estimating with an artilleryman's eye. His lantern jaw worked a moment, as if chewing sour cud, before he spoke:

"We can't go back the way we came, Commandant. That muck'll fall out all over those parts. We've got to keep headed this way and hope we can get out from under. Ask one of these yokels if he knows a decent southbound trail."

"Must we have a trail?" puffed Wildenvey. "Let's cut right through the woods."

"Listen to the for-Harry's-sake heathdweller talk!" jeered Kors. "Porkface, I grew up in the Ernshaw. Have you ever tried to run through underbrush?"

"Save your breath, you two," advised Raven. He loped a little faster until he joined Dawyd and Elfavy at the head of the line. Grass whispered under his boots, now and then a hobnail rang on a stone and sparks showered. The sky was dull brown, streaked with black, the light from it like tarnished brass and casting no shadows. The only bright things in the world were an occasional fire-spit from Mount Granis, and Elfavy's flying hair.

Raven put the question to her. He spaced his words with his breathing, which he kept in rhythm with his feet. The girl replied in the same experienced manner. "In this direction, all paths converge on the Holy City. We ought to be safe there, if we can reach it soon enough."

"Before Bale time?" exclaimed Dawyd.

"Is it forbidden?" asked Raven, and wondered if he would use his guns to enter a refuge tabooed.

"No...no rule of conduct... But nobody goes there outside Bale time!" Dawyd shook his head, bewildered. "It would be a meaningless act."

"Meaningless—to save our lives?" snapped Raven.

"Unsymbolic," said Elfavy. "It would fit into no pattern." She lifted her face to the spreading darkness and cried. "But what sense would it make to breathe that dust? I want to see Byord again!"

"Yes. So...so be it..." Dawyd then shut his mouth and concentrated on making speed.

Raven's eyes, watching the uneven ground, touched the girl's quick feet and stayed there. Not until he tripped on a vine did he remember exactly where he was. Then he swore and forced himself to think of the situation. Without analytical apparatus, he had no way to confirm that volcanic ash was as dangerous as Dawyd claimed; but it sounded reasonable on a planet like this. The first expedition had been warned about many vegetable species, which were poisonous to man simply because they grew in soil loaded with heavy elements. It wouldn't take a lot of inhaled metallic material to destroy you: radioactives, arsenates, perhaps elemental mercury liberated from its oxide by heat. A few gulps and you were done. Dying might take a while, prolonged by the medics' attempts to get a hopelessly big dose out of your body. Not that Raven intended to watch his own lungs and brain go rotten. His pistol could do him a final service. But Elfavy—

They stopped to rest at the head of a downward trail. One of the Gwydiona protested through a dried-out throat: "Not the Holy City! We'd destroy the whole meaning of Bale time!"

"No, we wouldn't." Dawyd, who had been thinking as he trotted, answered with an authority that pulled all their reddened eyes to him. "The eruption at the moment when we happened to be downwind was an accident so improbable it was senseless. Right? That Night Face called Chaos." Several men crossed themselves, but they all nodded. "If we redress the situation—restore the balance of events, of logical sequence—by entering the Focus of God (in our purely human persona, at that, which makes our act a parable of man's conscious reasoning powers, his science)—what could be more significant?"

They mulled it over while the gloom thickened and Mount Granis boomed at their backs. One by one, they murmured agreement. Tolteca whispered to Raven, in Ispanyo: "Oa, I do believe I see a new myth being born."

"Yes. They'll doubtless bring one of their quasi-gods into it, a few generations hence...while preserving an accurate historical account of what really happened!"

"But by all creation! Here they are, running from an unnecessarily horrible death, and they argue whether it would be artistic to shelter in this temple spot!"

"It makes more sense than you think," said Raven, somberly. "I remember once when I was a boy, my very first campaign in fact. A civil war, the Bitter Water clan against my own Ethnos. We boxed a regiment of them in the Stawr Hills, expecting them to dig in. They wouldn't, because there were brave men's graves all around, the Danoora who fell three hundred years ago. They came out prepared to be mowed down. When we grasped the situation, we let them go, gave them a day's head start. They reached their main body, which perhaps turned the course of the war. But that victory would have cost us too much."

Tolteca shook his head. "I don't understand you."

"You wouldn't."

"Any more than you would understand why men died to pull down the foreign castles on your planet."

"Well, maybe so."

Raven wondered how much lethal dust he was already breathing. Not enough to matter, yet. The air was still clean in his nostrils, he could still see far across hills and down forested slopes. The heavy particles and stones were not dangerous. It was the finely divided material slowly settling over many hectares that could kill men.

Like a mind reader, Dawyd said, "The Holy City will be almost ideal for us. Airflow patterns protect it from the ash—it lies right under the Steeps of Kolumkill, and never gets a south wind. The site was chosen with that in mind, even though our local volcanoes very rarely erupt. We shall have to wait there till the next heavy rain, which may take a few days at this season. That will carry down the last airborne dust leach from the soil what has fallen; wash the poison into the rivers and so into the sea, safely diluted. The City has ample food supplies, and I see no reason why we should not avail ourselves of them."

He stood up. "But first we must get there," he finished. "Does everyone have his breath back?"

The rest of the journey was little remembered. They went at a dogtrot, along well-kept trails, under cool leaves; they halted a few minutes at a time when it seemed indicated; but toward the end men lurched along in each other's arms. Three Namericans collapsed. Dawyd had poles chopped and raincoats spread to make litters for them. No one complained at the burden. But maybe that was because no breath was left to complain.

When he entered the Holy City, Raven himself scarcely saw it. He retained enough strength to spread a bedroll for Elfavy, who sprawled quietly down and passed out. He brought a cup of water for Dawyd, who lay on his back and stared with eyes emptied of awareness. He even washed the grime and sweat from himself before crawling into his own bag. But then darkness clubbed him.

When he awoke, it took a few seconds before he knew his own name, and a bit longer to fix his location. He rallied those drilled reflexes by which he could deny to himself that he was stiff and aching. Shadow from a wall covered him, but he looked straight up to the stars. Had he slept so long? The sky was utterly clear; men were indeed safe in this place. The constellations glittered in unfamiliar patterns. He could barely recognize that one they called The Plowman on Lochlann; its distortion made him feel cold and alone. The Nebula, dimming some parts of the sky and blotting out others, was somehow less alien.

He left his bag, crouched in the dark, and opened the packsack pillow with fingers too schooled to need light. Quickly he dressed. Dagger and pistol made a comforting drag on his flanks. He threw a wide-sleeved tunic over the drab route clothes, for it flaunted the crests of his family and nation, and glided between men still unconscious into the open.

The night was very quiet. He stood in a forum, if it could be so named. There was no paving in the Holy City, but thick pseudomoss lay cool and full of dew under his feet. On every side rose white marble buildings, long and low, fluted delicate porticos upholdings roofs where figures danced on friezes. They had wide, doorless main entrances atop mossy ramps, but the windows were mere slits. Colonnades and wings knitted them together into a labyrinthine unity. Behind them stood a ring of towers, airily slender, with bronze cupolas that must show a mellow green by daylight. The entire place was surrounded by an amphitheater or whatever you wanted to call it: low moss-carpeted tiers enclosing this miniature dell like the sides of a chalice. Trees grew thickly on its top.

Down here there were no trees; but many formal gardens—rather, a single, reticulated one, interwoven with the houses and the towers—held beds of Terran violets and thornless roses, native jule and sunbloom and baleflower and much else that Raven didn't recognize. Southward, those cliffs called the Steeps of Kolumkill, which the party had had to go around, shouldered against the stars.

He was able to see much detail, for the moon, She, was rising in the west. Its retrograde path would take it over the sky and through half a cycle of phases during half a night period. Already it was a white semicircle, a degree in angular diameter, filling the hollow with unreal light.

A fountain tinkled in the middle of the forum. Raven crossed to its little moss-grown bowl and swallowed until his mummy gullet felt alive again. The water gurgled back down a whimsical drainpipe, a grotesque fish face. Well, why shouldn't there be humor in the geometric center of sacredness thought Raven? The people of Gwydion laughed more than most, not raucously like a Namerican or wolfishly like a Lochlanna, but a gentle mirth, which found something comical in even the grandest things. The water must come from some woodland spring; it had a wild taste.

He heard a noise and whirled about, one hand on his gun. Elfavy entered the moonlight. "Oh," he said stupidly. "Are you awake, milady?"

She laughed. "No. I am sound asleep in my bed in Instar." Treading close, she said, "I woke up an hour ago or more, but didn't want to move. Not for a day, at least! Then I saw you here, and—" Her voice trailed off.

Raven directed his heartbeat to slow down. It obeyed poorly. "Someone should keep watch," he said. "May as well be me."

"No need, far-friend. There are no dangers here."

"Wild animals?"

"Robots keep them off. Other robots maintain the grounds." She pointed to a little wheeled machine weeding a rose bed with delicate tendrils.

Raven grinned. "Ah, but who maintains the robots?"

"Silly! An automatic unit, of course. Every ten years, local years, I mean, our engineers hold a midwinter ceremony where they inspect the facilities and bring in fresh supplies."

"I see. And otherwise no one ever comes here except at— uh—Bale time?"

She nodded. "No reason to. Shall we look around? Walking might get the cramp out of my legs." She could have been offering to show him any local curiosum.

Their feet fell noiseless on the moss. The buildings looked like faerie work, there under the brutal mass of Kolumkill; but as he reached a doorway, Raven saw that their walls were fused stone, thick and strong as all Gwydiona architecture. Light came from fluoros, recessed in the high ceiling: probably solar battery powered, he thought. It was dim, but there was little to see anyhow—a gracious anteroom, archways opening on corridors.

"We mustn't go very deeply in," said the girl, "or we will get lost and blunder around for hours till we find our way out. Look…" She pointed down a hall, toward an intersection whence five other passages radiated. "That is only the edge of the maze."

Raven touched a wall. It yielded to his fingers, the same rubbery gray substance that felt so pleasant under his feet. "What's this?" he asked. "A synthetic elastomer? Does it line the whole interior?"

"Yes," said Elfavy. Her tone grew indifferent. "Nothing in here, really. Let's go up in one of the towers, then you can see the total pattern."

"A moment, if you grant." Raven opened one of the doors that lined the nearest corridor. It was of typical steel construction, though coated with the universal soft plastic, and had an inside bolt. The room beyond was ventilated through a slit-window; a toilet and water tap were the only furnishings, but a heap of small shapeless bags filled one corner. "What's in those?" asked Raven.

"Food supplies, sealed in plastiskins," Elfavy answered. "An artificial food, which keeps indefinitely till opened. I'm afraid you won't find it very exciting, but it is nourishing."

"You seem to live rather austerely at Bale time," said Raven. He watched her from the edge of an eye.

"It is no time to worry about material needs. Instead, you grab a sack of food and slit it open with your thumbnail when hungry, drink from a tap or fountain when thirsty, flop down anywhere when sleepy."

"I see. But what is the important thing you do, to which keeping alive is so incidental?"

"I told you." She left the room with a quick nervous stride. "We are God."

47

"But when I asked you what you meant by that, you said you couldn't explain."

"I can't." She evaded his glance. Her voice was not perfectly level. "Don't you see, it goes beyond language. Any language. We employ several on Gwydion, you realize. Science is one, painting is another, music another, choreography another and so on. According to what you have told me, this seems to be the only planet where myth was also developed, deliberately and systematically, as still a different language—not by primitives who confused it with the scientific or the common-sense concepts, but by people trained in semantics, who knew that each language describes one single facet of reality, and wanted myth to help them talk about something for which all the others were inadequate. You can't believe, for instance, that mathematics and poetry are interchangeable!"

"No," said Raven.

She brushed back her tousled hair and went on, eager now, "Well, what happens at Bale time could only be described by a fusion of every language, including those no human being has yet imagined. And such a super-language is impossible, because it would be self-contradictory."

"Do you mean that at Bale time you perceive, or commune with, total reality?"

They came out into the open again. She hastened across the forum, through the barred shadows of a colonnade to the spires beyond. He had never seen anything so beautiful as the sight of her running in the moonlight. She pulled up short at a tower doorway, it cast a darkness over her and she said from the darkness, "That's merely another set of words, *liatha*. Not even a label. I wish you could be here yourself and know!"

They started upward. A padded ramp wound around small rooms. It was dimly lit and stuffy. Raven asked, after a silence, "What was it you called me just now?"

"What?" He couldn't be sure, but he thought her face was stained with quick color.

"*Liatha*...I don't know that word."

Her lashes fluttered down. "Nothing," she mumbled. "An expression."

"Ah, let me guess." He wanted to make a joke, to suggest that it perhaps meant oaf, barbarian, villain, swinedog but remembered that Gwydiona had no such terms. Since she looked at him with enormous expectant eyes he must blunder, "Darling, beloved—"

She stopped, shrinking back against the wall. "You said you didn't know!"

The discipline of a lifetime kept him walking. When she rejoined him he made himself say, lightly, through a clamor, "You are most kind, peacemaker, but I don't need any further flattery than the fact that you have time to spare for me."

"There will be time enough for everything else," she whispered, "after you are gone."

The highest room, just under the roof, was the only one that possessed a true window, rather than a slit. Moonlight cataracted past its bronze grille. The air was warm, but that light made Elfavy's hair seem to crackle with frost. She pointed out at the intricate interlocking of labyrinth, towers, and flowerbeds. "The hexagons inscribed in circles mean the laws of nature," she began in a small voice, "their regularity enclosed in some greater scheme. It is the sign of Owan the Sunsmith, who—" She stopped. Neither of them had been listening. They searched each other's faces under the fenced-off moon.

"Must you go?" she asked finally.

"I have made promises," he said.

"But after they are fulfilled?"

"I don't know." He considered the stranger sky. "I have known people from one place, one culture, who tried to settle into another. It rarely works."

"It might. If there was a willingness. A Gwydiona...for example...could be happy even on, well, on Lochlann."

"I wonder..."

"Will you do something for me? Now."

His pulses jumped. "If I can, milady."

"Sing me the rest of that song. The one you sang when we first met."

"But you couldn't—"

"I would like to try again. Please."

He hadn't brought his flute, but he sang low in the chilly night:

> "— *'Tis I, my love, sits on your grave*
> *And will not let you sleep;*
> *For I crave one kiss of your clay-cold lips,*
> *And that is all I seek.'*

> *'You crave one kiss of my clay-cold lips;*
> *But my breath smells earthy strong;*
> *If you have one kiss of my clay-cold lips*
> *Your time will not be long' —*"

"No," said Elfavy. She gulped and hugged herself, seeking warmth. "I'm sorry."

He recalled again that there was no tragic art on Gwydion. None whatsoever. He wondered why. He wondered what a *Lear* or an *Agamemnon* or an *Old Men at Centauri* might do to her. Or the real thing, even: Vard of Helldale rebelling for a family honor he didn't really believe in, defeated and slain by his own comrades; young Brand who broke his regimental oath, gave up friends and wealth and the mistress he loved more than the sun, to go live in a peasant's hut and tend his insane wife.

He wondered if he, himself, was healthy enough within his skull to live on Gwydion.

The girl rubbed her eyes. "Best we go down again," she said. "Others will soon be awake. They don't know what has become of us."

"We'll talk later," said Raven. "When we aren't so tired."

"Of course," she said.

CHAPTER SIX

Festival dwelt in Instar. Tolteca was reminded of Carnival Week on Nuevamerica—not the commercialized feverishness of the cities, but masquerade and street dancing in the hinterlands, where folk still made their own pleasure. Oddly enough, for a people otherwise so ceremonious, the Gwyndiona celebrated the time just before Bale by scrapping all formalism. Courtesy, honesty, nonviolence seemed too ingrained to lose. But men shouted and made horseplay, women dressed with a lavishness that would have been snickered at anytime else in the planet's long year, schools became playgrounds, each formerly simple meal was a banquet, and quite a few families broke out the wine and got humanly drunk. A garland of roses, jule, and pungent margwy herb hung on every door; no hour of day or night lacked music.

And so it was all over this world, thought Tolteca: in every town on every inhabited island, the year had turned green and the people were soon bound for their shrines.

He came striding down a gravel road. The sun stood at late morning and the boy Byord walked with a hand in his. Far and holy above western forests, the mountain peaks dreamed.

"What did you do then?" asked Byord, breathless.

"We stayed in the City till it rained," said Tolteca. "A couple of days, which we passed with games and stories. Then when it was safe, we proceeded to our goal, inspected it—a fine site indeed—and at last we came back here. We got in the day before yesterday, remember?"

"Gol! What's the City like?"

"Don't you know?"

" 'Course not 'cept they told us a little about it at school. I wasn't born, last Bale time. I'm going with my mother because I'm big enough."

"It's very beautiful," said Tolteca. He wondered how children this age fitted into a time of religious meditation if that was what it was, and how they kept so well afterward the secret of what happened.

"Tell me 'bout planets," said Byord. "When I get big, I want to be a spaceman. Like you."

"Why not?" said Tolteca. Byord could get as good a scientific education here as anywhere in the known galaxy. By the time he was old enough, the astro academies would doubtless be eager to enroll Gwydiona cadets. Gwydion itself would be more than a refueling stop, a decade hence. A people that gifted couldn't help themselves, they were certain to become curious about the universe (as if they weren't already so interested that only the intelligence of their questions made the number endurable) —and, yes, to influence it. The Empire had fallen; human society was once more in flux. What better ideal for the next civilization than Gwydion?

And why count myself out? thought Tolteca. *When we build our spaceports here, they'll require Namerican administrators, engineers, factors, liaicon officers. Why shouldn't I become one, and live my life under Ynis and She?*

He looked down at the tangled head near his waist. He'd always shuddered at the notion of acquiring a ready-made family. But why not? Byord was a polite and talented boy who still remained very much a boy. It would be a pleasure to take him fishing. Even today's outing—undertaken frankly to ingratiate one Miguel Tolteca with Elfavy and Simnon—had been a lot of fun.

When earlier, one of the Namerican spacemen had expressed a desire to settle here, Raven had warned him he'd go berserk in one standard year. But what did Raven know about it? The prediction was doubtless true enough for him. Lochlanna society, caste-ridden, haughty, ritualistic, and murderous has indeed nothing in common with Gwydion. *But Nueveramerica now—oh, I don't pretend I wouldn't miss the lights and tall buildings once in a while, but what's to prevent me and my family from taking vacation trips there? As for the rest, here are a calm, rational, but merry people with an ideal of beauty, uncrowded in a nature that has never been trampled on. And not static, either. They have their scientific research, innovations in the arts, engineering projects. Look how they welcome the idea of regular interstellar contact. How could I fail to fall in love with Gwydion?*

Specifically, with—Tolteca shut that thought off. He came from a civilization where all problems were practical problems. So let's not moon about, but rather take the indicated steps to get what we want. Since Byord was pestering him for yarns of other planets, he reminisced aloud, with some editing, and the rest of their walk passed quickly.

They entered the town. It looked deserted all at once. Where people had milled about a few hours ago, they now seemed to be indoors. Here and there a man hurried from one place to another, carrying some burden. It was quiet beneath the sun, but with an underlying murmur, voices behind walls.

Byord broke free and skipped in the street. "We're going soon, we're going soon," he caroled.

"How do you know?" asked Tolteca. He had been told long ago that there was no set date for Bale time.

Every freckle grinned. "I know, Adult Miguel! Aren't you comin' too?"

"I think I better stay and take care of your pets," said Tolteca. Byord maintained the usual small-boy zoo of bugs and amphibia.

"There's Granther! Hey, Granther!" Byord broke into a run. Dawyd, emerging from his house braced himself. When the small cyclone had struck him and been duly hugged, he pushed it toward the entrance.

"Go on inside, now," he said. "Your mother's making ready. She has to wash at least a few kilos of dirt off you and pack your lunch, before we start."

"Thanks, Adult Miguel!" Byord whoozed through the door.

Dawyd chuckled. "I hope you aren't too exhausted," he said.

"Not at all," Tolteca answered. "I enjoyed it. We went upstream to the House of the Philosophers. I never thought a

53

place devoted to abstract thinking would include picnic grounds and a carousel."

"Why not? Philosophers are human too, I'm told. It is refreshing for them to watch the children, romp with them…and perhaps a little respect for knowledge rubs off on the youngsters." Dawyd started down the street. "Would you like to accompany me? You being a technical man, this may interest you."

"Are you leaving now?" Tolteca fell into step.

"Yes. The signs have become clear, even to me. Older people are not so sensitive; the young adults have been wild all morning." Dawyd's eyes glittered, and his lined brown face held less than its normal serenity.

"It is about ten hours on foot to the Holy City," he added after a moment. "Less for a man unencumbered by children and aged. If you should, yourself, feel the time upon you, please do come after us."

Tolteca drew a long breath, as if to smell the tokens. The air was alive with the blooming of a hundred flowers, trees, bushes, vines; nectar-gathering insects droned in flooding sunlight. "You never told me what the signs are," he reminded.

At other times, Dawyd had been a little uneasy at such queries, and changed the subject—which was simple enough with so much to talk about, twelve hundred years of separate history. Now the physician laughed aloud. "I *can't* tell you," he said. "I know, that is all. How do buds know when to unfold?"

"But haven't you ever, in the rest of the year, made any scientific study of—"

"Here we are." Dawyd halted on the riverbank. The central fortress loomed square and bleak above them. Dawyd led the way inside, where long halls were cool and shadowy. Another man passed, holding a monkey wrench. Dawyd waved at him. "A technician," he explained. "Making a final check on the central power controls. Everything vital, or potentially dangerous, is stored here during Bale time: all motor vehicles in a garage down that way for instance. My own task—"

He opened a door, which gave on a huge and sunny room, gaily painted walls lined with cribs and playpens. A mobile robot stood by each, and a bright large machine murmured to itself in the center of the floor. Dawyd walked around, looking. "This is a routine and rather nominal inspection," he said. "The engineers have already overhauled everything. I have to certify the sanitation and pleasantness of the environment, but that has never been a problem."

"What is it for?" asked Tolteca.

"Do you not know? Why, to care for infants, those too young to accompany us to the Holy City. Byord is about as young as we ever dare take them. The hospital wing of this building has robots to nurse the sick and the very old during Bale time, but that is not under my supervision." Dawyd rubbed his chin. "What in the name of Chaos was I going to tell you? Oh, yes. In case you have not already been warned. The entire building is locked up during Bale. Automatic shock beams are fired at anyone—anything—that comes within ten meters. Any moving object that actually touches the outside wall is shot by the robots, flame blasts. Stay away from here!"

Tolteca stood quiet, for the last words had been alarmingly harsh.

Finally he ventured, "Isn't that rather extreme?"

"Bale time lasts about three of our days," said Dawyd, staring at a pen, the words tossed over his shoulder. "That's more than ten standard days. Plus the time to walk to the Holy City and back. We don't take chances."

"But—you've only carnivorous animals to fear, haven't you? A closed door, a barred window—"

Dawyd said, not entirely steadily, "We don't talk about it much. But Bale is, after all, when God comes, and God has Vwi Faces too. It isn't a safe time. Not everyone returns from the Holy City. Those who do, sometimes find that in spite of locks and shutters, there has been destruction. So we put our machines and our helpless people where nothing can enter till the time locks open themselves."

"Have you any idea," breathed Tolteca, "what causes...caused...the trouble?"

"No," said Dawyd. "We spend the entire time in the Holy City. It has been theorized, possibly the mountain ape is driven mad by the nearness of God, and comes down into the lowlands. Or conceivably, I don't know, conceivably we are not the only intelligent race on Gwydion. There are legends about underground creatures... But it is never a good idea to theorize in advance of the facts."

He continued his inspection with jerky movements, and in silence.

They were leaving the fortress when Tolteca suggested diffidently, "Perhaps we can observe what happens while you are gone."

Dawyd had cooled down again. "I doubt it," he said. "Many attempts were made in the past to plant cameras and other recording devices, but those were always evaded, or sometimes broken. I don't believe anything untoward will happen. Nothing has, for many years. Even in my own boyhood, a raid on a deserted town was a rare event. You must not believe this is a major problem for us.

Tolteca struck a cigarette. The streets were now entirely bare, save for himself and the older man. And yet the sun drenched them in light. It sharpened their desolation.

"I'm afraid you will have a dull time, actually." Dawyd was becoming more and more himself. "Everybody gone, everything locked up, all over the inhabited planet. Maybe you would like to fly down to the southern hemisphere, where no one lives, and explore a little."

"I think we'll just stay put and correlate our data," said Tolteca. "We have a lot. When you return—"

"We won't be worth much for a few days," said Dawyd. "It isn't easy for mortal flesh, being God."

They reached his house. He stopped at the door, embarrassed. "I should invite you in, but—"

"I understand. Family rites." Tolteca smiled. "I'll just stroll down to the park at town's end. You'll all pass by there on your way and I'll wave farewell."

"Thank you, far-friend."

The door closed. Tolteca stood a moment, inhaling deeply, before he ground the cigarette butt under his heel and walked off between shuttered walls.

The park was gay with flowers. A few of the expedition lounged under shade trees, also waiting to observe the departure. Tolteca saw Raven, and clamped lips together. *I will not lose my temper.* He approached and gave greeting.

Raven answered with Lochlanna formality. The mercenary was in full dress for the occasion, blouse, trousers, tooled leather boots, embroidered surcoat. He stood massive next to a baleflower bush as tall as himself. Its buds were opening in a riot of crimson blooms; they smelled like summer meadows and like something else almost but not quite remembered. The Siamese cat, Zio, nestled in Raven's arms; he stroked the beast with one hand and got a purr for answer.

Tolteca repeated Dawyd's warning about the fortress. Raven's dark head nodded. "I knew that. I'd do the same in their place."

"Yes, *you* would," said Tolteca. He remembered his resolution and added impersonally, "Such over-destructiveness doesn't seem characteristic of the Gwydiona, though."

"This isn't a characteristic season. Every five standard years, for about ten standard days, something happens to them, and I'd feel easier if I knew what."

"My guess—" Tolteca paused. He hated to say it aloud. But finally: "A dionysiac religion."

"I can't swallow that," said Raven. "These people know all about photosynthesis. They don't believe magic makes the earth fertile."

"They might employ such ceremonies anyhow." Tolteca winced, thinking of Elfavy, but if he didn't say it himself, someone else would; and he was mature enough, he insisted, to accept a person on her own cultural terms. "Orgiastic."

"No," said Raven. "They aren't an orgiastic folk. Not at any time of year. That cool, reasonable, humorous mentality couldn't take a free-for-all seriously enough. Someone would be bound to start laughing and spoil the whole effect."

Tolteca was happy to agree and to suggest: "Well, then, drugs? Hallucinogens? A lot of cultures, you know, some of them quite scientific, believe that peyote or lysergic acid or whatever reveals otherwise inaccessible truths."

"If that were so in this case," Raven answered, "they'd use the stuff oftener than once in five years. Nor would they make such a mystery of their religion; they'd tell us in plain polite words, we aren't initiates and it's none of our business what happens. Another trouble with your idea is that they shun drugs so completely in their everyday life. Do you know, this past day is the first instance I've seen or heard or read of any Gwydiona even getting high on alcohol?"

"Well," flared Tolteca, "suppose you tell me what they do!"

"I wish I could." Raven's troubled gaze went to the bale flower. "You said something about having this analyzed. Did you?"

"Yes. Orilla checked it out for me. Nothing special about it."

"Nothing at all?"

"Oa, its perfume does contain an indole, among other compounds, probably to attract pollinating insects. But quite harmless. If you breathed it at an extremely high concentration, you might get a little dizzy, I suppose, but you couldn't get a real jag."

Raven scowled. "And yet this bush is named for the festival. And alone on the whole planet, has no mythology."

"Xinguez and I threshed that out. He checked his linguistic references, bearing in mind that Gwydiona stems from a rather archaic dialect of Anglic, closely related to the original English. That word *bale* can mean several things, depending on ultimate derivation. It can be a bundle; a fire, especially a funeral pyre; an evil or sorrow; and, more remotely and with a different original spelling, *Baal* is an ancient word for a god."

Tolteca tapped a fresh cigarette on his thumbnail and struck it with a rough motion. "You can imagine how the Gwydiona would intertwine such multiple meanings," he continued. "What elaborate symbolisms they'd develop. Those flowers have long petals aimed upward; a bush in full bloom would look rather like a fire, I imagine. The Burning Bush of primitive religion. Hence, maybe, the name *bale*. But that could also mean 'God' and 'evil'. And it blooms just at Bale time. So because of all these coincidences, the bale flower symbolizes the Night Faces, the destructive aspect of reality...probably the most violent phase thereof, at that. Therefore, no one talks about it. The Gwydiona don't deny that evil and sorrow exist, but neither do they go out of their way to contemplate the fact."

"I know," said Raven. "In that respect, they're like Namericans."

"And in every other respect!" snapped Tolteca. "Including the fact that your bloody warlords are not going to carve up this planet!"

Raven turned his face to the engineer. So did Zio. It was disconcerting, for the cat's eyes were as cold and steady as the man's. "Are you quite certain," said Raven, "that these people are the same species as us?"

"Oa! If you think that just because they're too civilized to brew up war like you—" Tolteca advanced with fists cocked. *If Elfavy could only see!* it begged through the boiling within him. *If she could see what this animal really thinks of her!*

"Oh, quite possibly interbreeding is still feasible," said Raven. "We'll find that out soon enough."

Tolteca's fist leaped forward of itself.

Raven threw up an arm—Zio scampered to his shoulder—and blocked the blow. His hand slid down to seize Tolteca's own arm, his other hand got the Namerican's biceps, his foot scythed behind the oncoming ankles. Tolteca went on his back, pinned. The cat squalled and clawed at him.

"That isn't necessary, Zio." Raven let go. Several other men hurried up. He waved them away. "It was nothing," he called. "I was only demonstrating."

Kors looked dubious, but at that moment someone yelled, "They're coming," and attention went to the road.

Not that the parade was much to see. The Instar folk walked with an easy, distance-devouring stride. They were lightly clad; they carried the one lunch they would need on the way, spare garments, and nothing else. But their laughter and singing and rapid chatter were like a bird-flock, like sunlight on a windy lake, and now and then one of them danced among hurtling children. So they went past, a flurry of bright tunics, sunbrowned limbs, garlanded fair hair, up into the hills and the Holy City.

But Elfavy broke from them. She ran to Raven, caught both the soldier's hands in her own, and cried, "Come with us! Can't you feel it, *liatha?*"

He watched her a long while, his features wooden, before he shook his head. "No..."

Tears blurred her eyes, and that wasn't the way of Gwydion either. "You can never be God, then?" Her head drooped; the yellow mane hid her face. Tolteca stood staring. What else could he do?

"If I might give you the power," said Elfavy, "I would give up my own." She sprang free, raised hands to the sun and shouted, "But it's impossible that you can't feel it! God is here already, everywhere. I see Vwi shining from you, Raven! You must come!"

He folded his hands together within the surcoat sleeves. "Will you stay here with me?" he asked.

"Always, always."

"Now, I mean. During Bale time."

"What? Oh—no, yes—you are joking?"

He said slowly, "I'm told the Night Faces are also revealed, sometimes, under the Steeps of Kolumkill. That not everyone comes home every year."

Elfavy took a backward step from him. "God is more than good," she pleaded. "God is *real.*"

"Yes. As real as death."

"Great ylem!" exploded Tolteca. "What do you expect, man? Everybody who can walk goes up there. Some must have incipient disease, or weak old hearts, or old arteries. The excitement—"

Raven ignored him. "Is it a secret what happens, Elfavy?"

Her muscles untensed. Her laughter leaped forth. "No. It's only that words are such poor lame things."

"Well, tell me whatever words can, then. What do you do up there? What would a camera record?"

The blood drained from her face. She stood moveless. Eventually, out of a silence that grew and grew around her: "No. I can't."

"Or you mustn't?" Raven grabbed her bare shoulders so hard that his fingers sank in. She didn't seem to feel it. "You mustn't talk about it, or you won't, or you can't?" he roared. "Quick, now!"

Tolteca tried to stir, but his bones seemed locked together. The Instar people danced by, too lost in their joy to pay attention. The other Namericans looked indignant, but Wildenvey had drawn his gun, casually, and grinned in their faces. Elfavy shuddered. "I can't tell!" she gasped.

Raven's expression congealed. "You don't know," he said. "Is that it?"

"Let me go!"

He released her. She stumbled back against the bush. A moment she crouched, then drew a long breath. Tears caught sunlight on her cheeks, but she looked at the bruises on her skin, laughed, sprang forward, and kissed Raven on his unmoving lips. "Wait for me, then, *liatha!*" She whirled, ran, and was lost in the throng.

Raven gazed after them till they dwindled among the fields.

Tolteca said through a taste like vomit: "Well, are you satisfied?"

"In a way." Raven didn't stir. His words fell flat.

"Don't make too many assumptions," said Tolteca. "She's in an abnormal state. Wait till she comes back and is herself again, before you get your hopes up."

"What?" Raven turned his head, blinking wearily, and seemed to recognize Tolteca only after a few seconds. "Oh. But you're wrong. That's not an abnormal state."

"Huh?"

"Your planet has seasons. Do you consider spring fever a disease? Is it unnatural to feel brisk on a clear fall day?"

"Wait a minute. What are you hinting at?"

"Never mind." Raven lifted his shoulders and let them fall, an old man's gesture. "Come, Sir Engineer, we may as well go back to the ship."

"But— Oa!" Tolteca's finger stabbed at the Lochlanna. "Do you mean you've guessed—?"

"Yes. I may be wrong. Come, I say." Raven picked up Zio and became very busy making the cat comfortable in his sleeve.

"What?"

Raven started to go.

Tolteca caught him by the arm. Raven spun about. Briefly, the Lochlanna's face was drawn into such a snarl that the Namerican fell back. Raven clapped a hand to his dagger and whispered, "Don't ever do that again."

Tolteca braced his muscles. "What's your idea?" he demanded. "If Bale time really is dangerous—"

Raven leashed himself. "I see your thought. You want to go up there and stand by to protect her, don't you?"

"Yes. Suppose they do lie around in a comatose state. Some animal might sneak past the guard robots and—"

"No. You will stay down here. Everyone will. That's a direct order under my authority as military commander." Raven wet his lips. "Don't you see," he added, "this has been going on for more than a thousand years. By now they have evolved a system that minimizes the hazard. *Most* of them survive. The ancestors alone know what delicate balance you may upset by blundering in there."

After another pause: "I've been through this sort of thing before. Sent out men according to the best possible plan, and then sat and waited, knowing my own attempt to help could only throw askew the statistics of their survival. It's even harder to deal with God, who can wear any face." He started trudging. "You'll stay here and wait, like the rest of us."

Tolteca stared after him. Thought trickled into his consciousness. *The hell I will.*

CHAPTER SEVEN

Raven awoke more slowly than usual. He glanced at the clock. Death and plunder, had he been eleven hours asleep? Like a drugged man, too. He still felt tired. Perhaps because there had been evil dreams, he couldn't remember exactly what but they had left a scum of sadness in him. He sat on his bunk edge, rested head in hands, and tried to think. All he seemed able to do, though, was recall his father's castle, hawks nesting in the bell tower, himself about to ride forth and pausing to look down the mountainside, fells and woods and the peasants' enslaved fields, then everything hazed into blue hugeness. The wind had tasted of glaciers.

He pushed the orderly buzzer. Kors' big ugly nose came through the door.

"Tea," said Raven.

He scalded his mouth on it, but enough sluggishness departed him that he could will relaxation. His brain creaked into gear. It wasn't wise after all, simply to wait till the Instar people came home. He'd been too abrupt with Tolteca; but his knowledge had been too new in him. Now he felt able to discuss it. Not that he wanted to. What right had a storeful of greasy Namerican merchants to such a truth? But it was certain to be discovered sometime, by some later expedition; maybe a decent secrecy could be achieved, if an aristocrat made the first explanation.

Zio pattered after him as he left his cabin and went down a short passageway to Tolteca's. He knocked, but got no answer. Well, try the saloon... Captain Utiel sat there with a cigar and an old letter; he became aware of Raven by stages. "No, Commandant," he replied, "I haven't seen Sir Engineer Tolteca for, oh, two or three hours. He was going out to observe high tide from the dike-top, he said, and wouldn't be back for some time. Is it urgent?"

Raven stood motionless before answering, "Possibly. Did he have anyone with him? Or any instruments that you noticed?"

"No. Just a lunch and his sidearm." Bitterness uncoiled in Raven. "Did you seriously believe he was making a technical survey?"

"Why…well…I didn't really think about it… Well, he may simply have gone to admire the sight. The tide is impressive, you know."

Raven glanced at his watch. "Won't be high tide for hours."

Utiel sat up straight. "What's the matter?"

"Listen carefully," said Raven. "I am going out too. Stand by to lift ship. Keep someone on the radio. If I don't return, or haven't sent directions to the contrary, within—oh—thirty hours, go into orbit. In that event, and only in that event, one of my men will hand over to you a tape I've left in his care, with an explanation. Do you understand?"

Utiel rose. "I will not be treated in this fashion!" he barked.

"I didn't ask you that, Captain," said Raven. "I asked if you understood my orders."

Utiel grew rigid. "Yes, Commandant," he got out.

Raven went swiftly from the saloon. Once in the corridor, he ran. Kors gaped outside his cabin. "Fetch Wildenvey," said Raven. He clipped a tape to his personal recorder, dictated, released it, and sealed its container with wax and his family signet. Wildenvey knocked as he was slipping a midget transceiver into his pocket. Raven gave him the tape, with instructions, and added, "See if you can find Miguel Tolteca anywhere about. Roust the whole guard to help. If you do, call me on the radio and I'll head back."

"Where are you going, sir?" asked Kors.

"Into the hills. I am not to be followed."

Kors curled his lip and spat between two long yellow teeth. The gob clanged on a disposer chute. "Very good, sir. Let's go."

"You stay here and take care of my effects."

"Any obscene child of impropriety can do that, sir," said Kors, looking hurt.

Raven glanced at the man and felt his own mouth drawn faintly upward. "As you will, then. But if ever you speak a word about this, I'll yank out your tongue with my bare fingers."

"Aye, sir," Kors opened a drawer and took out a couple of field belts, with supplies and extra ammunition in the pouches.

Raven set Zio carefully on the bunk and stroked him under the chin. Zio purred. He tried to follow the men. Raven pushed him back and closed the door in his face. Zio scolded him in absentia for several minutes.

Emerging from the spaceship, Raven saw that dusk was upon the land. The sky was deeply blue-black, early stars in the east, a last sunset cloud above the western mountains like a streak of clotting blood. He thought he could hear the sea bellow beyond the dike.

"We going far, Commandant?" asked Kors.

"Maybe as far as the Holy City," said Raven. "On the double."

"Holy muck balls!" Kors clipped a flash beam to his belt and began jogging.

The first hour they went through open fields. Here and there stood an outlying house, black under blackening heaven. They heard livestock low, and the whir of machinery tending empty farms. If no one ever came back, wondered Raven, how long would the robots continue their routines? How long would the cattle stay tame, the infants alive?

The road ended, the ground rose in waves, only a trail pierced through boles and brush. The Lochlanna halted for a breather. "You're chasing Tolteca, aren't you, Commandant?" asked Kors. "Shall I kill the son of a bitch when we catch him, or do you want to?"

"*If* we catch him," corrected Raven. "He has a long head start, even though we can travel a good deal faster. No, don't shoot unless he resists arrest." He stopped a second, to underline what followed. "Don't shoot any Gwydiona. Under any circumstances whatsoever."

He fell silent, slumping against a tree in total muscular relaxation, trying to blank his mind. After ten minutes they resumed the march.

Trees and bushes walled either side of the trail, leaves made a low roof over head. It was very dark, only the bobbing light of Kors' flash picked stones and dust into relief. Beyond the soft thud of their feet, they could hear rustlings, creakings, distant chirps and croaks, the cold tinkle of a brook. Once an animal screamed. The air cooled as they climbed, but it always remained mild, and it overflowed with odors. Raven thought he could distinguish the smells of earth and green growth, the damp smell of water when a rivulet crossed the trail, certain individual flower scents; but the rest was unfamiliar. Smell is the most evocative sense, and forgotten things seemed to move below Raven's awareness, but he couldn't identify them. Overriding all else was the clear brilliant odor of bale flower. In the past few hours, every bush had come to full bloom.

Seen by daylight, tomorrow, the land would look as if it burned.

Time faded. That was a trick you learned early, from the regimental bronzes who instructed noblemen's sons. You needed it, to survive the waiting and the waiting of war without your sanity cracking open. You turned off your conscious mind. Part of it might revive during pauses in the march. Surely it was hard to stop at the halfway point for a drink of water and a bite of field ration, and not think about Elfavy. But it could be done, since it must.

The moon rose over Mount Granis. Passing an open patch of ground and looking downward, Raven saw the whole world turned to silver treetops. Then the forest gulped him again.

Some eight or nine hours after departure, Kors halted with an oath. His flashbeam picked out a thing that scuttled on spider like legs, a steel carapace, and arms ending in sword blades.

" 'S guts!" Raven heard a gun clank from a holster. The thing met the light with impersonal lens eyes, then slipped into the brush.

"Guard robot," said Raven. "It won't attack humans. We're close now, so douse that flash and shut up."

He led the way, cat-cautious in darkness, thinking that Tolteca must indeed have beaten him here. Though probably not by very long. Maybe the situation could still be rescued. He topped the final steep climb and poised on the upper edge of the great amphitheater.

For a moment the moonlight blinded him. She hung gibbous over the Steeps, turning them bone color and drowning stars. Then piece by piece Raven made out detail: mossy tiers curving downward to the valley floor, the ring of towers enclosing the ring-shaped labyrinth, even the central fountain and its thin mercury-like jet. Even the gardens full of bale flower, though they looked black against all that slender white. He heard a mumbling down in the forum, but couldn't see what went on. With great care he padded forward into the open.

"Hee-ee," said a man who sat on an upper terrace. "That's hollow, Bale-friend."

Raven stopped dead. Kors said something raw at his back. Slowly, Raven turned to face the man. He had seen him before, in Instar. Now he sat hugging his knees and grinning. There was blood on his mouth.

"It is, you know," he said. "Hollow. Hollow is God. I hail hollow, hollow hallow hullo."

Raven looked into the man's eyes, but the moonlight was so reflected from them that they stared blank. "Where did the blood come from?" he asked most quietly.

"She was empty," said the man. "Empty and so small. It wasn't good for her to grow up and be hollow. Was it? That much more nothing?" He rubbed his chin, regarded the wet fingers, licked them, and said plaintively, "The machines took her away. That wasn't fair. She was only a year and a half hollow."

Raven started down into the chalice.

"She came up about to my waist," said the voice behind him. "I think once, very long ago, before the hollow, I taught her to laugh. I even gave her a name once, and the name was Wormwood." Raven heard him begin to weep.

Kors took out his machine pistol, unclipped the holster, and clamped it on as a rifle stock. "Easy there," said Raven, not looking back but recognizing the noise. "You won't need that."

"The muck I won't," said Kors.

"We aren't going to fire on *any* Gwydiona. And I doubt if Tolteca will give trouble."

They reached level sward and passed under a tower. Raven remembered it was the one he had climbed before. A child stood in the uppermost window, battering herself against the grille and uttering no sound.

Raven went through a colonnade. Just beyond, at the edge of the forum, some fifty Instar people were gathered, mostly men. Their clothes were torn, and even in the moonlight, across meters of distance, Raven could see unshaven chins.

Miguel Tolteca confronted them. "But he killed that little girl!" Tolteca shouted. "He killed her with his bare hands and ran away wiping his mouth. And the robots took the body away. And all you do is stare!"

A man trod forth. Awe blazed on his face. "Under She," he called, his voice rising and falling, with something of the remote quality of a voice heard through fever. "And She is the cold reflector of Ynis, and Ynis Burning Bush, though we taste the river. If the river gives light, O look how my shadow dances!"

"As Gonril danced for his mother," said the one next to him. "Which is joy, since man comes from darkness when he is born."

"Night are Day Faces are God!"

"Dance, God!"

"Howl for God, Vwi burns!"

An old man turned to a young girl, knelt before her and said, "Give me your blessing, Mother." She touched his head with an infinite tenderness.

"But are you all crazy?" wailed Tolteca.

It snarled in the crowd of them. Those who had begun to dance stopped. A man with tangled gray hair advanced on Tolteca, who made a whimpering noise and retreated. Raven recognized Dawyd.

"What do you mean?" asked Dawyd. His tone was metal.

"I mean... I want to say... I don't understand—"

"No," said Dawyd. "What do you *mean*? What is your significance? Why are you here?"

"T-t-to help—"

They began circling about, closing off Tolteca's retreat. He fumbled after his sidearm, but blindly, as if knowing how few he could shoot before they dragged him down.

"You wear the worst of the Night Faces," groaned Dawyd. "For it is no face at all. It is Chaos. It is Emptiness. It is Meaninglessness."

"Hollow," whispered the crowd. "Hollow, hollow, hollow."

Raven squared his shoulders. "Stick close and keep your mouth shut," he ordered Kors. He stepped from the colonnade shadows, into open moonlight, and approached the mob.

Someone on its fringe was first to see him: a big young man, who turned with a bear's growl and shambled to meet the newcomers. Raven halted and let the Gwydiona walk into him. A crook-fingered hand swiped at his eyes. He evaded it, gave a judo twist, and sent the man spinning across the forum.

"He dances!" cried Raven from full lungs. "Dance with him!" He snatched a woman and whirled her away. "Dance on the bridge from Yin to Yang!"

They didn't—quite. They stood quieter than it seemed possible men could stand. Tolteca's mouth fell open. His face was a moonlit lake of sweat. "Raven," he choked, "Oa, ylem, Raven—"

"Shut up," muttered the Lochlanna. He edged next to the Namerican. "Stick by me. No sudden movements, and not a word."

Dawyd cringed. "I know you," he said. "You are my soul. And eaten with forever darkness and ever and no, no, no."

Raven raked his memory. He had heard so many myths, there must be one he could use...yes, maybe... His tones rolled out to fill the space within the labyrinth:

"There was a time when the Sunsmith ran in the shape of a harbuck with silver horns. A hunter saw him and pursued him. They fled up a mountainside, which was all grown over with crisflower, and wherever the harbuck's hoofs touched earth the crisflower bloomed, but wherever the hunter ran it withered. And at last they came to the top of the mountain, whence a river of fire flowed down a sheer cliff. The chasm beyond was cold, and so misty that the hunter could not even see if it had another side. But the harbuck sprang out over the abyss, and sparks showered where his hoofs struck—"

He held himself as still as they, but his eyes flickered back and forth, and he saw in the moonlight how they began to ease. The tiniest thawing stirred within him. He had not been sure he had grasped the complex symbolism of the myth he retold. Certainly he understood its meaning only in a vague way. But it was the right story. It could be interpreted to fit this situation, and thus turn his escape into a dance, which would lead men back into those rites that had evolved out of uncounted manslayings.

Still talking, he backed off, step by infinitesimal step, as if survival possessed its own calculus. Kors drifted beside him, screening Tolteca's shivers from their eyes.

But they followed. And others began to come from the buildings—from the towers, when they had passed through the colonnade again. When Raven put his feet on the first upward tier, a thousand faces must have been turned to him. None said a word, but he could hear them breathing, a sound like the sea beyond Instar's dike.

But now the myth was ended. He climbed another step, and another, always facing back to their upturned eyes. It seemed to him that She had grown more full since he descended into this valley. But it couldn't have taken that long. Could it?

Tolteca grasped his hand. The Namerican's fingers were ice. Kors' voice would have been inaudible a meter away: "Can we keep on retreating, sir, or d' you think those gooks will rush us?"

"I wish I knew," Raven answered. Even then, he was angered at the word Kors used.

Dawyd spread his arms. "Dance the Sunsmith home!" he shouted.

The knowledge of victory went through Raven like a knife. Nothing but discipline kept him erect. He saw the crowd swirl outward, forming a series of interlocked rings, and hissed to Kors: "We've made it, if we're careful. We have to continue backing up, slowly, waiting between every step, while they dance. If we disappear into the woods at the very end, I think they'll be satisfied."

"What's happening?" The words grated in Tolteca's throat.

"Quiet, I told you!" Raven felt the man stagger against him. Well, he thought, it had been a vicious shock, especially for someone with no real training in death. Talk might keep Tolteca from collapse, and the dancers below—now starting to tread a stately measure, absorbed in it as children—wouldn't be aware that the symbols above them whispered together.

"All right." Raven felt the rhythm of the dance indicate a backward step for him. He guided Tolteca with a hand to the elbow. "You came here with some idiotic notion of protecting Elfavy. What then?"

"I, I, I went down…to the plaza… They were—all mumbling—it didn't make sense, it was ghastly—"

"Not so loud!"

"I saw Dawyd. Tried to talk to him. They all, all got more and more excited. A little girl yelled and ran from me. That man, her father, I swear he was her father, killed her. The cleaning robots s-s-simply carried off the body. They began...closing in on me—"

"Enough. Now, steady. Another backward step. Halt." Raven stood as if cast in metal, for many heads turned his way. At this distance under the moon, they lacked faces.

When their attention had drifted back to the dance, Raven said, "It must be a mutation. Mutation and genetic drift, acting on a small initial population. Maybe that story of theirs is true, they're all descended from one man and two women—though it sounds like a myth— Their metabolism changed. They're all violently allergic to tobacco, for instance. Not that the change was great, in glandular terms. They may well be interfertile with us, biologically speaking. Though culturally, no, I don't believe they are the same species. Not anymore."

"Baleflower?" asked Tolteca. His tone was thin and shaky, like a hurt child's.

"Yes. You told me it emits an indole when it blooms. Not one that affects the normal human being's biochemistry; but still, chemically related to the substances associated with schizophrenia. *They* are susceptible. Every Gwydiona springtime, they go insane."

The soundless dance below jarred into a quicker, staccato beat. Raven used the chance to climb several tiers in a hurry.

"It's a wonder they survived the first few generations," he said when he must stop again. "Somehow, they did, and began the slow, painful adaptation. Naturally, they don't remember the insane episodes. They don't dare. That's the underlying reason why they've never made a scientific investigation of Bale, or taken the preventive measures that look so obvious to us. Instead, they built a religion and a way of life around it. But only in the first exuberant flush of the season are they even able to admit to themselves that they don't consciously know what happens. They worked out their culture, trial and error, through centuries, until they reached a point where little damage is done in their madness.

"Remember, their psychology isn't truly human. You and I are mixtures, good, bad, indifferent; our conflicts have we always with us. The Gwydiona seem to concentrate all their troubles into these few days. That's why there used to be so much destruction, till they stumbled into ways to cope with it. That's why they are so sane most of the year. In fact, they are so well adapted now that they don't, they can't colonize the rest of the planet. They don't know why, but I do; no bale flower. I wonder what would happen to a Gwydiona taken away from his periodic dementia. I suspect it would be rather horrible.

"Their material organization protects them: strong buildings, no isolated homes, no firearms, no atomic energy, everything that might be harmful or harmed locked away for the duration of hell. The Holy City there, every such spot on the planet, I suppose, is built like a warren, full of places to run and dodge and hide and lock yourself away when homicidal fury breaks loose. The walls are padded; the ground is soft. But of course, the main bulwark is psychological. Myths, symbols, rites, so much a part of their lives that even in their lunacy they remember. Probably more than in their sanity: things they dare not recall when conscious, the wild and tragic symbols, the Night Faces that aren't talked about. Slowly, over the generations, they've groped their way to a system that keeps their world somewhat meaningful, somewhat orderly, while the bale flower blooms. Which actually channels the mania, so that very few people get hurt anymore; so they act out their hates and fear, dance them out, believing their myths are true...instead of clawing each other in the physical eyes."

The dance was losing pattern. It wouldn't end after all, Raven thought, but merely dissolve into aimlessness. Well, that would serve, if he could disappear and be forgotten.

He said to Tolteca, "You had to come bursting into their dream universe and unbalance it. You killed that little girl."

"Oa, name of mercy." The engineer covered his face.

Raven sighed. "Forget it. Partly my fault. I should have told you at once what I surmised."

They were halfway up the terraces when someone broke through the dancers and came bounding toward them. Two, Raven saw, his heart gone hollow. The moonlight cascaded over their blond hair, turning it to frost.

"Stop," called Elfavy, low and with laughter. "Stop, Regan."

He wondered what sort of destiny the accidental likeness of his name to that of a myth would prove to be.

She paused a few steps below him. Byord clutched her hand, looking about from bright soulless eyes. Elfavy brushed a lock off her forehead, a gesture he remembered. "Here is the River Child, Regan," she called. "And you are the rain. And I am the Mother, and darkness in me."

Beyond her shoulder, he saw that others had heard. They were halting in the dance, one by one, and staring up.

"Welcome, then," said Raven. "Go back to your home in the meadows, River Child. Take him home, Bird Maiden."

Byord's small face opened. He screamed.

"Don't eat me, mother!"

Elfavy bent down and embraced him. "No," she crooned, "oh, no, no, no. You shall come to me. Don't you recall it? I was in the ground, and rain fell on me, and it was dark where I was. Come with me, River Child."

Byord shrieked and tried to break free. She dragged him up toward Raven. From the crowd below, a deep voice lifted: "And the earth drank the rain, and the rain was the earth, and the Mother was the Child and carried Ynis in her arms."

"Jingleballs!" muttered Kors. His scarecrow form slouched forward, to stand between the Commandant and those below. "That tears it."

"I'm afraid so," said Raven.

Dawyd sprang onto the lowest tier. His tone rang like a trumpet: "They came from the sky and violated the Mother! Can you hear the leaves weep?"

"Now what?" Tolteca glared at them, where they surged and shouted. "What do they mean? It's a nightmare, it doesn't make sense!"

"All nightmares make sense," Raven answered. The homicidal urge is awake and looking for something to destroy. And it has just figured out what, too."

"The ship, huh?" Kors hefted his gun.

"Yes," said Raven. "Rainfall is a fertility symbol. So what kind of symbol do you think a spaceship landing on your home soil and discharging its crew is? What would you do to a man who attacked your mother?"

"I'd hate to shoot those unarmed bastards," said Kors, "but—"

Raven snarled like an animal. "If you do, I'll kill you myself!"

He regained control and drew out his mini radio. "I'll warn Utiel. There mustn't be any spaceship for them to attack when they get there. Then we'll see if we can save our own hides."

Elfavy reached him. She flung Byord at his feet, where the boy sobbed in his terror, having insufficient mythic training to give pattern to that which stirred within him. Elfavy fixed her gaze wide upon Raven. "I know you," she panted. "You sat on my grave once, and I couldn't sleep."

He thumbed the minirad switch and put the little box to his lips. Her fingernails gashed his hand, which opened in sheer reflex. She snatched the box and flung it from her, further than he would have believed a woman could throw. "No!" she cried, "Don't leave the darkness in me, Regan! You woke me up once!"

Kors started forward. "I'll get it," he snapped. Elfavy pulled his knife from its sheath as he passed and thrust it between his ribs. He sank on all fours, astonished in the moonlight.

Down below, the howl of amok broke loose as they saw. Dawyd shuffled to the minirad box, picked it up, gaped at it, tossed it back into the mob. They halted a moment, a millrace.

Raven stooped over Kors. The soldier bubbled blood: "Get started, Commandant. I'll hold 'em." He picked up his gun and took an unsteady aim.

"No." Raven snatched it from him. "It's us who came to them."

"Horse apples," said Kors, and died.

Raven straightened. He handed Tolteca the gun and the withdrawn dagger, and added his own weapons. "On your way," he said. "You have to reach the ship before they do."

"You go!" Tolteca screamed.

"I'm trained in unarmed combat," said Raven. "I can hold them a good deal longer than you, clerk."

He stood thinking. Elfavy knelt beside him. She clasped his hand. Byord trembled at his feet.

"You might bear in mind next time," said Raven, "that a Lochlanna has obligations."

He gave Tolteca a shove. The Namerican drew a deep breath and ran.

"O the harbuck at the cliff's edge!" called Dawyd joyously. "The arrows of the sun are in him!" He went after Tolteca like a streak. Raven pulled loose from Elfavy, intercepted the older man, and stiff-armed him. Dawyd rolled down the green steps, into the band of men that yelped, and there they tore him apart.

Raven went back to Elfavy. She still knelt, holding her son, and he had never seen anything so gentle as her smile. "We're next," he said. "But you've time to get away. Run. Lock yourself in a tower room."

Her hair swirled about her shoulders with the gesture of negation. "Sing me the rest."

"You can save Byord too," he begged.

"It's such a beautiful song," said Elfavy.

Raven watched the men of Instar feasting. He hadn't much voice left, but he did his lame best.

> *"— 'Tis down in yonder garden green,*
> *Love, where we used to walk,*
> *The finest flower that e'er was seen*
> *Is withered to a stalk.*
> *The stalk is withered dry, my love,*
> *So will our hearts decay;*
> *So make yourself content, my love,*
> *Till God calls you away.' "*

"Thank you, Regan," said Elfavy.

"Will you go now?" he asked.

"I," she said. "How could I? We are the Three."

He sat down beside her, and she leaned against him. His free hand stroked the boy's damp hair.

Presently the crowd uncoiled itself and lumbered up the steps. Raven arose. He moved away from Elfavy, who remained where she was. If he could hold all their attention, she might survive the night.

And not remember.

THE END

If you've enjoyed this book, you will not want to miss these terrific titles…

ARMCHAIR MYSTERY-CRIME DOUBLE NOVELS, $12.95 each

B-16   **KISS AND KILL** by Richard Deming
         THE DEAD STAND-IN by Frank Kane

B-17   **DANGEROUS LADY** by Octavus Roy Cohen
         ONE HOUR LATE by William O'Farrell

B-18   **LOVE ME AND DIE!** by Day Keene
         YOU'LL GET YOURS by Thomas Wills

B-19   **EVERYBODY'S WATCHING ME** by Mickey Spillane
         A BULLET FOR CINDERELLA by John D. MacDonald

B-20   **WILD OATS** by Harry Whittington
         MAKE WAY FOR MURDER by A. A. Marcus

B-21   **THE ART STUDIO MURDERS** by Edward Ronns
         THE CASE OF JENNIE BRICE by Mary Roberts Rinehart

B-22   **THE LUSTFUL APE** by Bruno Fisher
         KISS THE BABE GOODBYE by Bob McKnight

B-23   **SARATOGA MANTRAP** by Dexter St. Claire
         CLASSIFICATION: HOMICIDE by Jonathan Craig

ARMCHAIR SCI-FI & HORROR DOUBLE NOVELS, $12.95 each

E-5   **THE IDOLS OF WULD** by Milton Lesser
         PLANET OF THE DAMNED by Harry Harrison

E-6   **BETWEEN WORLDS** by Garret Smith
         PLANET OF THE DEAD by Rog Phillips

E-7   **DAUGHTER OF THOR** by Edmond Hamilton
         TALENTS, INCORPORATED by Murray Leinster

E-8   **ALL ABOARD FOR THE MOON** by Harold M. Sherman
         THE METAL EMPEROR by Raymond A. Palmer

E-9   **DEATH HUNT** by Robert Gilbert
         THE BEST MADE PLANS by Everett B. Cole

E-10   **GIANT KILLER** by Dwight V. Swain
         GOLDEN AMAZONS OF VENUS by John Murray Reynolds

ARMCHAIR SCI-FI & HORROR GEMS SERIES, $12.95 each

G-21   **SCIENCE FICTION GEMS, Vol. Eleven**
         Rog Phillips and others

G-22   **HORROR GEMS, Vol. Eleven**
         Thorp McClusky and others

If you've enjoyed this book, you will not want to miss these terrific titles…

ARMCHAIR SCI-FI & HORROR DOUBLE NOVELS, $12.95 each

D-181   **THE LADY OF LIGHT** by Jack Williamson
        THE SWORDSMAN OF PIRA by Charles Recour

D-182   **A TWELVEMONTH AND A DAY** by Poul Anderson
        PREFERRED RISK by Lester Del Rey & Frederik Pohl

D-183   **PLANET OF THE KNOB-HEADS** by Stanton A. Coblentz
        OUT OF THE VOID by Leslie F. Stone

D-184   **DIVIDED WE FALL** by Raymond F. Jones
        VASSALS OF THE LODE-STAR by Gardner F. Fox

D-185   **THE ANT WITH THE HUMAN SOUL** by Bob Olsen
        NIGHT OF THE TROLLS by Keith Laumer

D-186   **GATEWAY TO INFINITY** Milton Lesser
        AROUND THE UNIVERSE by Ray Cummings

D-187   **WEST POINT, 3000 A. D.** by Manly Wade Wellman
        HOLY CITY OF MARS by Ralph Milne Farley

D-188   **M'BONG-AH** by Rog Phillips
        MERCENARY by Mack Reynolds

D-189   **THE GREAT MIRROR** by Arthur J. Burks
        TERROR FROM THE ABYSS by John Fletcher

D-190   **SINBAD: THROUGH TIME AND SPACE** by Chester S. Geier
        THE ENORMOUS ROOM by H. L. Gold and Robert W. Krepps

ARMCHAIR SCIENCE FICTION CLASSICS, $12.95 each

C-71   **WORLD'S FAIR, 1992**
       by Robert Silverberg

C-72   **THE PROFESSOR JAMESON SAGA, Book Three**
       by Neil R. Jones

C-73   **THAT WORLDS MAY LIVE**
       by Nelson S. Bond

ARMCHAIR SCI-FI & HORROR GEMS SERIES, $12.95 each

G-23   **SCIENCE FICTION GEMS, Vol. Twelve**
       Theodore Sturgeon and others

G-24   **HORROR GEMS, Vol. Twelve**
       Allison V. Harding and others

HUMANITY FACED A DARK FUTURE

The Company was a powerful, efficient, and monstrous organization that controlled the entire world, scientifically regulating everything in life: war, epidemics, one-a-day food pills, and test-tube sex…all through the use of its patented, terrifying human deep-freeze vault.

"Preferred Risk" is an extraordinary, prophetic novel of the world of tomorrow from two ingenious science fiction masters, Frederik Pohl and Lester del Rey. "Preferred Risk" was also the winner of the $6,500 Galaxy-Simon & Schuster novel-writing contest of 1955. It is a taut science fiction suspense story that asks the challenging question: how dangerous would it be to live in a rigidly risk-free world?

ORIGINAL COVER

Galaxy
SCIENCE FICTION

JUNE 1955

35¢

$6,500.00 PRIZE WINNING STORY

STARTS IN THIS ISSUE

"Preferred Risk" by Frederik Pohl & Lester del Rey; cover story to the June 1955 issue of Galaxy Science Fiction.

PREFERRED RISK

RISK

By
FREDERIK POHL & LESTER DEL REY

ARMCHAIR FICTION
PO Box 4369, Medford, Oregon 97504

*For more information about Armchair Books and products, visit our website
at…*

www.armchairfiction.com

Or email us at…

armchairfiction@yahoo.com

CHAPTER ONE

The liner from Port Lyautey was comfortable and slick, but I was leaning forward in my seat as we came in over Naples. I had been on edge all the way across the Atlantic. Now as the steward came through the compartments to pick up our Blue Plate ration coupons for the trip, I couldn't help feeling annoyed that I hadn't eaten the food they represented. For the Company wanted everyone to get the fullest possible benefit out of his policies—not only the food policies, but Blue Blanket, Blue Bolt and all the others.

We *whooshed* in to a landing at Carmody Field, just outside of Naples. My baggage was checked through, so I didn't expect to have any difficulty clearing past the truce-team Customs inspectors. It was only a matter of turning over my baggage checks, and boarding the *rapido* that would take me into Naples.

But my luck was low. The man before me was a fussbudget who insisted on carrying his own bags, and I had to stand behind him a quarter of an hour, while the truce-teams geigered his socks and pajamas.

While I fidgeted, though, I noticed that the Customs shed had, high up on one wall, a heroic-sized bust of Millen Carmody himself. Just standing there, under that benevolent smile, made me feel better. I even managed to nod politely to the traveler ahead of me as he finally got through the gate and let me step up to the uniformed Company expediter who checked my baggage tickets.

And the expediter gave me an unexpected thrill. He leafed through my papers, then stepped back and gave me a sharp military salute. "Proceed, Adjuster Wills," he said, returning my travel orders. It hadn't been like that at the transfer point at Port Lyautey—not even back at the Home Office in New York. But here we were in Naples, and the little war was not yet forgotten; we were under Company law, and I was an officer of the Company.

It was all I needed to restore my tranquility. But it didn't last.

The *rapido* took us through lovely Italian countryside, but it was in no hurry to do it. We were late getting into the city itself, and I found myself almost trotting out of the little train and up into the main waiting room where my driver would be standing at the Company desk.

I couldn't really blame the Neapolitans for the delay—it wasn't their fault that the Sicilians had atomized the main passenger field at Capodichino during the war, and the *rapido*wasn't geared to handling that volume of traffic from Carmody Field. But Mr. Gogarty would be waiting for me, and it wasn't my business to keep a Regional Director waiting.

I got as far as the exit to the train shed. There was a sudden high, shrill blast of whistles and a scurrying and, out of the confusion of persons milling about, there suddenly emerged order.

At every doorway stood three uniformed Company expediters; squads of expediters formed almost before my eyes all over the train shed; single expediters appeared and took up guard positions at every stairwell and platform head. It was a triumph of organization; in no more than ten seconds, a confused crowd was brought under instant control.

But why?

There was a babble of surprised sounds from the hurrying crowds; they were as astonished as I. It was reasonable enough that the Company's expediter command should conduct this sort of surprise raid from time to time, of course. The Company owed it to its policyholders; by insuring them against the hazards of war under the Blue Bolt complex of plans, it had taken on the responsibility of preventing war when it could. And ordinarily it could, easily enough.

How could men fight a war without weapons—and how could they buy weapons, particularly atomic weapons, when the Company owned all the sources and sold only to whom it pleased, when it pleased, as it pleased? There were still occasional outbreaks—witness the recent strife between Sicily and Naples itself—but the principle remained… Anyway, surprise raids were well within the Company's rights.

I was mystified, though—I could not imagine what they were looking for here in the Naples railroad terminal; with geigering at

Carmody Field and every other entry point to the Principality of Naples, they should have caught every fissionable atom coming in, and it simply did not seem reasonable that anyone in the principality itself could produce nuclear fuel to make a bomb.

Unless they were not looking for bombs, but for people who might want to use them. But that didn't tie in with what I had been taught as a cadet at the Home Office.

There was a crackle and an unrecognizable roar from the station's public-address system. Then the crowd noises died down as people strained to listen, and I began to understand the words: "...Where you are in an orderly fashion until this investigation is concluded. You will not be delayed more than a few minutes. Do not, repeat, *do not* attempt to leave until this man has been captured. Attention! Attention! All persons in this area! Under Company law, you are ordered to stop all activities and stand still at once. An investigation is being carried out in this building. All persons will stand still and remain where you are in an orderly fashion until this investigation..."

The mounting babble drowned the speaker out again, but I had heard enough.

I suppose I was wrong, but I had been taught that my duty was to serve the world, by serving the Company, in all ways at all times. I walked briskly toward the nearest squad of expediters, who were already breaking up into detachments and moving about among the halted knots of civilians, peering at faces, asking questions.

I didn't quite make it; I hadn't gone more than five yards when a heavy hand fell on my shoulder, and a harsh voice snarled in the Neapolitan dialect, "Halt, you! Didn't you hear the orders?"

I spun, staggering slightly, to face an armed expediter-officer. I stood at attention and said crisply, "Sorry. I'm Thomas Wills, Claims Adjuster. I thought I might be able to help."

The officer stared at me for a moment. His cheeks moved; I had the impression that, under other circumstances, he would have spat on the floor at my feet. "Papers!" he ordered.

I passed him my travel orders. He looked them over briefly, then returned them. Like the Customs expediter at Carmody Field, he gave me a snap salute, militarily precise and, in a way I could not quite define, contemptuous. "You should just stay here, Adjuster

Wills," he advised—in a tone that made it a command. "This will be over in a moment."

He was gone, back to his post. I stood for a moment, but it was easier to listen to his orders than to obey them; the Neapolitan crowd didn't seem to take too well to discipline, and though there was no overt resistance to the search squads, there was a sort of Brownian movement of individuals in the throng that kept edging me back and away from where I had been standing. It made me a little uncomfortable; I was standing close to the edge of a platform, and a large poster announced that the Milan Express was due to arrive on that track at any moment. In fact, I could hear the thin, effeminate whistle of its Diesel locomotive just beyond the end of the platform. I tried to inch my way from the edge. I dodged around an electric baggage-cart, and trod heavily on someone's foot.

"PREFERRED RISK"

By Frederik Pohl
& Lester del Rey

Interior illustrations
by Sanford Kossin

"Excuse me," I said quickly, looking at the man. He glared back at me. There was a bright spark in his eyes; I could tell little about his expression because, oddly enough in that country of clean-shaven faces, he wore a heavy, ragged, clipped beard. He wore the uniform of a porter. He mumbled something I could not quite catch, and moved as if to push me away. I suppose I put up my arm. My papers, with the Company seal bright gold upon them, were still in my hand, and the bearded man caught sight of them.

If there had been anger in his eyes before, there was now raging fury. He shrilled, "Beast! Animal!" He thrust at me blindly and leaped past me, out of the shelter of the bags; he went spinning furiously through the crowd, men and women ricocheting off him.

I heard a harsh bellow: "There he goes! Zorchi! Zorchi!" And I could hear the bearded man shrieking curses as he hurtled up the platform, up toward the oncoming train, over to the edge—and off the platform to the tracks!

He fell less than a yard in front of the slim nose of the Diesel. I don't suppose the speed of the train was even five miles an hour, but the engineer hadn't a chance in the world to stop.

While I watched, struck motionless, along with all the others on that platform, the engine passed over the huddled form. The brakes were shrieking, but it was much, much too late. Even in that moment I thought he would not be killed—not instantly, at least, unless he died of loss of blood. The trunk of his body was safely in the well between the tracks. But his legs were sprawled over a rail. And the slow click-click of the wheels didn't stop until his uniformed body was far out of sight.

It was shocking, sickening, unbelievable.

And it didn't stop there. A strange thing happened. When the man had dived into the path of the train, there was a sudden fearful hush; it had happened too suddenly for anyone to cry out. And when the hush ended, there was only a momentary, instinctive gasp of horror. Then there was a quick, astonished babble of voices— and then cheers! And applause, and ringing bravos!

I didn't understand.

The man had thrown himself deliberately under the train. I was sure of it.

Was that something to cheer?

I finally made it to where the Regional Director was waiting for me—nearly an hour late.

It was at a hotel overlooking the Bay, and the sight was thrilling enough to put the unpleasant accident I had seen out of my mind for a moment. There was nothing so beautiful in all the world, I thought, as the Bay of Naples at sunset. It was not only my own opinion; I had seen it described many times in the travel folders I had pored over, while my wife indulgently looked over my shoulder, back in those remote days of marriage. "La prima vista del mundo," the folders had called it—the most beautiful sight of the world. They had said: "See Naples, and die."

I hadn't known, of course, that Marianna would die first...

But that was all behind me. After Marianna's death, a lot of things had happened, all in a short time, and some of them very bad. But good or bad, I had laid down a law for myself: I would not dwell on them. I had started on a new life, and I was going to put the past in a locked compartment in my mind. I had to!

I was no longer an ordinary civilian, scraping together his Blue Heaven premiums for the sake of a roof over his head, budgeting his food policies, carrying on his humdrum little job. I was a servant of the human race and a member of the last surviving group of gentleman-adventurers in all the world: I was an Insurance Claims Adjuster for the Company!

All the same, I couldn't quite forget some of the bad things that had happened, as I walked into the hotel dining room to meet the Regional Director.

Regional Director Gogarty was a huge, pale balloon of a man. He was waiting for me at a table set for four. As he greeted me, his expression was sour. "Glad to meet you, Wills. Bad business, this. Bad business. He got away with it again."

I coughed. "Sir?" I asked.

"Zorchi!" he snapped. And I remembered the name I had heard on the platform. The mad-man! Zorchi, Luigi Zorchi, the human jellyfish. "Wills, do you know that that man has just cashed in on his *twelfth* disability policy? And not a thing we could do to stop him! You were there. You saw it, didn't you?"

"Well, yes, but—"

"Thought so. The twelfth! And your driver said on the phone it was both legs this time. Both legs—and on a common carrier. Double indemnity!" He shook his enormous head. "And with a whole corps of expediters standing by to stop him!"

I said with some difficulty, "Sir, do you mean that the man I saw run over by the train was—"

"Luigi Zorchi. That's who he was. Ever hear of him, Wills?"

"Can't say I have."

Gogarty nodded his balloon-like head. "The Company has kept it out of the papers, of course, but you can't keep anything from being gossiped about around here. This Zorchi is practically a national hero in Naples. He's damn near a millionaire by now, I guess, and every lira of it has come right out of the Company's indemnity funds. And do you think we can do anything about it? Not a thing! Not even when we're tipped off ahead of time—when, what, and where!

"He just laughs at us. I know for a fact," Gogarty said bitterly, "that Zorchi knew we found out he was going to dive in front of that express tonight. He was just daring us to stop him. We should have! We should have figured he might disguise himself as a porter. We should—"

I interrupted, "Mr. Gogarty, are you trying to tell me this man *deliberately* maims himself for the accident insurance?" Gogarty nodded sourly. "Good heavens," I cried, "that's disloyal!"

Gogarty laughed sharply and brought me up standing. There was a note to the way he laughed that I didn't like; for a moment there, I thought he was thinking of my own little—well, indiscretion. But he said only, "It's expensive, too." I suppose he meant nothing by it. But I was sensitive on the subject.

Before I could ask him any more questions, the massive face smoothed out in a smile. He rose ponderously, greeting someone. "Here they are, Wills," he said jovially. "The girls!"

The headwaiter was conducting two young ladies toward us. I remembered my manners and stood up, but I confess I was surprised. I had heard that discipline in the field wasn't the same as at the Home Office, but after all—Gogarty was a Regional Director!

It was a little informal of him to arrange our first meeting at dinner, in the first place. But to make a social occasion of it was—in the straitlaced terms of the Home Office where I had been trained—almost unthinkable.

And it was apparent that the girls were mere decoration. I had a hundred eager questions to ask Gogarty—about this mad Zorchi, about my duties, about Company policy here in the principality of

Naples—but it would be far out of line to bring up Company matters with these females present. I was not pleased, but I managed to be civil.

The girls were decorative enough, I had to admit.

Gogarty said expansively, all trace of ill humor gone, "This is Signorina dell'Angela and Miss Susan Manchester. Rena and Susan, this is Tom Wills."

I said stiffly, "Delighted."

Susan was the blonde one, a small plump girl with the bubbly smile of a professional model. She greeted Gogarty affectionately. The other was dark and lovely, but with a constant shadow, almost glowering, in her eyes.

So we had a few drinks. Then we had a few more. Then the captain appeared with a broad menu, and I found myself in an embarrassing position. For Gogarty waved the menu aside with a gesture of mock disgust. "Save it for the peasants," he ordered. "We don't want that Blue Plate slop. We'll start with those little baby shrimps like I had last night, and then an antipasto and after that—"

I broke in apologetically, "Mr. Gogarty, I have only a Class-B policy."

Gogarty blinked at me. "What?"

I cleared my throat. "I have only Class-B coverage on my Blue Plate policy," I repeated. "I, uh, I never went in much for such—"

He looked at me incredulously. "Boy," he said, "this is on the Company. Now relax and let me order. Blue Plate coverage is for the peasants; I eat like a human being."

It shook me a little. Here was a Regional Director talking about the rations supplied under the Company's Blue Plate coverage as "slop." Oh, I wasn't naive enough to think that no one talked that way. There were a certain number of malcontents anywhere. I'd heard that kind of talk, and even worse, once in a while from the Class-D near-uninsurables, the soreheads with a grudge against the world who blamed all their troubles on the Company and bleated about the "good old days." Mostly they did their bleating when it was premium time, I'd noticed.

But I certainly never expected it from Gogarty.

Still—it was his party. And he seemed like a pretty nice guy. I had to allow him the defects of his virtues, I decided. If he was less reverent to the Company than he should have been, at least by the same token he was friendly and democratic. He had at least twenty years seniority on me, and back at the Home Office a mere Claims Adjuster wouldn't have been at the same table with a Regional Director.

And here he was feeding me better than I had ever eaten in my life, talking as though we were equals, even (I reminded myself) seeing to it that we had the young ladies to keep us company.

We were hours at dinner, hours and endless glasses of wine, and we talked continually. But the conversation never came close to official business.

The girl Rena was comfortable to be with, I found. There was that deep, eternal sadness in her eyes, and every once in a while I came up against it in the middle of a laugh; but she was soft-voiced and pleasant, and undeniably lovely. Marianna had been prettier, I thought, but Marianna's voice was harsh Midwest while Rena's—

I stopped myself.

When we were on our after-dinner liqueurs, Rena excused herself for a moment and, after a few minutes, I spotted her standing by a satin-draped window, looking wistfully out over a balcony. Gogarty winked.

I got up and, a little unsteadily, went over to her. "Shall we look at this more closely?" I asked her. She smiled and we stepped outside.

Again I was looking down on the Bay of Naples—a scene painted in moonlight this time, instead of the orange hues of sunset. It was warm, but the Moon was frosty white in the sky. Even its muddled reflection in the slagged waters was grayish white, not yellow. There was a pale orange halo over the crater of Mount Vesuvius, to our left; and far down the coast a bluish phosphorescence, over the horizon, marked Pompeii. "Beautiful," I said.

She looked at me strangely. All she said was, "Let's go back inside."

Gogarty greeted us. "Looking at the debris?" he demanded jovially. "Not much to see at night. Cheer up, Tom. You'll see all the damage you want to see over the next few days."

I said, "I hope so, sir."

Gogarty shook his head reprovingly. "Not 'sir,' Tom. Save that for the office. Call me Sam." He beamed. "You want to know what it was like here during the war? You can ask the girls. They were here all through. Especially Susan—she was with the Company's branch here, even before I took over. Right, Susan?"

"Right, Sam," she said obediently.

Gogarty nodded. "Not that Rena missed much either, but she was out of town when the Sicilians came over. Weren't you?" he demanded, curiously intent. Rena nodded silently. "Naples sure took a pasting," Gogarty went on. "It was pretty tough for a while. Did you know that the Sicilians actually made a landing right down the coast at Pompeii?"

"I saw the radioactivity," I said.

"That's right. They got clobbered, all right. Soon's the barges were in, the Neapolitans let them have it. But it cost them. The Company only allowed them five A-bombs each, and they had to use two more to knock out Palermo. And—well, they don't like to tell this on themselves, but one of the others was a dud. Probably the only dud A-bomb in history, I guess."

He grinned at Rena. Astonishingly, Rena smiled back.

She was, I thought, a girl of many astonishing moments; I had not thought that she would be amused at Gogarty's heavy-handed needling.

Gogarty went on and on. I was interested enough—I had followed the Naples-Sicily war in the papers and, of course, I'd been briefed at the Home Office before coming over—but the girls seemed to find it pretty dull. By the time Gogarty finished telling me about the Sicilian attempt to trigger Mt. Vesuvius by dropping an A-bomb into its crater, Rena was frankly bored and even Susan was yawning behind her palm.

We finally wound up under the marquee of the restaurant. Gogarty and the blonde politely said good night, and disappeared into a cab. It was clearly up to me to take Rena home.

I hailed a cab. When I made up my new insurance schedule at the Home Office before coming over, I splurged heavily on transportation coverage. Perhaps I was making up for the luxuries of travel that life with Marianna hadn't allowed me. Anyway, I'd taken out Class AA policies. And as the cab driver clipped my coupons he was extremely polite.

Rena lived a long way from the hotel. I tried to make small talk, but she seemed to have something on her mind. I was in the middle of telling her about the terrible "accident" I had seen that evening at the station—suitably censored, of course—when I observed she was staring out the window.

She hadn't been paying attention while I talked, but she noticed the silence when I stopped. She gave a little shake of the head and looked at me. "I'm sorry, Mr. Wills," she said. "I am being rude."

"Not at all," I said gallantly.

"Yes." She nodded and smiled, but it was a thoughtful, almost a sad, smile. "You are too polite, you gentlemen of the Company. Is that part of your training?"

"It's easy to be polite to you, Miss dell'Angela," I said by rote. Yes, it was part of our training: *A Claims Adjuster is always courteous.* But what I said was true enough, all the same. She was a girl that I enjoyed being polite to.

"No, truly," she persisted. "You are an important officer in the Company, and you must have trained long for the post. What did they teach you?"

"Well—" I hesitated. "Just the sort of thing you'd expect, I guess. A little statistical mathematics—enough so we can understand what the actuaries mean. Company policies, business methods, administration. Then, naturally, we had a lot of morale sessions. A Claims Adjuster—" I cleared my throat, feeling a little self-conscious. "A Claims Adjuster is supposed to be like Caesar's wife, you know. He must always set an example to his staff and to the public. I guess that sounds pretty stuffy. I don't mean it to be. But there is a lot of emphasis on tradition and honor and discipline."

She asked, rather oddly, "And is there a course in loyalty?"

"Why, I suppose you might say that. There are ceremonies, you know. And it's a matter of cadet honor to put the Company ahead of personal affairs."

"And do all Claims Adjusters live by this code?"

For a moment I couldn't answer. It was like a blow in the face. I turned sharply to look at her, but there was no expression on her face, only a mild polite curiosity.

I said with difficulty, "Miss dell'Angela, what are you getting at?"

"Why, nothing!" Her face was as angelic as her name.

"I don't know what you mean or what you may have heard about me, Miss dell'Angela, but I can tell you this, if you are interested. When my wife died, I went to pieces. I admit it. I said a lot of things I shouldn't have, and some of them may have reflected against the Company. I'm not trying to deny that but, you understand, I was upset at the time. I'm not upset now." I took a deep breath. "To me, the Company is the savior of humanity. I don't want to sound like a fanatic, but I am loyal to the Company, to the extent of putting it ahead of my personal affairs, to the extent of doing whatever job the Company assigns to me. And, if necessary, to the extent of dying for it if I have to. Is that clear?"

Well, that was a conversation-stopper, of course. I hadn't meant to get all wound up about it, but it hurt to find out that there had been gossip. The dell'Angela girl merely said: "Quite clear."

We rode in silence for a while. She was staring out the window again, and I didn't especially want to talk just then. Maybe I was too sensitive. But there was no doubt in my mind that the Company was the white hope of the world, and I didn't like being branded a traitor because of what I'd said after Marianna died. I was, in a way, paying the penalty for it—it had been made pretty clear to me that I was on probation. That was enough.

As I said, she lived a long way from the Gran Reale. I had plenty of time for my flare-up, and for brooding, and for getting over it.

But we never did get around to much idle conversation on that little trip. By the time I had simmered down, I began to have disturbing thoughts. It suddenly occurred to me that I was a man, and she was a girl, and we were riding in a cab.

I don't know how else to say it. At one moment I was taking her home from a dinner; and at the next, I was taking her home from a date. Nothing had changed—except the way I looked at it.

All of a sudden, I began to feel as though I were fourteen years old again. It had been quite a long time since I had had the duty of escorting a beautiful girl—and by then I realized this was a really *beautiful* girl—home at the end of an evening. And I was faced with the question that I had thought would never bother me again at least a decade before. Should I kiss her good night?

It was a problem, and I thought about it, feeling a little foolish but rather happy about it. But all my thinking came to nothing. She decided for me.

The cab stopped in front of a white stucco wall. Like so many of the better Italian homes, the wall enclosed a garden, and the house was in the middle of the garden. It was an attractive enough place—Class A at least, I thought—though it was hard to tell in the moonlight.

I cleared my throat and sort of halfway leaned over to her.

Then she turned and was looking up at me, and the moonlight glinted brightly off what could only have been tears in her eyes.

I stared.

She didn't say a word. She shook her head briefly, opened the door and was gone behind the gate.

It was a puzzlement. Why had she been crying? What had I done?

I reviewed my conduct all the way back to the hotel, but nothing much came of it. Perhaps I had been brusque—but brusque enough to bring tears? I couldn't believe it.

Curious new life! I fell asleep with the pale moon shining in the window, brooding about the life I was just beginning, and about the old life behind me that was buried in the same grave with Marianna.

CHAPTER TWO

The Naples branch of the Company lay in the heart of the city. I took a cab to a sort of dome-roofed thing called a *galleria*, and walked under its skeletal steel ceiling to my new office. Once the *galleria* had been roofed with glass, but the glass had powdered down from the concussion of the Mt. Vesuvius bomb, or the Capodichino bomb, or one of the other hammerblows the Sicilians had rained on the principality of Naples in the recent unpleasantness.

I entered the office and looked around. The blonde girl named Susan appeared to double as the office receptionist. She nodded efficiently and waved me to a fenced-off enclosure where Sam Gogarty sat, plump and untroubled, at an enormous desk.

I pushed open the swinging gate.

Gogarty looked at me icily. "You're late," he said.

He had no hangover, it was clear. I said apologetically, "Sorry, I'm—"

"Never mind. Just don't let it happen again." It was clear that, in the office, business was business; the fact that we had been drinking together the night before would not condone liberties the morning after. Gogarty said, "Your desk is over there, Wills. Better get started."

I felt considerably deflated as I sat down at my desk and stared unhappily at the piles of blue and yellow manifolds before me.

The Company had trained me well. I didn't need to be coached in order to get through the work; it was all a matter of following established techniques and precedents. I checked the coverage, reduced the claim to tape-code, fed the tapes into a machine.

If the claim was legitimate, the machine computed the amounts due and issued a punch-card check. If there was anything wrong, the machine flashed a red light and spat the faulty claim out into a hopper.

And there were plenty of claims. Every adult in Naples, of course, carried the conventional War-and-Disaster policy—the so-called Blue Bolt coverage. Since few of them had actually been injured in the war, the claims were small—mostly for cost of premiums on other policies, under the disability clauses. (For if war prevented a policyholder from meeting his Blue Plate premiums, for instance, the Company itself under Blue Bolt would keep his policies paid—and the policyholder fed.)

But there were some big claims, too. The Neapolitan government had carried the conventional Blue Bolt policies and, though the policy had been canceled by the Company before hostilities broke out—thus relieving the Company of the necessity of paying damages to the principality of Naples itself—still there were all the subsidiary loss and damage claims of the Neapolitan government's bureaus and departments, almost every one of them non-canceling.

It amounted to billions and billions of lire. Just looking at the amounts on some of the vouchers before me made my head swim. And the same, of course, would be true in Sicily. Though that would naturally be handled by the Sicilian office, not by us.

However, the cost of this one brief, meager little war between Naples and Sicily, with less than ten thousand casualties, lasting hardly more than a week, must have set the Company's reserves back hundreds of millions of dollars.

And to think that some people didn't like the Company! Why, without it, the whole peninsula of Italy would have been in financial ruin, the solvent areas dragged down with the combatants!

Naturally, the Regional Office was understaffed for this volume of work—which is why they had flown in new Adjusters like myself.

I looked up from my desk, surprised. Susan was standing next to me, an aspirin and a paper cup of water in her hand. "You look like you might need this," she whispered. She winked and was gone.

I swallowed it gratefully, although my hangover was almost gone. I was finding in these dry papers all the romance and excitement I had joined the Company's foreign service for. Here before me were human lives, drama, tragedy, even an occasional touch of human-interest comedy.

For the Company was supporting most of Naples and whatever affected a Neapolitan life showed up somehow in the records of the Company.

It was a clean, *dedicated* feeling to work for the Company. The monks of the Middle Ages might have had something of the same positive conviction that their work in the service of a mighty churchly empire was right and just, but surely no one since.

I attacked the mountain of forms with determination, taking pleasure in the knowledge that every one I processed meant one life helped by the Company.

It was plain in history, for all to see. Once the world had been turbulent and distressed, and the Company had smoothed it out. It had started with fires and disease. When the first primitive insurance companies—there were more than one, in the early days—began offering protection against the hazards of fire, they had found it wise to try to prevent fires. There were the advertising campaigns with their wistful-eyed bears pleading with smokers not to drop their lighted cigarettes in the dry forest; the technical bureaus like the Underwriter's Laboratory, testing electrical equipment, devising intricate and homely gimmicks like the underwriter's knot; the Fire Patrol in the big cities that followed up the city-owned Fire Department; the endless educational sessions in the schools... And fires decreased.

Then there was life insurance. Each time a death benefit was paid, a digit rang up on the actuarial scoreboard. Was tuberculosis a major killer? Establish mobile chest X-rays; alert the people to the meaning of a chronic cough. Was it heart disease? Explain the dangers of overweight, the idiocy of exercise past forty. People lived longer.

Health insurance followed the same pattern. It had begun by paying for bills incurred during sickness, and ended by providing full medical sickness prevention and treatment for all. Elaborate research programs reduced the danger of disease to nearly nothing. Only a few rare cases, like that of Marianna...

I shook myself away from the thought. Anyway, it was neither fire nor health insurance that concerned me now, but the Blue Bolt anti-war complex of the Company's policies. It was easy enough to see how it had come about. For with fire and accident and disease ameliorated by the strong protecting hand of the Company, only one major hazard remained—war.

And so the Company had logically and inevitably resolved to wipe out war.

I looked up. It was Susan again, this time with a cardboard container of coffee.

"You're an angel," I said. She set the coffee down and turned to go. I looked quickly around to make sure that Gogarty was busy, and stopped her. "Tell me something?"

"Sure."

"About this girl, Rena. Does she work for the Company?"

Susan giggled. "Heavens, no. What an idea!"

"What's so strange about it?"

She straightened out her face. "You'd better ask Sam—Mr. Gogarty, that is. Didn't you have a chance to talk to her last night? Or were you too busy with other things?"

"I only want to know how she happened to be with you."

Susan shrugged. "Sam thought you'd like to meet her, I guess. Really, you'll have to ask him. All I know is that she's been in here quite a lot about some claims. But she doesn't work here, believe me." She wrinkled her nose in amusement. "And I won't work here either, if I don't get back to my desk."

I took the hint. By lunch time, I had got through a good half of the accumulation on my desk. I ate briefly and not too well at a nearby *trattoria* with a "B" on the Blue Plate medallion in its window. After the dinner of the night before, I more than half agreed with Gogarty's comments about the Blue Plate menus.

Gogarty called me over when I got back to the office. He said, "I haven't had a chance to talk to you about Luigi Zorchi."

I nodded eagerly. I had been hoping for some explanations.

Gogarty went on, "Since you were on the scene when he took his dive, you might as well follow up. God knows you can't do worse than the rest of us."

I said dubiously, "Well, I saw the accident, if that's what you mean."

"Accident! What accident? This is the twelfth time he's done it, I tell you." He tossed a file folder at me. "Take a look! Loss of limbs—four times. Internal injuries—six times. Loss of vision, impaired hearing, hospitalization and so on—good lord, I can't count the number of separate claims. And, every one, he has collected on. Go ahead, look it over."

I peered at the folder. The top sheet was a field report on the incident I had watched, when the locomotive of the Milan express had severed both legs. The one below it, dated five weeks earlier, was for flash burns suffered in the explosion of a stove, causing the loss of the right forearm nearly to the elbow.

Curious, I thought, I hadn't noticed anything when I saw the man on the platform. Still, I hadn't paid too much attention to him at first, and modern prosthetic devices were nearly miraculous. I riffled through the red-bordered sheets. The fifth claim down, nearly two years before, was—

I yelped, "Mr. Gogarty! This is a fraud!"

"What?"

"Look at this! 'On 21st October, the insured suffered severe injuries while trapped in a rising elevator with faulty safety equipment, resulting in loss of both legs above knees, multiple lacerations of—' Well, never mind the rest of it. But look at that, Mr. Gogarty! He already lost both legs! He can't lose them twice, can he?"

Gogarty sat back in his chair, looking at me oddly. "You startled me," he complained. "Wills, what have I been trying to tell you? That's the whole point, boy! No, he didn't lose his legs twice. It was *five* times!"

I goggled at him. "But—"

"But, but. But he did. Wait a minute—" He held up a hand to stop my questions. "Just take a look through the folder. See for yourself." He waited while, incredulously, I finished going through the dossier. It was true. I looked at Gogarty wordlessly.

He said resentfully, "You see what we're up against? And none of the things you are about to say would help. There is no mistake in the records—they've been double and triple-checked. There is no possibility that another man, or men, substituted for Zorchi— fingerprints have checked every time. The three times he lost his arms, retina-prints checked. There is no possibility that the doctors were bribed, or that he lost a little bit more of his leg, for instance, in each accident—the severed sections were recovered, and they were complete. Wills, *this guy grows new arms and legs like a crab!*"

I looked at him in a daze. "What a fantastic scientific discovery!" I said.

He snorted. "Fantastic pain in the neck! Zorchi can't go on like this; he'll bankrupt the Company. We can't stop him. Even when we were tipped off this time—we couldn't stop him. And I'll tell you true, Wills, that platform was loaded with our men when Zorchi made his dive. You weren't the only Adjuster of the Company there."

He picked a folded sheet of paper out of his desk. "Here. Zorchi is still in the hospital; no visitors allowed today. But I want you to take these credentials and go to see him tomorrow. You came to us with a high recommendation from the Home Office, Wills—" That made me look at him sharply, but his expression was innocent. "You're supposed to be a man of intelligence and resourcefulness. See if you can come up with some ideas on dealing with that situation. I'd handle it myself, but I've got..." He grimaced. "...certain other minor administrative difficulties to deal with. Oh, nothing important, but you might as well know that there appears to be a little, well, popular underground resentment toward the Company around here."

"Incredible!" I said.

He looked at me thoughtfully for a moment. "Well," he said, "it's quitting time. See you in the morning."

I had a lonely dinner at the same cheap restaurant where I'd had my lunch. I spent an hour in my room with my Company-issued *Adjuster's Handbook*, looking for some precedent that had some sort of bearing on the case of a man who could grow new arms and legs. There wasn't anything, of course. I went out for a walk...and still it wasn't nearly time for me to retire to bed.

So I did what I had been avoiding doing. I looked in the phone book for Rena dell'Angela's number. There was, it developed, a Benedetto dell'Angela at the address she'd given the cab driver; but the phone was disconnected.

So I wandered around some more, and then I went to sleep, dreaming about Benedetto dell'Angela. I saw him as a leather-faced, white-bearded and courtly old gentleman. Rena's father, surely. Possibly even her elder brother. Certainly not her husband.

It was a dull finish to the first full day of my rich, exciting new life...

The "minor administrative difficulties" got major. So I didn't get to see Zorchi the next day, after all.

A Junior Adjuster named Hammond—he was easily sixty, but the slow-moving, unenterprising type that would stay junior till the day he died—came white-faced into the office a few minutes after opening and huddled with Gogarty for a quarter of an hour.

Then Gogarty called me over. He said, "We're having a spot of trouble. Hammond needs a little help; you're elected. Draw what you need, take a couple of expediters along, report back to me this evening."

Hammond and I stopped at the cashier's office to draw three dispatch-cases full of lira-notes. Outside, an armored car was waiting for us, with a full crew of six uniformed expediters. We raced off down the narrow streets with the sirens wailing, climbing the long hill road past the radioactive remains of Capodichino, heading out toward the farmlands.

Hammond worriedly filled me in on the way. He had got in early to his branch office that morning, but no earlier than the first of a long line of policyholders. There had, it appeared, been some kind of rumor spread that the Company was running out of money. It was preposterous on the face of it—after all, who *printed* the money?—but you can't argue with a large group of people and, before the official hour of opening the branch, there were more than a hundred in the knotted line outside the door.

Hammond had rushed into the Naples office for help, leaving his staff to do the best they could. He said gloomily, staring out through the view-slits at the farmlands and vineyards we were passing through, "I just hope we still have a branch office. This is a bad spot, Wills. Caserta. It got bombed out, you know; the whole southern end of the town is radioactive. And it has a long history of trouble. Used to be the summer royal seat of the old Italian monarchy; then the Americans used it for a command headquarters in the war Mussolini got into—the first atom war. It's been fought over time and again."

I said reasonably, "But don't they know the Company has all the resources in the world?"

"Sure they do—when they're thinking. Right now they're not thinking. They've got it in their heads that the Company isn't going to pay off. They're scared. You can't tell them anything. You can't even give them checks—they want cash on the line."

I said, "That's pretty silly, isn't it? I mean—ugh!" I retched, as I suddenly got a whiff of the most unpleasant and penetrating odor I had ever encountered in my life. It was like death and destruction in gaseous form; a sickly sweet, clinging stink that oozed in through the pores of my skin to turn my stomach. "Wow!" I said, gasping.

Hammond looked at me in bewilderment; then he grinned sourly. "New here, aren't you?" he inquired. "That's hemp. They grow the stuff for the fibers; and to get the fibers out, they let it get good and rotten. You'll get used to it," he promised.

I tried. I tried pretty hard to get used to it; I hardly heard a word he said all the rest of the way in to Caserta, I was trying so hard. But I didn't get used to it.

Then I had my mind taken off my troubles. The branch was still doing business when we got there, though there were easily three or four hundred angrily shouting policyholders milling around in front of it. They scattered before us as the armored car came racing in; we skidded to a stop, siren blasting, and the expediters leaped out with their weapons at the ready.

Hammond and I climbed out of the armored car with our bags of money. There was an audible excitement in the crowd as the word spread back that the Company had brought in enormous stores of lire, more than any man had ever seen, to pay off the claims. We could hear the chatter of many voices, and we almost could feel the tension slack off.

It looked like the trouble was over.

Then there was a shrill whistle. It sounded very much like the alarm whistle of one of our expediters but, thinking back, I have never been sure.

Perhaps it was a nervous expediter, perhaps it was an agent provocateur in the crowd. But, whoever pulled the trigger, the explosion went off.

There was a ragged yell from the crowd, and rocks began whizzing through the air. The pacifists in the mob began heading for the doorways and alleys around; women screamed, men shouted and bellowed, and for a moment it looked like we would be swamped. For not very many of them were pacifists, and there were at least a hundred screaming, gesticulating men lunging at us.

One cobblestone shattered the theoretically unbreakable windshield of the truck next to my head; then the expediters, gas guns spitting, were ringing around us to protect the money.

It was a short fight but vicious. By the time the first assault was repulsed there were at least fifty persons lying motionless in the street.

I had never seen that sort of violence before. It did something to my stomach. I stood weaving, holding to the armored car, while the expediters circled the area around the branch office, firing hurry-up shots at the running rioters. Hammond looked at me questioningly.

"That smell," I said apologetically.

He said only, "Sure." True, the fetid aroma from the hemp fields was billowing all around us, but he knew as well as I that it was not the smell that was bothering me.

In a few moments, as we were locking the bags of money into the office safe, red-crossed vehicles bearing the Company insignia appeared in the street outside, and medics began tending to the victims. Each one got a shot of something—an antidote to the sleep-gas from the expediters' guns, I guessed—and was loaded unceremoniously into the ambulances.

Hammond appeared beside me. "Ready for business?" he asked. "They'll be back any minute now, the ones that can still walk. We'll be paying off until midnight, the way it looks."

I said, "Sure. That—that gas doesn't hurt them any, does it? I mean, after they go to the hospital they'll be all right, won't they?"

Hammond, twirling a pencil in his fingers, stared broodingly at the motionless body of one policyholder. He was a well-dressed man of fifty or so, with a reddish mustache, unusual in that area, and shattered rimless glasses. Not at all the type I would expect to see in a street fight; probably, I thought, a typical innocent bystander.

Hammond said absently, "Oh, sure. They'll be all right. Never know what hit them." There was a tiny sharp *crack* and the two halves of the pencil fell to the floor. He looked at it in surprise. "Come on, Wills. Let's get to work."

CHAPTER THREE

Of course I still believed in the Company.

But all the same, it was the first time since I went to work for the Company that I had even had to ask myself that question.

That long, long day in Hammond's puny little branch office, sweltering in the smell of the hemp fields, pushing across the mountains of lire to the grim-faced policyholders left me a little less sure of things. Nearly all of the first hundred or so to pass my desk had been in the crowd that the expediters had fired on. A few had fresh bandages to show where stones had missed the expediters, but found targets all the same. Nearly all of them were hostile. There was no casual conversation, very few "*Grazies*" as they received their payments.

But at last the day was at an end. Hammond snapped an order to one of the clerks, who shoved his way through the dwindling line to close the door and bang down the shutters. I put through the last few applications, and we were through.

It was hot and muggy out in the streets of New Caserta. Truce teams of expediters were patrolling the square, taken off their regular assignments of enforcing the peace between Naples and Sicily to keep down Caserta's own mobs. Hammond suggested dinner, and we went to a little Blue Plate in the palace itself.

Hammond held Class-A food policies, but he was politeness itself; he voluntarily led the way to the Class-B area. We presented our policy-cards to the waiter for canceling, and sat back to enjoy the air conditioning.

I was still troubled over the violence. I said, "Has there been any trouble around here before?"

Hammond said ruefully, "Plenty. All over Europe, if you want my opinion. Of course, you never see it in the papers, but I've heard stories from field workers. They practically had a revolution in the Sudeten strip after the Prague-Vienna affair." He stopped talking as the waiter set his Meal-of-the-Day in front of him. Hammond looked at it sourly. "Oh, the hell with it, Wills," he said. "Have a drink with me to wash this stuff down."

We ordered liquor, and Hammond shoved his Class-A card at the waiter. I am not a snoop, but I couldn't help noticing that the liquor coupons were nearly all gone; at his present rate, Hammond would use up his year's allotment by the end of the summer, and be paying cash for his drinks.

Dinner was dull. Hammond made it dull, because he was much more interested in his drinking than in me. Though I was never much of a drinker, I'd had a little experience in watching others tank up; Hammond I classified as the surly and silent type. He wasn't quite rude to me, but after the brandy with his coffee, and during the three or four straight whiskies that followed that, he hardly spoke to me at all.

We left the Blue Plate in a strained silence and, after the cooled restaurant, the heat outside was painful. The air was absolutely static, and the odor from the hemp fields soaked into our clothes like a bath in a sewer.

Overhead it was nearly dark, and there were low black clouds. "We'd better get going," I ventured. "Looks like rain."

Hammond said nothing, only grunted. He lurched ahead of me toward the narrow street that led back to the branch office, where our transport was waiting.

The distance was easily half a mile. Now I am not terribly lazy, and even in the heat I was willing enough to walk. But I didn't want to get caught in a rain. Maybe it was superstition on my part—I knew that the danger was really slight—but I couldn't forget that three separate atomic explosions had gone off in the area around Caserta and Naples within only a very few months, and

there was going to be a certain amount of radioactivity in every drop of rain that fell for a hundred miles around.

I started to tell Hammond about it, but he made a disgusted noise and stumbled ahead.

It wasn't as if we had to walk. Caserta was not well equipped with cabs, but there were a few; and both Hammond and myself ranked high enough in the Company to have been able to get a lift from one of the expediter cars that were cruising about.

There was a flare of lightning over the eastern mountains and, in a moment, the pounding roll of thunder. And a flat globule of rain splattered on my face.

I said, "Hammond, let's wait here for a lift."

Surprisingly he came along with me.

If he hadn't, I would have left him in the street.

We were in a street of tenements. It was almost deserted; I rapped on the nearest door. No answer, no sound inside. I rapped again, then tried the door. It was locked

The next door—ancient and rickety as the first—was also locked, and no one answered. The third door, no one answered. By then it was raining hard; the knob turned under my fingers, and we stepped inside.

We left the door ajar, on the chance that a squad car or cab might pass, and for light. It was almost dark outside, apart from the light from the lightning flashes, but even so it was darker within. There was no light at all in the narrow, odorous hall; not even a light seeping under the apartment doors.

In the lightning flare, Hammond's face was pale. He was beginning to sober up, and his manner was uneasy.

We were there perhaps half an hour in that silent hall, watching the rain sleet down and the lightning flare and listening to the thunder. Two or three times, squad cars passed, nosing slowly down the drenched streets, but though Hammond looked longingly at them, I still didn't want to get wet.

Then the rain slowed and almost simultaneously a civilian cab appeared at the head of the block. "Come on," I said, tugging at his arm.

He balked. "Wait for a squad car," he mumbled.

"Why? Come on, Hammond, it may start to pour again in a minute."

"No!"

His behavior was exasperating me. Clearly it wasn't that he was too niggardly to pay for the cab; it was almost as if he were delaying going back to the branch office for some hidden reason. But that was ridiculous, of course.

I said, "Look, you can stay here if you want to, but I'm going." I jumped out of the doorway just in time to flag the cab; it rolled to a stop, and the driver backed to where I was standing. As I got in, I looked once more to the doorway where Hammond was standing, his face unreadable.

He made a gesture of some sort, but the lightning flashed again and I skipped into the cab. When I looked again he was invisible inside the doorway, and I told the driver to take me to the branch office of the Company.

Curious; but it was not an end to curious things that night. At the branch office, my car was waiting to take me back to Naples.

I surrendered my travel coupons to the cab driver and jumped from one vehicle to the other.

Before my driver could start, someone appeared at the window of the car and a sharp voice said, "Un momento, Signore 'Ammond!"

I stared at the man, a rather badly dressed Neapolitan. I said angrily, "Hammond isn't here!"

The man's expression changed. It had been belligerent; it now became astonished and apologetic. "A thousand times excuse me," he said. "The Signore 'Ammond, can you say where he is?"

I hesitated, but only for a moment. I didn't like the little man peering in my window, however humble and conciliatory he had become. I said abruptly, "No." And my driver took off, leaving the man standing there.

I turned to look back at him as we drove off.

It was ridiculous, but the way he was standing as we left, holding one hand in his pocket, eyes narrowed and thoughtful, made me think that he was carrying a gun.

But, of course, that was impossible. The Company didn't permit lethal weapons, and who in all the world would challenge a rule of the Company?

When I showed up in the Naples office the next morning, Susan had my coffee ready and waiting for me. I said gratefully, "Bless you."

She chuckled. "That's not all," she said. "Here's something else you might like. Just remember though, if anyone asks, you got it out of the files yourself."

She slipped a folder under the piles of forms on my desk and disappeared. I peered at it curiously. It was labeled: "Policy BNT-3KT-890776, Blue Bolt Comprehensive. Insuree: Renata dell'Angela."

I could have been no more grateful had she given me the Company Mint.

But I had no chance to examine it. Gogarty was calling for me. I hastily swallowed my coffee and reported for orders.

They were simple enough. The appointment with Zorchi that I hadn't been able to keep the day before was set up for right then. I was already late and I had to leave without another glance at Rena's file.

The hospital Zorchi honored with his patronage was a marble-halled palace on the cliffs that rimmed the southern edge of the Bay of Naples. It was a luxurious, rich man's hospital, stuffy with its opulence; but the most opulent of all was the plush-lined three-room suite where Zorchi was.

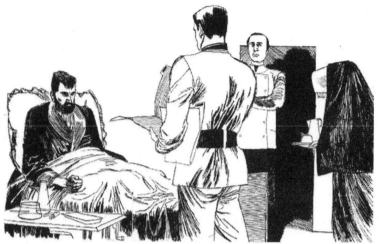

A white-robed sister of some religious order led me into a silent elevator and along a statued hall. She tapped on a door, and left me in the care of a sharp-faced young man with glasses who introduced himself as Mr. Zorchi's secretary.

I explained my business. He contemptuously waved me to a brocaded chair, and left me alone for a good half hour.

By the time Zorchi was ready to see me, I was boiling. Nobody could treat a representative of the Company like an errand boy! I did my best to take into consideration the fact that he had just undergone major surgery—first under the wheels of the train, then under the knives of three of Naples' finest surgeons.

I said as pleasantly as I could, "I'm glad to see you at last."

The dark face on the pink embroidered pillow turned coldly toward me. "Che volete?" he demanded. The secretary opened his mouth to translate.

I said quickly, "Scusí; parlo un po' la lingua. Non bisogno un traduttore."

Zorchi said languidly in Italian, "In that case, Mario, you may go. What do you want with me, Weels?"

I explained my duties as a Claims Adjuster for the Company, pointing out that it was my task, indeed my privilege, to make settlement for injuries covered by Company policies. He listened condescendingly. I watched him carefully while I talked, trying to estimate the approach he might respond to if I was to win his confidence.

He was far from an attractive young man, I thought. No longer behind the shabby porter's uniform he had worn on the platform of the station, he still had an unkempt and slipshod appearance, despite the heavy silken dressing gown he wore and the manifest costliness of his room. The beard was still on his face; it, at least, had not been a disguise. It was not an attractive beard. It had been weeks, at the least, since any hand had trimmed it to shape and his hair was just as shaggy.

Zorchi was not impressed with my friendly words. When I had finished, he said coldly, "I have had claims against the Company before, Weels. Why is it that this time you make speeches at me?"

I said carefully, "Well, you must admit you are a rather unusual case."

"Case?" He frowned fiercely. "I am no case, Weels. I am Zorchi, if you please."

"Of course, of course. I only mean to say that—"

"That I am a statistic, eh?" He bobbed his head. "Surely. I comprehend. But I am not a statistic, you see. Or, at best, I am a statistic which will not fit into your electronic machines, am I not?"

I admitted, "As I say, you are a rather unusual ca—a rather unusual person, Mr. Zorchi."

He grinned coldly. "Good. We are agreed. Now that we have come to that understanding, are we finished with this interview?"

I coughed. "Mr. Zorchi, I'll be frank with you." He snorted, but I went on, "According to your records, this claim need not be paid. You see, you already have been paid for total disability, both a lump sum and a continuing settlement. There is no possibility of two claims for the loss of your legs, you must realize."

He looked at me with a touch of amusement. "I must?" he asked. "It is odd. I have discussed this, you understand, with many attorneys. The premiums were paid, were they not? The language of the policy is clear, is it not? My legs—would you like to observe the stumps yourself?"

He flung the silken covers off. I averted my eyes from the white-bandaged lower half of his torso, hairy and scrawny and horribly *less* than a man's legs should be.

I said desperately, "Perhaps I spoke too freely. I do not mean, Mr. Zorchi, that we will not pay your claim. The Company *always* lives up to the letter of its contracts."

He covered himself casually. "Very well. Give the check to my secretary, please. Are you concluded?"

"Not quite." I swallowed. I plunged right in. "Mr. Zorchi, what the hell are you up to? How do you do it? There isn't any fraud, I admit it. You really lost your legs—more than once. You grew new ones. But how? Don't you realize how important this is? If you can do it, why not others? If you are in some way pecu—that is, if the structure of your body is in some way different from that of others, won't you help us find out how so that we can learn from it? It isn't necessary for you to live as you do, you know."

He was looking at me with a hint of interest in his close-set, dull eyes. I continued, "Even if you can grow new legs, do you *enjoy* the pain of having them cut off? Have you ever stopped to think that some day, perhaps, you will miscalculate, and the wheels of the train, or the truck, or whatever you use, may miss your legs and kill you? That's no way for a man to live, Mr. Zorchi. Why not talk freely to me, let me help you? Why not take the Company into your confidence, instead of living by fraud and deceit and—"

I had gone too far. Livid, he snarled, "Ass! That will cost your Company, I promise. Is it fraud for me to suffer like this? Do I enjoy it, do you think? Look, ass!" He flung the covers aside again, ripped at the white bandages with his hands—Blood spurted. He uncovered the raw stumps and jerked them at me.

I do not believe any sight of my life shocked me as much as that; it was worse than the Caserta hemp fields, worse than the terrible *gone* moment when Marianna died, worse than anything I could imagine.

He raved, "See this fraud, look at it closely! Truly, I grow new legs, but does that make it easier to lose the old? It is the pain of being born, Weels, a pain you will never know! I grow legs, I grow arms, I grow eyes. I will never die! I will live on like a reptile or a fish."

His eyes were staring. Ignoring the blood spurting from his stumps, ignoring my attempts to say something, he pounded his abdomen. "Twelve times I have been cut—do you see even a scar? My appendix, it is bad; it traps filth, and the filth makes me sick. And I have it cut out—and it grows again; and I have it cut out again, and it grows back. And the pain, Weels, the pain never stops!" He flung the robe open, slapped his narrow, hairy chest.

I gasped. Under the scraggly hair was a rubble of boils and wens, breaking and matting the hair as he struck himself in frenzy. "Envy me, Weels!" he shouted. "Envy the man whose body defends itself against everything! I will live forever, I promise it, and I will always be in pain, and someone will pay for every horrible moment of it! Now get out, get out!"

I left under the hating eyes of the sharp-faced secretary who silently led me to the door.

I had put Zorchi through a tantrum and subjected myself to as disagreeable a time as I'd ever had. And I hadn't accomplished a thing. I knew that well enough. And if I hadn't known it by myself, I would have found out.

Gogarty pointed it out to me, in detail. "You're a big disappointment to me," he moaned sourly. "Ah, the hell with it. What were you trying to accomplish, anyway?"

I said defensively, "I thought I might appeal to his altruism. After all, you didn't give me very explicit instructions."

"I didn't tell you to remember to wipe your nose either," he said bitterly. He shook his head, the anger disappearing. "Well," he said disconsolately, "I don't suppose we're any worse off than we were. I guess I'd better try this myself." He must have caught a hopeful anticipatory gleam in my eye, because he said quickly, "Not right now, Wills. You've made that impossible. I'll just have to wait until he cools off."

I said nothing; just stood there waiting for him to let me go. I was sorry things hadn't worked out but, after all, he had very little to complain about. Besides, I wanted to get back to my desk and the folder about Rena dell'Angela. It wasn't so much that I was interested in her as a person, I reminded myself. I was just curious…

Once again, I had to stay curious for a while. Gogarty had other plans for me. Before I knew what was happening, I was on my way out of the office again, this time to visit another Neapolitan hospital, where some of the severely injured in the recent war were waiting final settlement of their claims. It was a hurry-up matter, which had been postponed too many times already; some of the injured urgently required major medical treatment, and the hospital was howling for approval of their claims before they'd begin treatment.

This one was far from a marble palace. It had the appearance of a stucco tenement, and all of the patients were in wards. I was a little surprised to see expediters guarding the entrance.

I asked one of them, "Anything wrong?"

He looked at me with a flicker of astonishment, recognizing the double-breasted Claim Adjuster uniform, surprised, I think, at my asking him a question. "Not as long as we're here, sir," he said.

"I mean, I was wondering what you were doing here."

The surprise became overt. "Vaults," he said succinctly.

I prodded no further. I knew what he meant by vaults, of course. It was part of the Company's beneficent plan for ameliorating the effects of even such tiny wars as the Naples-Sicily affair that those who suffered radiation burns got the best treatment possible. And the best treatment, of course, was suspended animation. The deadly danger of radiation burns lay in their cumulative effect; the first symptoms were nothing, the man was well and able to walk about. Degeneration of the system followed soon, the marrow of the bone gave up on its task of producing white corpuscles, the blood count dropped, the tiny radiant poisons in his blood spread and worked their havoc. If he could be gotten through the degenerative period he might live. But, if he lived, he would still die. That is, if his life processes continued, the radiation sickness would kill him. The answer was to stop the life process, temporarily, by means of the injections and deep-freeze in the vaults. It was used for more than radiation, of course. Marianna, for instance—

Well, anyway, that was what the vaults were. These were undoubtedly just a sort of distribution point, where local cases were received and kept until they could be sent to the main Company vaults up the coast at Anzio.

I wasn't questioning the presence of vaults there; I was only curious why the Company felt they needed guarding.

I found myself so busy, though, that I had no time to think about it. A good many of the cases in this shabby hospital really needed the Company's help. But a great many of them were obvious attempts at fraud.

There was a woman, for instance, in the maternity ward. During the war, she'd had to hide out after the Capodichino bombing and hadn't been able to reach medical service. So her third child was going to be a girl, and she was asking indemnity under the gender-guarantee clause. But she had only Class-C coverage and her first two had been boys; a daughter was permissible in any of the first four pregnancies. She began swearing at me before I finished explaining these simple facts to her.

I walked out of the ward, hot under the collar. Didn't these people realize we were trying to help them? They didn't appear to be aware of it. Only the terribly injured, the radiation cases, the amputees, the ones under anesthetic—only these gave me no arguments, mainly because they couldn't talk.

Most of them were on their way to the vaults, I found. My main job was revision of their policies to provide for immobilization. Inevitably, there are some people who will try to take advantage of anything.

The retirement clause in the basic contract was the joker here. Considering that the legal retirement age under the universal Blue Heaven policy was seventy-five years—calendar years, not metabolic years—there were plenty of invalids who wanted a few years in the vaults for reasons that had nothing to do with health. If they could sleep away two or three decades, they could, they thought, emerge at a physical age of forty or so and live idly off the Company the rest of their lives.

They naturally didn't stop to think that if any such practice became common the Company would simply be unable to pay claims. And they certainly didn't think, or care that, if the Company went bankrupt, the world as we knew it would end.

It was a delicate problem; we couldn't deny them medical care, but we couldn't permit them the vaults unless they were either in clearly urgent need, or were willing to sign an extension waiver to their policies…

I saw plenty of that, that afternoon. The radiation cases were the worst, in that way, because they still could talk and argue. Even while they were being loaded with drugs, even while they could see with their own eyes the blood-count graph dipping lower and lower, they still complained at being asked to sign the waiver.

There was even some fear of the vaults themselves—though every living human had surely seen the Company's indoctrination films that showed how the injected drugs slowed life processes and inhibited the body's own destructive enzymes; how the apparently lifeless body, down to ambient air temperature, would be slipped into its hermetic plastic sack and stacked away, row on row, far underground, to sleep away the months or years or, if necessary, the centuries. Time meant nothing to the suspendees. It was hard to imagine being afraid of as simple and natural a process as that!

Although I had to admit that the vaults looked a lot like morgues…

I didn't enjoy it. I kept thinking of Marianna. She had feared the vaults too, in the childish, unreasoning, feminine way that was her characteristic. When the Blue Blanket technicians had turned up the diagnosis of leukemia, they had proposed the sure-thing course of putting her under suspension while the slow-acting drugs—specially treated to operate even under those conditions—worked their cure, but she had refused. There had been, they admitted, a ninety-nine and nine-tenths per cent prospect of a cure without suspension…

It just happened that Marianna was in the forlorn one-tenth that died.

I couldn't get her out of my mind. The cases who protested or whined or pleaded or shrieked that they were being tortured and embalmed alive didn't help. I was glad when the afternoon was over and I could get back to the office.

As I came in the door, Gogarty was coming in, too, from the barbershop downstairs. He was freshly shaved and beaming.

"Quitting time, Tom," he said amiably, though his eyes were memorizing the pile of incomplete forms on my desk. "All work and no play, you know." He nudged me. "Not that you need reminding, eh? Still, you ought to tell your girl that she shouldn't call you on office time, Tom."

"Call me? Rena called me?"

He nodded absently, intent on the desk. "Against Company rules, you know. Say, I don't like to push you, but aren't you running a little behind here?"

I said with some irritation, "I don't have much chance to catch up, the way I've been racing around the country, you know. And there's plenty to be done."

He said soothingly, "Now, take it easy, Tom. I was only trying to say that there might be some easier way to handle these things." He speared a form, glanced over it casually. He frowned. "Take this, for instance. The claim is for catching cold as a result of exposure during the evacuation of Cerignola. What would you do with that one?"

"Why—pay it, I suppose."

"And put in the paper work? Suppose it's a phony, Tom? Not one case of coryza in fifty is genuine."

"What would you do?" I asked resentfully.

He said without hesitation, "Send it back with Form CBB-23A192. Ask for laboratory smear-test reports."

I looked over the form. A long letter was attached; it said in more detail than was necessary that there had been no laboratory service during the brief war, at least where the policyholder happened to be, and therefore he could submit only the affidavits of three registered physicians. It looked like a fair claim to me. If it was up to me, I would have paid it automatically.

I temporized. "Suppose it's legitimate?"

"Suppose it is? Look at it this way, Tom. If it's phoney, this will scare him off, and you'd be saving the Company the expense and embarrassment of paying off a fraudulent claim. If it's legitimate, he'll resubmit it—at a time when, perhaps, we won't be so busy. Meanwhile that's one more claim handled and disposed of, for our progress reports to the Home Office."

I stared at him unbelievingly. But he looked back in perfect calm, until my eyes dropped. After all, I thought, he was right in a way. The mountain of work on my desk was certainly a log-jam, and it had to be broken somehow. Maybe rejecting this claim would work some small hardship in an individual case, but what about the hundreds and thousands of others waiting for attention? Wasn't it true that no small hardship to an individual was as serious as delaying all those others?

It was, after all, that very solicitude for the people at large that the Company relied on for its reputation—that, and the iron-clad guarantee of prompt and full settlement.

I said, "I suppose you're right."

He nodded, and turned away. Then he paused. "I didn't mean to bawl you out for that phone call, Tom," he said. "Just tell her about the rule, will you?"

"Sure. Oh, one thing." He waited. I coughed. "This girl, Rena. I don't know much about her, you know. Is she, well, someone you know?"

He said, "Heavens, no. She was making a pest out of herself around here, frankly. She has a claim, but not a very good one. I don't know all the details, because it's encoded, but the machines turned it down automatically. I do know that she, uh..." He sort of half winked. "...wants a favor. Her old man is in trouble. I'll look it up for you some time, if you want, and get the details. I think he's in the cooler—that is, the clinic—up at Anzio."

He scratched his plump jowls. "I didn't think it was fair to you for me to have a girl at dinner and none for you; Susan promised to bring someone along, and this one was right here, getting in the way. She said she liked Americans, so I told her you would be assigned to her case." This time he did wink. "No harm, of course. You certainly wouldn't be influenced by any, well, personal relationship, if you happened to get into one. Oh, a funny thing. She seemed to recognize your name."

That was a jolt. "She what?"

Gogarty shrugged. "Well, she reacted to it. 'Thomas Wills,' I said. She'd been acting pretty stand-offish, but she warmed up quick. Maybe she just likes the name, but right then is when she told me she liked Americans."

I cleared my throat. "Mr. Gogarty," I said determinedly, "please get me straight on something. You say this girl's father is in some kind of trouble, and you imply she knows me. I want to know if you've ever had any kind of report, or even heard any kind of rumor, that would make you think that I was in the least sympathetic to any anti-Company groups? I'm aware that there were stories—"

He stopped me. "I never heard any, Tom," he said definitely.

I hesitated. It seemed like a good time to open up to Gogarty; I opened my mouth to start, but I was too late. Susan called him off for what she claimed was an urgent phone call and, feeling letdown, I watched him waddle away.

Because it was, after all, time that I took down my back hair with my boss.

Well, I hadn't done anything too terribly bad—anyway, I hadn't *meant* to do anything bad. And the circumstances sort of explained it, in a way. And it was all in the past, and—

And nothing. I faced the facts. I had spent three solid weeks getting blind drunk, ranting and raving and staggering up to every passer-by who would listen and whining to him that the Company was evil, the Company was murderous, the Company had killed my wife.

There was no denying it. And I had capped it all off one bleary midnight, with a brick through the window of the Company branch office that served my home. It was only a drunken piece of idiocy, I kept telling myself. But it was a drunken piece of idiocy that landed me in jail, that had been permanently indorsed on every one of my policies, that was in the confidential pages of my Company service record. It was a piece of idiocy that anyone might have done. But it would have meant deep trouble for me, if it hadn't been for the intercession of my wife's remote relative, Chief Underwriter Defoe.

It was he who had bailed me out. He had never told me how he had found out that I was in jail. He appeared, read the riot-act to me and got me out. He put me over the coals later, yes, but he'd bailed me out. He'd told me I was acting like a child—and convinced me of it, which was harder. And when he was convinced I had snapped out of it, he personally backed me for an appointment to the Company's school as a cadet Claims Adjuster.

I owed a considerable debt of gratitude to my ex-remote-in-law, Chief Underwriter Defoe.

While I still was brooding, Gogarty came back. He looked unhappy. "Hammond," he said bitterly. "He's missing. Look, was he drunk when you left him last night?" I nodded. "Thought so. Never showed up for work. Not at his quarters. The daily ledger's still open at his office, because there's no responsible person to sign it. So naturally I've got to run out to Caserta now, and what Susan will say—" He muttered away.

I remembered the file that was buried under the papers on my desk, when he mentioned Susan's name.

As soon as he was out of the office, I had it open.

And as soon as I had it open, I stared at it in shock.

The title page of the sheaf inside was headed: Signorina Renata dell'Angela. Age 22; daughter of Benedetto dell'Angela; accepted to general Class-AA; no employment. There were more details.

But across all, in big red letters, was a rubber stamp: *Policy Canceled. Reassigned Class-E.*

It meant that the sad-eyed Rena was completely uninsurable.

CHAPTER FOUR

Phone or no phone, I still had her address.

It was still daylight when I got out of the cab, and I had a chance for a good look at the house. It was a handsome place by day; the size of the huge white stucco wall didn't fit the *uninsurable* notation on Rena's claim. That wall enclosed a garden; the garden could hardly hold less than an AA house. And Class-Es were ordinarily either sent to public hostels—at the Company's expense, to be sure—or existed on the charity of friends or relatives. And Class-Es seldom had friends in Class-AA houses.

I knocked at the gate. A fat woman, age uncertain but extreme, opened a little panel and peered at me. I asked politely, "Miss dell'Angela?"

The woman scowled. "Che dice?"

I repeated: "May I see Miss dell'Angela? I'm a Claims Adjuster for the Company. I have some business with her in connection with her policies."

"Ha!" said the woman. She left it at that for a moment, pursing her lips and regarding me thoughtfully. Then she shrugged apathetically. "Momento," she said wearily, and left me standing outside the gate.

From inside there was a muttering of unfamiliar voices. I thought I heard a door open, and the sound of steps, but when the fat woman came back she was alone.

Silently she opened the door and nodded me in. I started

automatically up the courtyard toward the enclosed house, but she caught my arm and motioned me toward another path. It led down a flowered lane through a grape arbor to what might, at one time, have been a caretaker's hut.

I knocked on the door of the hut, comprehending where Rena dell'Angela lived as a Class-E uninsurable.

Rena herself opened it, her face flushed, her expression surprised—apprehensive, almost, I thought at first. It was the first time I had seen her by daylight. She was—oh, there was no other word. She was lovely.

She said quickly, "Mr. Wills! I didn't expect you."

I said, "You phoned me. I came as soon as I could."

She hesitated. "I did," she admitted. "It was—I'm sorry, Mr. Wills. It was an impulse. I shouldn't have done it."

"What was it, Rena?"

She shook her head. "I am sorry. It doesn't matter. But I am a bad hostess; won't you come in?"

The room behind the door was long and narrow, with worn furniture and a door that led, perhaps, to another room behind. It seemed dusty and, hating myself as a snooping fool, I took careful note that there was a faint aroma of tobacco. I had been quite sure that she didn't smoke, that evening we had met.

She gestured at a chair—there only were two, both pulled up to a crude wooden table, on which were two poured cups of coffee. "Please sit down," she invited.

I reminded myself that it was, after all, none of my business if she chose to entertain friends—even friends who smoked particularly rancid tobacco. And if they preferred not to be around when I came to the door, why, that was their business, not mine. I said cautiously, "I didn't mean to interrupt you."

"Interrupt me?" She saw my eyes on the cups. "Oh—oh, no, Mr. Wills. That other cup is for you, you see. I poured it when Luisa told me you were at the gate. It isn't very good, I'm afraid," she said apologetically.

I made an effort to sip the coffee; it was terrible. I set it down. "Rena, I just found out about your policies. Believe me, I'm sorry. I hadn't known about it, when we had dinner together; I would have—Well, I don't know what I would have done. There isn't much I can do, truthfully; I don't want you thinking I have any great power. But I wish I had known—I might not have made you cry, at any rate."

She smiled an odd sort of smile. "That wasn't the reason, Mr. Wills."

"Please call me Tom. Well, then, why did you cry?"

"It is of no importance. Please."

I coughed and tried a different tack. "You understand that I do have *some* authority. And I would like to help you if I can—if you'll let me."

"Let you? How could I prevent it?"

Her eyes were deep and dark. I shook myself and pulled the notes I'd made on her policies from my pocket. In the most official voice I could manage, I said, "You see, there may be some leeway in interpreting the facts. As it stands, frankly, there isn't much hope. But if you'll give me some information—"

"Certainly."

"All right. Now, your father—Benedetto dell'Angela. He was a casualty of the war with Sicily; he got a dose of radiation, and he is at present in a low-metabolism state in the clinic at Anzio, waiting for the radiogens to clear out of his system. Is that correct?"

"It is what the Company's report said," she answered.

Her tone was odd. Surely she wasn't doubting a Company report!

"As his dependent, Rena, you applied for subsistence benefits on his Blue Blanket policies, as well as war-risk benefits under the Blue Bolt. Both applications were refused; the Blue Blanket because your father is technically not hospitalized; the Blue Bolt, as well as all your other personal policies, was cancelled, because of…" I stuttered over it, "…of activities against the best interest of the Company. Specifically, giving aid and comfort to a known troublemaker whose name is given here as Slovetski." I showed her the cancellation sheet I had stolen from the files.

She shrugged. "This much I know, Tom," she said.

"Why?" I demanded. "This man is believed to have been instrumental in inciting the war with Sicily!"

She flared, "Tom, that's a lie! Slovetski is an old friend of my father's—they studied together in Berlin, many years ago. He is utterly, completely against war—any war!"

I hesitated. "Well, let's put that aside. But you realize that, in view of this, the Company can maintain—quite properly in a technical sense—that you contributed to the war, and therefore you can't collect Blue Bolt compensation for a war you helped bring about. You were warned, you see. You can't even say that you didn't know what you were doing."

"Tom," Rena's voice was infinitely patient and sad. "I knew what I was doing."

"In that case, Rena, you have to admit that it seems fair enough. Still, perhaps we can get something for you—even if only a refund of your premiums. The Company doesn't always follow the letter of the law, there are always exceptions, so—"

Her expression stopped me. She was smiling, but it was the tortured smile of Prometheus contemplating the cosmic jest that was ripping out his vitals.

I asked uncertainly, "Don't you believe me?"

"Believe you, Tom? Indeed I do." She laughed out loud that time. "After what happened to my father, I assure you, Tom, I am certain that the Company doesn't always follow the law."

I shook my head quickly. "No, you don't understand. I—"

"I understand quite well." She studied me for a moment, then patted my hand. "Let us talk of something else."

"Won't you tell me why your policy was cancelled?"

She said evenly, "It's in the file. Because I was a bad girl."

"But why? Why—"

"Because, Tom. Please, no more. I know you are trying to be just as helpful as you can, but there is no help you can give."

"You don't make it easy, Rena."

"It can't be easy! You see, I admit everything. I was warned. I helped an old friend whom the Company wanted to—shall we say—treat for radiation sickness? So there is no question that my policy can be cancelled. All legal. It is not the only one of its kind, you know. So why discuss it?"

"Why shouldn't we?"

Her expression softened. "Because—because we do not agree. And never shall."

I stared at her blankly. She was being very difficult. Really, I shouldn't be bothering with her, someone I barely knew, someone I hadn't even heard of until—

That reminded me. I said, "Rena, how did you know my name?"

Her eyes went opaque. "Know your name, Tom? Why, Mr. Gogarty introduced us."

"No. You knew of me before that. Come clean, Rena. Please."

She said flatly, "I don't know what you mean." She was beginning to act agitated. I had seen her covertly glancing at her watch several times; now she held it up openly—ostentatiously, in fact. "I am sorry, but you'd better go," she said with a hint of anxiety in her voice. "Please excuse me."

Well, there seemed no good reason to stay. So I went—not happily; not with any sense of accomplishment; and fully conscious of the figure I cut to the unseen watcher in the other room, the man whose coffee I had usurped.

Because there was no longer a conjecture about whether there had been such a person or not. I had heard him sneeze three times.

Back at my hotel, a red light was flashing on the phone as I let myself in. I unlocked the play-back with my room key and got a recorded message that Gogarty wanted me to phone him at once.

He answered the phone on the first ring, looking like the wrath of God. It took me a moment to recognize the symptoms; then it struck home.

The lined gray face, the jittery twitching of the head, the slow, tortured movements; here was a man with a classic textbook case of his ailment. The evidence was medically conclusive. He had been building up to a fancy drinking party, and something made him stop in the middle.

There were few tortures worse than a grade-A hangover, but one of those that qualified was the feeling of having the drink die slowly, going through the process of sobering up without the anesthetic of sleep.

He winced as the scanning lights from the phone hit him. "Wills," he said sourly. "About time. Listen, you've got to go up to Anzio. We've got a distinguished visitor, and he wants to talk to you."

"Me?"

"You! He knows you—his name is Defoe."

The name crashed over me; I hadn't expected that, of all things. He was a member of the Council of Underwriters! I thought they never ventured far from the Home Office. In fact, I thought they never had a moment to spare from the awesome duties of running the Company.

Gogarty explained. "He appeared out of nowhere at Carmody Field. I was still in Caserta! Just settling down to a couple of drinks with Susan, and they phoned me to say Chief Underwriter Defoe is on my doorstep!"

I cut in, "What does he want?"

Gogarty puffed his plump cheeks. "How do I know? He doesn't like the way things are going, I guess. Well, I don't like them either! But I've been twenty-six years with the Company, and if he thinks... Snooping and prying. There are going to be some changes in the office, I can tell you. Somebody's been passing on all kinds of lying gossip and—" He broke off and stared at me calculatingly as an idea hit him.

Then he shook his head. "No. Couldn't be you, Wills, could it? You only got here, and Defoe's obviously been getting this stuff for weeks. Maybe months. Still—Say, how did you come to know him?"

It was none of his business. I said coldly, "At the Home Office. I guess I'll take the morning plane up to Anzio, then."

"The hell you will. You'll take the night train. It gets you there an hour earlier." Gogarty jerked his head righteously—then winced and clutched his temple. He said miserably, "Oh, damn. Tom, I don't like all of this. I think something happened to Hammond."

I repeated, "Happened? What could happen to him?"

"I don't know. But I found out a few things. He's been seen with some mighty peculiar people in Caserta. What's this about somebody with a gun waiting at the office for him when you were there?"

It took a moment for me to figure out what he was talking about. "Oh," I said, "you mean the man at the car? I didn't know he had a gun, for certain."

"I do," Gogarty said shortly. "The expediters tried to pick him up today, to question him about Hammond. He shot his way out."

I told Gogarty what I knew, although it wasn't much. He listened abstractedly and, when I had finished, he sighed. "Well, that's no help," he grumbled. "Better get ready to catch your train."

I nodded and reached to cut off the connection. He waved half-heartedly. "Oh, yes," he added, "give my regards to Susan if you see her."

"Isn't she here?"

He grimaced. "Your friend Defoe said he needed a secretary. He requisitioned her."

I boarded the Anzio train from the same platform where I had seen Zorchi dive under the wheels. But this was no sleek express; it was an ancient three-car string that could not have been less than fifty years out of date. The cars were not even air-conditioned.

Sleep was next to impossible, so I struck up a conversation with an expediter-officer. He was stand-offish at first but, when he found out I was a Claims Adjuster, he mellowed and produced some interesting information.

It was reasonable that Defoe would put aside his other duties and make a quick visit to Anzio, because Anzio seemed to need someone to do something about it pretty badly. My officer was part of a new levy being sent up there; the garrison was being doubled; there had been trouble. He was vague about what kind of "trouble" it had been, but it sounded like mob violence. I mentioned Caserta and the near-riot I had been in; the officer's eyes hooded over, and about five minutes after that he pointedly leaned back and pulled his hat over his eyes. Evidently it was not good form to discuss actual riots.

I accepted the rebuke, but I was puzzled in my mind as I tried to get some sleep for myself.

What kind of a place was this Naples, where mobs rioted against the Company and even intelligent-seeming persons like Renata dell'Angela appeared to have some reservations about it?

CHAPTER FIVE

I slept, more or less, for an hour or so in that cramped coach seat. I was half asleep when the train-expediter nudged my elbow and said, "Anzio."

It was early—barely past daybreak. It was much too early to find a cab. I got directions from a drowsing stationmaster and walked toward the vaults.

The "clinic," as the official term went, was buried in the feet of the hills just beyond the beaches. I was astonished at the size of it. Not because it was so large; on the contrary. It was, as far as I could see, only a broad, low shed.

Then it occurred to me that the vaults were necessarily almost entirely underground, for the sake of economy in keeping them down to the optimum suspendee temperature. It was safe enough and simple enough to put a man in suspended animation but, as I understood it, it was necessary to be sure that the suspendees never got much above fifty degrees temperature for any length of time. Above that, they had an unwelcome tendency to decay.

This was, I realized, the first full-scale "clinic" I had ever seen. I had known that the Company had hundreds, perhaps thousands, of them scattered all over the world.

I had heard that the Company had enough of them, mostly in out-of-the-way locations, to deep-freeze the entire human race at once, though that seemed hardly reasonable.

I had even heard some ugly, never-quite-made-clear stories about *why* the Company had so many clinics…but when people began hinting at such ridiculous unpleasantness, I felt it was my duty to make it clear that I wanted to hear no subversive talk. So I had never got the details—and certainly would never have believed them for a moment if I had.

It was very early in the morning, as I say, but it seemed that I was not the first to arrive at the clinic. On the sparse grass before the main entrance, half a dozen knots of men and women were standing around apathetically. Some of them glared at me as I came near them, for reasons I did not understand; others merely stared.

I heard a hoarse whisper as I passed one group of middle-aged women. One of them was saying, "Benedetto non é morte." She seemed to be directing it to me; but it meant nothing. The only comment that came to my somewhat weary mind was, "So what if Benedetto isn't dead?"

A huge armed expediter, yawning and scratching, let me in to the executive office. I explained that I had been sent for by Mr. Defoe. I had to wait until Mr. Defoe was ready to receive me and was finally conducted to a suite of rooms.

This might have once been an authentic clinic; it had the aseptic appearance of a depressing hospital room. One for, say, Class-Cs with terminal myasthenia. Now, though, it had been refitted as a private guest suite, with an attempt at luxurious drapes and deep stuffed armchairs superimposed on the basic adjustable beds and stainless steel plumbing.

I hadn't seen Defoe in some time, but he hadn't changed at all. He was, as always, the perfect model of a Company executive of general-officer rank. He was formal, but not unyielding. He was tall, distinguished-gray at the temples, spare, immaculately outfitted in the traditional vest and bow tie.

I recalled our first meeting. He was from the side of Marianna's family that she talked about, and she fluttered around for three whole days, checking our Blue Plate policies for every last exotic dish we could squeeze out to offer him, planning the television programs allowed under our entertainment policies, selecting the most respectable of our friends—"acquaintances" would be a better description; Marianna didn't make friends easily—to make up a dinner party. He'd arrived at the stroke of the hour he was due, and had brought with him what was undoubtedly his idea of a princely gift for newly-weds—a paid-up extra-coverage maternity benefit rider on our Blue Blanket policies.

We thanked him effusively. And, for my part, sincerely. That was before I had known Marianna's views on children; she had no intentions of raising a family.

As I walked in on Defoe in his private suite at the clinic, he was standing with his back to me, at a small washstand, peering at his reflection in a mirror. He appeared to have finished shaving. I rubbed my own bristled chin uneasily.

He said over his shoulder, "Good morning, Thomas. Sit down."

I sat on the edge of an enormous wing chair. He pursed his lips, stretched the skin under his chin and, when he seemed perfectly satisfied the job was complete, he said as though he were continuing a conversation, "Fill me in on your interview with Zorchi, Thomas."

It was the first I'd known he'd ever *heard* of Zorchi. I hesitantly began to tell him about the meeting in the hospital. It did not, I knew, do me very much credit, but it simply didn't occur to me to try to make my own part look better. I suppose that if I thought of the matter at all, I simply thought that Defoe would instantly detect any attempt to gloss things over. He hardly seemed to be paying attention to me, though; he was preoccupied with the remainder of his morning ritual—slowly massaging his face with something fragrant, brushing his teeth with a maddening, old-fashioned insistence on careful strokes, combing his hair almost strand by strand.

Then he took a small bottle with a daub attached to the stopper and touched it to the distinguished gray at his temples.

I spluttered in the middle of a word; I had never thought of the possibility that the handsomely grayed temples of the Company's senior executives, as inevitable as the vest or the watch chain, were equally a part of the uniform! Defoe gave me a long inquiring look in the mirror; I coughed and went on with a careful description of Zorchi's temper tantrum.

Defoe turned to me and nodded gravely. There was neither approval nor disapproval. He had asked for information and the information had been received.

He pressed a communicator button and ordered breakfast. The microphone must have been there, but it was invisible. He sat down at a small, surgical-looking table, leaned back and folded his hands.

"Now," he said, "tell me what happened in Caserta just before Hammond disappeared."

Talking to Defoe had something of the quality of shouting down a well. I collected my thoughts and told him all I knew on the riot at the branch office.

While I was talking, Defoe's breakfast arrived. He didn't know I hadn't eaten anything, of course—I say "of course" because I know he couldn't have known, he didn't ask. I looked at it longingly, but all my looking didn't alter the fact that there was only one plate, one cup, one set of silverware.

He ate his breakfast as methodically as he'd brushed his teeth. I doubt if it took him five minutes. Since I finished the Caserta story in about three, the last couple of minutes were in dead silence, Defoe eating, me sitting mute as a disconnected jukebox.

Then he pushed the little table away, lit a cigarette and said, "You may smoke if you wish, Thomas. Come in, Susan."

He didn't raise his voice; and when, fifteen seconds later, Susan Manchester walked in, he didn't look at all impressed with the efficiency of his secretary, his intercom system, or himself. The concealed microphone, it occurred to me, had heard him order breakfast and request his secretary to walk in. It had undoubtedly heard—and most probably recorded—every word I had said.

How well they did things on the upper echelon of the Company!

Susan looked—different. She was as blonde and pretty as ever. But she wasn't bubbly. She smiled at me in passing and handed Defoe a typed script, which he scanned carefully.

He asked, "Nothing new on Hammond?"

"No, sir," she said.

"All right. You may leave this." She nodded and left. Defoe turned back to me. "I have some news for you, Thomas. Hammond has been located."

"That's good," I said. "Not too badly hung over, I hope."

He gave me an arctic smile. "Hardly. He was found by a couple of peasants who were picking grapes. He's dead."

CHAPTER SIX

Hammond dead! He had had his faults, but he was an officer of the Company and a man I had met. Dead!

I asked, "How? What happened?"

"Perhaps you can tell me that, Thomas," said Defoe.

I sat startledly erect, shocked by the significance of the words. I said hotly, "Damn it, Mr. Defoe, you know I had nothing to do with this! I've been all over the whole thing with you and I thought you were on my side! Just because I said a lot of crazy things after Marianna died doesn't mean I'm anti-Company—and it certainly doesn't mean I'd commit murder. If you think that, then why the devil did you put me in cadet school?"

Defoe merely raised his hand by bending the wrist slightly; it was enough to stop me, though. "Gently, Thomas. I don't think you did it—that much should be obvious. And I put you in cadet school because I had work for you."

"But you said I knew something I was holding back."

Defoe waggled the hand reprovingly. "I said you might be able to tell me who killed Hammond. And so you might—but not yet. I count heavily on you for help in this area, Thomas. There are two urgent tasks to be done. Hammond's death..." He paused and shrugged, and the shrug was all of Hammond's epitaph, "...is only an incident in a larger pattern; we need to work out the pattern itself."

He glanced again at the typed list Susan had handed him. "I find that I can stay in the Naples area for only a short time; the two tasks must be done before I leave. I shall handle one myself. The other I intend to delegate to you.

"First we have the unfortunate situation in regard to the state of public morale. Unfortunate? Perhaps I should say disgraceful. There is quite obviously a nucleus of troublemakers at work, Thomas, and Gogarty has not had the wit to find them and take the appropriate steps. Someone else must. Second, this Zorchi is an unnecessary annoyance. I do not propose to let the Company be annoyed, Thomas. Which assignment would you prefer?"

I said hesitantly, "I don't know if Mr. Gogarty would like me to—"

"Gogarty is an ass! If he had not blundered incessantly since he took over the district, I should not have had to drop important work to come here."

I thought for a second. Digging out an undercover ring of troublemakers didn't sound particularly easy. On the other hand, I had already tried my luck with Zorchi.

"Perhaps you'd better try Zorchi," I said.

"Try?" Defoe allowed himself to look surprised. "As you wish. I think you will learn something from watching me handle it, Thomas. Shall we join Signore Zorchi now?"

"He's *here*?"

Defoe said impatiently, "Of course, Thomas. Come along."

Zorchi's secretary was there, too. He was in a small anteroom, sitting on a hard wooden chair; as we passed him, I saw the hostility in his eyes. He didn't say a word.

Beyond him, in an examination room, was Zorchi, slim, naked and hideous, sitting on the edge of a surgical cot and trying not to look ill at ease. He had been shaved from head to knee stumps. Esthetically, at least, it had been a mistake. I never saw such a collection of skin eruptions on a human.

He burst out, faster than my language-school Italian could follow, in a stream of argument and abuse. Defoe listened icily for a moment, then shut him up in Italian as good as his own. "Answer questions; otherwise keep quiet. I will not warn you again."

I don't know if even Defoe could have stopped Zorchi under normal conditions. But there is something about being naked in the presence of fully dressed opponents that saps the will; and I guessed, too, that the shaving had made Zorchi feel nakeder than ever before in his life. I could see why he'd worn a beard and I wished he still had it.

"Dr. Lawton," said Defoe, "have you completed your examination of the insured?"

A youngish medical officer of the Company said, "Yes, sir. I have the slides and reports right here; they just came up from the laboratory." He handed a stapled collection of photographic prints and papers to Defoe, who took his own good time to examine them while the rest of us stood and waited.

Defoe finally put the papers down and nodded. "In a word, this bears out our previous discussion."

Lawton nodded. "If you will observe his legs, you will see that the skin healing is complete; already a blastema has formed and—"

"I know," Defoe said impatiently. "Signore Zorchi, I regret to say that I have bad news for you."

Zorchi waved his hand defiantly. "*You* are the bad news."

Defoe ignored him. "You have a grave systemic imbalance. There is great danger of serious ill effects."

"To what?" snarled Zorchi. "The Company's bank account?"

"No, Zorchi. To your life." Defoe shook his head. "There are indications of malignancy."

"Malignancy?" Zorchi looked startled. "What kind? Do you mean cancer?"

"Exactly." Defoe patted his papers. "You see, Zorchi, healthy human flesh does not grow like a salamander's tail."

The phone rang; impeccable in everything, Defoe waited while Dr. Lawton nervously answered it. Lawton said a few short words, listened for a moment and hung up, looking worried.

He said: "The crowd outside is getting rather large. That was the expediter-captain from the main gate. He says—"

"I presume he has standing orders," Defoe said. "We need not concern ourselves with that, need we?"

"Well—" The doctor looked unhappy.

"Now, Zorchi," Defoe went on, dismissing Lawton utterly, "do you enjoy life?"

"I despise it!" Zorchi spat to emphasize how much.

"But you cling to it. You would not like to die, would you? Worse still, you would not care to live indefinitely with carcinoma eating you piece by piece."

Zorchi just glowered suspiciously.

"Perhaps we can cure you, however," Defoe went on reflectively. "It is by no means certain. I don't want to raise false hopes. But there is the possibility—"

"The possibility that you will cure me of collecting on my policies, eh?" Zorchi demanded belligerently. "You are crazy, Defoe. Never!"

Defoe looked at him for a thoughtful moment. To Lawton, he said: "Have you this man's claim warranty? It has the usual application for medical treatment, I presume?" He nodded as Lawton confirmed it. "You see, Mr. Zorchi? As a matter of routine, no claim can be paid unless the policyholder submits to our medical care. You signed the usual form, so—"

"One moment! You people never put me through this before! Did you change the contract on me?"

"No, Signore Zorchi. The same contract, but this time we will enforce it. I think I should warn you of something, though."

He riffled through the papers and found a photographic print to show Zorchi. "This picture isn't you, Signore. It is a picture of a newt. The doctor will explain it to you."

The print was an eight-by-ten glossy of a little lizard with something odd about its legs. Puzzled, Zorchi held it as though the lizard were alive and venomous. But as the doctor spoke, the puzzlement turned into horror and fury.

"What Mr. Defoe means," said Lawton, "is that totipotency— that is, the ability to regenerate lost tissues, as you can, even when entire members are involved—is full of unanswered riddles. We have found, for instance, that X-ray treatment on your leg helps a new leg to form rapidly, just as it does on the leg of the salamanders. The radiation appears to stimulate the formation of the blastema, which—well, never mind the technical part. It speeds things up."

His eyes gleamed with scientific interest. "But we tried the experiment of irradiating limbs that had not been severed. It worked the same way, oddly enough. New limbs were generated *even though the old ones were still there.* That's why the salamander in the photo has four hands on one of its limbs—nine legs altogether, counting that half-formed one just beside the tail. Curious-looking little beast, isn't it?"

Defoe cleared his throat. "I only mention, Signore, that the standard treatment for malignancy is X-radiation."

Zorchi's eyes flamed—rage battling it out with terror. He said shrilly, "But you can't make a laboratory animal out of me! I'm a policyholder!"

"Nature did it, Signore Zorchi, not us," Defoe said.

Zorchi's eyes rolled up in his head and closed; for a moment, I thought he had fainted and leaped forward to catch him rather than let his legless body crash to the floor. But he hadn't fainted. He was muttering, half aloud, sick with fear, "For the love of Mary, Defoe! Please, please, I beg you! Please!"

It was too much for me. I said, shaking with rage, "Mr. Defoe, you can't force this man to undergo experimental radiation that might make a monster out of him! I insist that you reconsider!"

Defoe threw his head back. "*What, Thomas?*" he snapped.

I said firmly, "He has no one here to advise him—I'll take the job. Zorchi, listen to me! You've signed the treatment application and he's right enough about that—you can't get out of it. *But you don't have to take this treatment!* Every policyholder has the right to refuse any new and unguaranteed course of treatment, no matter what the circumstances. All you've got to do is agree to go into suspension in the va—in the clinic here, pending such time as your condition can be infallibly cured. Do it, man! Don't let them make you a freak—demand suspension! What have you got to lose?"

I never saw a man go so to pieces as Zorchi, when he realized how nearly Defoe had trapped him into becoming a guinea pig. Whimpering thanks to me, he hastily signed the optional agreement for suspended animation and, as quickly as I could, I left him there.

Defoe followed me. We passed the secretary in the anteroom while Dr. Lawton was explaining the circumstances to him; the man was stricken with astonishment, almost too paralyzed to sign the witnessing form Defoe had insisted on. I knew the form well—I had been about to sign one for Marianna when, at the last moment, she decided against the vaults in favor of the experimental therapy that hadn't worked.

Outside in the hall, Defoe stopped and confronted me. I braced myself for the blast to end all blasts.

I could hardly believe my eyes. The great stone face was smiling!

"Thomas," he said inexplicably, "that was masterful. I couldn't have done better myself."

CHAPTER SEVEN

We walked silently through the huge central waiting room of the clinic.

There should have been scores of relatives of suspendees milling around, seeking information—there was, I knew, still a steady shipment of suspendees coming in from the local hospitals;

I had seen it myself. But there were hardly more than a dozen or so persons in sight, with a single clerk checking their forms and answering their questions.

It was too quiet. Defoe thought so, too; I saw his frown.

Now that I had had a few moments to catch my breath, I realized that I had seen a master judoist at work. It was all out of the textbooks—as a fledgling Claims Adjuster, I had had the basic courses in handling difficult cases—but not one man in a million could apply textbook rules as skillfully and successfully as Defoe did with Zorchi.

Push a man hard and he will lunge back; push him hard enough and persistently enough, and he will lunge back farther than his vision carries him, right to the position you planned for him in the first place. And I, of course, had been only a tool in Defoe's hand; by interceding for Zorchi, I had tricked the man into the surrender Defoe wanted.

And he had complimented me for it!

I couldn't help wondering, though, whether the compliment Defoe gave me was part of some still subtler scheme…

Defoe nodded curtly to the expediter-captain at the door, who saluted and pressed the teleswitch that summoned Defoe's limousine.

Defoe turned to me. "I have business in Rome and must leave at once. You will have to certify Zorchi's suspension this afternoon; since I won't be here, you'll have to come back to the clinic for it. After that, Thomas, you can begin your assignment."

I said uncertainly, "What—where shall I begin?"

One eyebrow lifted a trifle. "Where? Wherever you think proper, Thomas. Or must I handle this myself?"

The proper answer, and the one I longed to make, was "Yes." Instead I said, "Not at all, Mr. Defoe. It's only that I didn't even know there was an undercover group until you told me about it a few moments ago; I don't know exactly where to start. Gogarty never mentioned—"

"Gogarty," he cut in, "is very likely to be relieved as District Administrator before long. I should like to replace him with someone already on the scene…" He glanced at me to be sure I understood. "Provided, that is, that I can find someone of proven competence. Someone who has the ability to handle this situation without the necessity of my personal intervention."

The limousine arrived then, with an armed expediter riding beside the chauffeur. Defoe allowed me to open the door for him and follow him in.

"Do you understand me?" he asked as the driver started off.

"I think so," I said.

"Good. I do not suppose that Gogarty has given you any information about the malcontents in this area."

"No."

"It may be for the best; his information is clearly not good." Defoe stared broodingly out the window at the silent groups of men and women on the grass before the clinic. "Your information is there," he said as they passed out of sight. "Learn what you can. Act when you know enough. And, Thomas—"

"Yes?"

"Have you given thought to your future?"

I shifted uncomfortably. "Well, I've only been a Claims Adjuster a little while, you know. I suppose that perhaps I might eventually get promoted, even become a District Administrator—"

He looked at me impersonally. "Dream higher," he advised.

I stood watching after Defoe's limousine, from the marquee of the hotel where he had left me to take a room and freshen up. *Dream higher.* He had the gift of intoxication.

Higher than a District Administrator! It could mean only—the Home Office.

Well, it was not impossible, after all. The Home Office jobs had to go to someone; the super-men who held them now—the Defoes and the Carmodys and the dozen or more others who headed up departments or filled seats on the Council of Underwriters—couldn't live forever. And the jobs had to be filled by someone.

Why not me? Only one reason, really. I was not a career man. I hadn't had the early academy training from adolescence on; I had come to the service of the Company itself relatively late in life. The calendar legislated against me.

Of course, I thought to myself, I was in a pretty good position, in a way, because of Defoe's evident interest in me. With him helping and counseling me, it might be easier.

I thought that and then I stopped myself, shocked. I was thinking in terms of personal preferment. That was not the Company way! If I had learned anything in my training, I had learned that Advancement was on merit alone.

Advancement *had* to be on merit alone...else the Company became an oligarchy, deadly and self-perpetuating.

Shaken, I sat in the dingy little hotel room that was the best the town of Anzio had for me and opened my little Black Book. I thumbed through the fine-printed pages of actuarial tables and turned to the words of Millen Carmody, Chief Underwriter, in the preface. They were the words that had been read to me and the others at our graduation at the Home Office, according to the tradition:

Remember always that the Company serves humanity, not the reverse. The Company's work is the world's work. The Company can end, forever, the menace of war and devastation; but it must not substitute a tyranny of its own. Corruption breeds tyrants. Corruption has no place in the Company.

They were glorious words. I read them over again, and stared at the portrait of Underwriter Carmody that was the frontispiece of the handbook. It was a face to inspire trust—wise and human, grave, but with warmth in the wide-spaced eyes.

Millen Carmody was not a man you could doubt. As long as men like him ran the Company—and he was the boss of them all, *the* Chief Underwriter, the highest position the Company had to offer—there could be no question of favoritism or corruption.

After eating, I shaved, cleaned up a little and went back to the clinic.

There was trouble in the air, no question of it. More expediters were in view, scattered around the entrance, a dozen, cautious yards away from the nearest knots of civilians. Cars with no official company markings, but with armor-glass so thick that it seemed yellow, were parked at the corners. And people were everywhere.

People who were quiet. Too quiet. There were some women—but not enough to make the proportion right. And there were no children.

I could almost feel the thrust of their eyes as I entered the clinic.

Inside, the aura of strain was even denser. If anything, the place looked more normal than it had earlier; there were more people. The huge waiting room was packed and a dozen sweating clerks were interviewing long lines of persons. But here, as outside, the feeling was wrong; the crowds weren't noisy enough; they lacked the nervous boisterousness they should have had.

Dr. Lawton looked worried. He greeted me and showed me to a small room near the elevators. There was a cocoon of milky plastic on a wheeled table; I looked closer, and inside the cocoon, recognizable through the clear plastic over the face, was the waxlike body of Luigi Zorchi. The eyes were closed and he was completely still. I would have thought him dead if I had not known he was under the influence of the drugs used in the suspension of life in the vaults.

I said: "Am I supposed to identify him or something?"

"We know who he is," Lawton snorted. "Sign the commitment, that's all."

I signed the form he handed me, attesting that Luigi Zorchi, serial number such-and-such, had requested and was being granted immobilization and suspension in lieu of cash medical benefits. They rolled the stretcher-cart away, with its thick foam-plastic sack containing the inanimate Zorchi.

"Anything else?" I asked.

Lawton shook his head moodily. "Nothing you can help with. I told Defoe this was going to happen!"

"What?"

He glared at me. "Man, didn't you just come in through the main entrance? Didn't you see that mob?"

"Well, I wouldn't call it a mob," I began.

"You wouldn't *now*," he broke in. "But you will soon enough. They're working themselves up. Or maybe they're waiting for something. But it means trouble, I promise, and I warned Defoe about it. And he just stared at me as if I was some kind of degenerate."

I said sharply, "What are you afraid of? Right outside, you've got enough expediters to fight a war."

"Afraid? Me?" He looked insulted. "Do you think I'm worried about my own skin, Wills? No, sir. But do you realize that we have suspendees here who need protection? Eighty thousand of them. A mob like that—"

"Eighty *thousand?*" I stared at him. The war had lasted only a few weeks!

"Eighty thousand. A little more, if anything. And every one of them is a ward of the Company as long as he's suspended. Just think of the damage suits, Wills."

I said, still marveling at the enormous number of casualties out of that little war, "Surely the suspendees are safe here, aren't they?"

"Not against mobs. The vaults can handle anything that might happen in the way of disaster. I don't think an H-bomb right smack on top of them would disturb more than the top two or three decks at most. But you never know what mobs will do. If they once get in here—And Defoe wouldn't listen to me!"

As I went back into the hall, passing the main entrance, the explosion burst.

I stared out over the heads of the dreadfully silent throng in the entrance hall, looking toward the glass doors, as was everyone else inside. Beyond the doors, an arc of expediters was retreating toward us; they paused, fired a round of gas-shells over the heads of the mob outside, and retreated again.

Then the mob was on them, in a burst of screaming fury. Hidden gas guns appeared, and clubs, and curious things that looked like slingshots. The crowd broke for the entrance. The line of expediters wavered but held. There was a tangle of hand-to-hand fights, each one a vicious struggle. But the expediters were professionals; outnumbered forty to one, they savagely chopped down their attackers with their hands, their feet and the stocks of their guns. The crowd hesitated. No shot had yet been fired, except toward the sky.

The air whined and shook. From low on the horizon, a needle-nosed jet thundered in. A plane! Aircraft never flew in the restricted area over the Company's major installations. Aircraft didn't barrel in at treetop height, fast and low, without a hint of the recognition numbers every aircraft had to carry.

From its belly sluiced a silvery milt of explosives as it came in over the heads of the mob, peeled off and up and away, then circled out toward the sea for another approach. A hail of tiny blasts rattled in the clear space between the line of expediters and the entrance. The big doors shook and cracked.

The expediters stared white-faced at the ship. And the crowd began firing. An illegal hard-pellet gun peppered the glass of the doors with pock-marks. The guarding line of expediters was simply overrun.

Inside the waiting room, where I stood frozen, hell broke out. The detachment of expediters, supervising the hundreds inside leaped for the doors to fight back the surging mob. But the mob inside the doors, the long orderly lines before the interviewing clerks, now split into a hundred screaming, milling centers of panic. Some rushed toward the doors; some broke for the halls of the vaults themselves. I couldn't see what was going on outside any more. I was swamped in a rush of women panicked out of their senses.

Panic was like a plague. I saw doctors and orderlies struggling against the tide, a few scattered expediters battling to turn back the terrified rush. But I was swept along ahead of them all, barely able to keep my feet. An expediter fell a yard from me. I caught up his gun and began striking out. For this was what Lawton had feared—the mob loose in the vaults!

I raced down a side corridor, around a corner, to the banked elevators that led to the deeps of the clinic. There was fighting there, but the elevator doors were closed. Someone had had the wit to lock them against the mob. But there were stairs; I saw an emergency door only a few yards away. I hesitated only long enough to convince myself, through the fear, that my duty was to the Company and to the protection of its helpless wards below. I bolted through the door and slammed it behind me, spun the levers over and locked it. In a moment, I was running down a long ramp toward the cool immensities of the vaults.

If Lawton had not mentioned the possible consequences of violence to the suspendees, I suppose I would have worried only about my own skin. But here I was. I stared around, trying to get my bearings. I was in a sort of plexus of hallways, an open area with doors on all sides leading off to the vaults. I was alone; the noise from above and outside was cut off completely.

No, I was not alone! I heard running footsteps, light and quick, from another ramp. I turned in time to see a figure speed down it, pause only a second at its base, and disappear into one of the vaults. It was a woman, but not a woman in nurse's uniform. Her back had been to me, yet I could see that one hand held a gas gun, the other something glittering and small.

I followed, not quite believing what I had seen. For I had caught only a glimpse of her face, far off and from a bad angle—but I was as sure as ever I could be that it was Rena dell'Angela!

She didn't look back. She was hurrying against time, hurrying toward a destination that obsessed her thoughts. I followed quietly enough, but I think I might have thundered like an elephant herd and still been unheard.

We passed a strange double-walled door with a warning of some sort lettered on it in red; then she swung into a side corridor where the passage was just wide enough for one. On either side were empty tiers of shelves waiting for suspendees. I speeded up to reach the corner before she could disappear.

But she wasn't hurrying now. She had come to a bay of shelves where a hundred or so bodies lay wrapped in their plastic sacks, each to his own shelf. Dropping to her knees, she began checking the tags on the cocoons at the lowest level.

She whispered something sharp and imploring. Then, straightening abruptly, she dropped the gas gun and took up the glittering thing in her other hand. Now I could see that it was a hypodermic kit in a crystal case. From it she took a little flask of purplish liquid and, fingers shaking, shoved the needle of the hypodermic into the plastic stopper of the vial.

Moving closer, I said: "It won't work, Rena."

She jumped and swung to face me, holding the hypodermic like a stiletto. Seeing my face, she gasped and wavered.

I stepped by her and looked down at the tag on the cocooned figure. *Benedetto dell'Angela, Napoli*, it said, and then the long string of serial numbers that identified him.

It was what I had guessed.

"It won't work," I repeated. "Be smart about this, Rena. You can't revive him without killing him."

Rena half-closed her eyes. She whispered, "Would death be worse than this?"

I hadn't expected this sort of superstitious nonsense from her. I started to answer, but she had me off guard. In a flash, she raked the glittering needle toward my face and, as I stumbled back involuntarily, her other hand lunged for the gas gun I had thrust into my belt.

Only luck saved me. Not being in a holster, the gun's front sight caught and I had the moment I needed to cuff her away. She gasped and spun up against the tiers of shelves. The filled hypodermic shattered against the floor, spilling the contents into a purple, gleaming pool of fluorescence.

Rena took a deep breath and stood erect. There were tears in her eyes again.

She said in a detached voice: "Well done, Mr. Wills."

"Are you crazy?" I crackled. "This is your father. Do you want to kill him? It takes a doctor to revive him. You're an educated woman, Rena, not a witch-ridden peasant! You know better than this!"

She laughed—a cold laugh. "Educated! A peasant woman would have kicked you to death and succeeded. I'm educated, all right! Two hundred men, a plane, twenty women risking themselves up there to get me through the door. All our plans—and I can't remember a way to kill you in time. I'm too educated to hate you, Claims Adjuster Wills!" She choked on the words. Then she shook her head dully. "Go ahead, turn me in and get it over with."

I took a deep breath. Turn her in? I hadn't thought that far ahead. True, that was the obvious thing to do; she had confessed that the whole riot outside was a diversion to get her down in the vaults, and anyone who could summon up that sort of organized anti-Company violence was someone who automatically became my natural enemy.

But perhaps I was too educated and too soft as well. There had been tears on her face, over her father's body. I could not remember having heard that conspirators cried.

And I sympathized a little. I had known what it was like to weep over the body of someone I loved. Despite our difficulties, despite everything, I would have done anything in the world to bring Marianna back to life. I couldn't. Rena—she believed—could revive her father.

I didn't want to turn her in.

I *shouldn't* turn her in. It was my duty *not* to turn her in, for hadn't Defoe himself ordered me to investigate the dissident movement of which she was clearly a part? Wouldn't it be easier for me to win her confidence, and trick her into revealing its secrets, than to have her arrested?

The answer, in all truth, was *No*. She was not a trickable girl, I was sure. But it was, at least, a rationale, and I clung to it.

I coughed and said: "Rena, will you make a bargain?"

She stared drearily. "Bargain?"

"I have a room at the Umberto. If I get you out of here, will you go to my room and wait for me there?"

Her eyes narrowed sharply for a second. She parted her lips to say something, but only nodded.

147

"Your word, Rena? I don't want to turn you in."

She looked helplessly at the purple spilled pool on the floor, and wistfully at the sack that held her father. Then she said, "My word on it. But you're a fool, Tom!"

"I know it!" I admitted.

I hurried her back up the ramp, back toward the violence upstairs. If it was over, I would have to talk her out of the clinic, somehow cover up the fact that she had been in the vaults. If it was still going on, though—

It was.

We blended ourselves with the shouting, rioting knots. I dragged her into the main waiting room, saw her thrust through the doors. Things were quieting even then. And I saw two women hastening toward her through the fight, and I do not think it was a coincidence that the steam went out of the rioters almost at once.

I stayed at the clinic until everything was peaceful again, though it was hours.

I wasn't fooling myself. I didn't have a shred of real reason for not having her arrested. If she had information to give, I was not the type to trick it out of her—even if she really was waiting at the Umberto, which was, in itself, not likely. If I had turned her in, Defoe would have had the information out of her in moments; but not I.

She was an enemy of the Company.

And I was unable to betray her.

CHAPTER EIGHT

Dr. Lawton, who seemed to be Chief Medical Officer for Anzio Clinic, said grimly: "This wasn't an accident. It was planned. The question is, why?"

The expediters had finished driving the rioters out of the clinic itself, and gas guns were rapidly dispersing the few left outside the entrance. At least thirty unconscious forms were scattered around—and one or two that were worse than unconscious.

I said, "Maybe they were hoping to loot the clinic." It wasn't a very good lie. But then, I hadn't had much practice in telling lies to an officer of the Company.

Lawton pursed his lips and ignored the suggestion. "Tell me something, Wills. What were you doing down below?"

I said quickly, "Below? You mean a half an hour ago?"

"That's what I mean." He was gentle, but—well, not exactly suspicious. Curious.

I improvised: "I—I thought I saw someone running down there. One of the rioters. So I chased after her—after *him*," I corrected, swallowing the word just barely in time.

He nodded. "Find anything?"

It was a tough question. Had I been seen going in or coming out? If it was coming out—Rena had been with me.

I took what we called a "calculated risk"—that is, I got a firm grip on my courage and told a big fat and possibly detectable lie. I said, "Nobody that I could find. But I still think I heard something. The trouble is, I don't know the vaults very well. I was afraid I'd get lost."

Apparently it was on the way in that I had been spotted, for Lawton said thoughtfully, "Let's take a look."

We took a couple of battered expediters with us—I didn't regard them as exactly necessary, but I couldn't see how I could tell Lawton that. The elevators were working again, so we came out in a slightly different part of the vaults than I had seen before; it was not entirely acting on my part when I peered around.

Lawton accepted my statement that I wasn't quite sure where I had heard the noises, without argument. He accepted it all too easily; he sent the expediters scouring the corridors at random.

And, of course, one of them found the pool of spilled fluorescence from the hypodermic needle I had knocked out of Rena's hand.

We stood there peering at the smear of purplish color, the shattered hypodermic, Rena's gas gun.

Lawton mused, "Looks like someone's trying to wake up some of our sleepers. That's our standard antilytic, if I'm not mistaken." He scanned the shelves. "Nobody missing around here. Take a look in the next few sections of the tiers."

The expediters saluted and left.

"They won't find anyone missing," Lawton predicted. "And *that* means we have to take a physical inventory of the whole damn clinic. Over eighty thousand suspendees to check." He made a disgusted noise.

I said, "Maybe they were scared off before they finished."

"Maybe. Maybe not. We'll have to check, that's all."

"Are you sure that stuff is to revive the suspendees?" I persisted. "Couldn't it just have been someone wandering down here by mistake during the commotion and—"

"And carrying a hypodermic needle by mistake, and armed with a gas gun by mistake. Sure, Wills."

The expediters returned and Lawton looked at them sourly.

They shook their heads. He shrugged. "Tell you what, Wills," he said. "Let's go back to the office and—"

He stopped, peering down the corridor. The last of our expediters was coming toward us—not alone.

"Well, what do you know!" said Lawton. "Wills, it looks like he's got your fugitive!"

The expediter was dragging a small writhing figure behind him; we could hear whines and pleading. For a heart-stopping second, I thought it was Rena, against all logic.

But it wasn't. It was a quavery ancient, a bleary-eyed wreck of a man, long past retirement age, shabbily dressed and obviously the sort who cut his pension policies to the barest minimum—and then whined when his old age was poverty-stricken.

Lawton asked me: "This the man?"

"I—I couldn't recognize him," I said.

Lawton turned to the weeping old man. "Who were you after?" he demanded. All he got was sobbing pleas to let him go; all he was likely to get was more of the same. The man was in pure panic.

We got him up to one of the receiving offices on the upper level, half carried by the expediters. Lawton questioned him mercilessly for half an hour before giving up. The man was by then incapable of speech.

He had said, as nearly as we could figure it out, only that he was sorry he had gone into the forbidden place, he didn't mean to go into the forbidden place, he had been sleeping in the shadow of the forbidden place when fighting began and he fled inside.

It was perfectly apparent to me that he was telling the truth—and, more, that any diversionary riot designed to get *him* inside with a hypodermic and gas gun would have been planned by maniacs, for I doubted he could have found the trigger of the gun. But Lawton seemed to think he was lying.

It was growing late. Lawton offered to drive me to my hotel, leaving the man in the custody of the expediters. On the way, out of curiosity, I asked: "Suppose he had succeeded? Can you revive a suspendee as easily as that, just by sticking a needle in his arm?"

Lawton grunted. "Pretty near, that and artificial respiration. One case in a hundred might need something else—heart massage or an incubator, for instance. But most of the time an antilytic shot is enough."

Then Rena had not been as mad as I thought.

I said: "And do you think that old man could have accomplished anything?"

Lawton looked at me curiously. "Maybe."

"Who do you suppose he was after?"

Lawton said off-handedly. "He was right near Bay 100, wasn't he?"

"Bay 100?" Something struck a chord; I remembered following Rena down the corridor, passing a door that was odd in some way. Was the number 100 on that door? "Is that the one that's locked off, with the sign on it that says anybody who goes in is asking for trouble?"

"That's the one. Though," he added, "nobody is going to get in. That door is triple-plate armor; the lock opens only to the personal fingerprint pattern of Defoe and two or three others."

"What's inside it that's so important?"

He said coldly, "How would I know? I can't open the door." And that was the end of the conversation. I knew *he* was lying.

I had changed my bet with myself on the way. I won it. Rena was in the room waiting for me. She was sound asleep, stretched out on the bed. She looked as sober-faced and intent in her sleep as a little girl—a look I had noticed in Marianna's sleeping face once.

It was astonishing how little I thought about Marianna any more.

I considered very carefully before I rang for a bellboy, but it seemed wisest to let her sleep and take my chances with the house detective, if any. There was none, it turned out. In fact, the bellboy hardly noticed her—whether out of indifference or because he was well aware that I had signed for the room with an official travel-credit card of the Company, it didn't much matter. He succeeded in conveying, without saying a word, that the Blue Sky was the limit.

I ordered dinner, waving away the menu and telling him to let the chef decide. The chef decided well. Among other things, there was a bottle of champagne in a bucket of ice.

Rena woke up slowly at first, and then popped to a sitting position, eyes wide. I said quickly, "Everything's all right. No one saw you at the clinic."

She blinked once. In a soft voice, she said, "Thank you." She sighed a very small sigh and slipped off the bed.

I realized as Rena was washing up, comparisons were always odious, but—Well, if a strange man had found Marianna with her dress hitched halfway up her thigh, asleep on his bed, he'd have been in for something. What the "something" would be might depend on circumstances; it might be a raging order to knock before he came in, it might only be a storm of blushes and a couple of hours of meticulously prissy behavior. But she wouldn't just let it slide. And Rena, by simply disregarding it, was as modest as any girl could be.

After all, I told myself, warming to the subject, it wasn't as if I were some excitable adolescent. I could see a lovely girl's legs without getting all stirred up. For that matter, I hardly even noticed them, come to think of it. And if I *did* notice them, it was certainly nothing of any importance; I had dismissed it casually, practically forgotten it, in fact.

She came back and said cheerfully, "I'm hungry!" And so, I realized, was I.

We started to eat without much discussion, except for the necessary talk of the table. I felt very much at ease sitting across from her, in spite of the fact that she had placed herself in opposition to the Company. I felt relaxed and comfortable; nothing bothered me. Certainly, I went on in my mind, I was as free and easy with her as with any man; it didn't matter that she was an attractive girl at all. I wasn't thinking of her in that way, only as someone who needed some help.

I came to. She was looking at me with friendly curiosity. She said, "Is that an American idiom, Tom, when you said, 'Please pass the legs'?"

We didn't open the champagne: it didn't seem quite appropriate. We had not discussed anything of importance while we were eating, except that I had told her about the old man; she evidently knew nothing about him. She was concerned, but I assured her he was safe with the Company—what did she think they were, barbarians? She didn't answer.

But after dinner, with our coffee, I said: "Now let's get down to business. What were you doing in the clinic?"

"I was trying to rescue my father," she said.

"Rescue, Rena? Rescue from what?"

"Tom, please. You believe in the Company, do you not?"

"Of course!"

"And I do not. We shall never agree. I am grateful to you for not turning me in, and I think perhaps I know what it cost you to do it. But that is all, Tom."

"But the Company—"

"When you speak of the Company, what is it you see? Something shining and wonderful? It is not that way with me; what I see is—rows of my friends, frozen in the vaults or the expediters and that poor old man you caught."

There was no reasoning with her. She had fixed in her mind that all the suspendees were the victims of some sinister brutality. Of course, it wasn't like that at all.

Suspension wasn't death; everyone knew that. In fact, it was the antithesis of death. It *saved* lives by taking the maimed and sick and putting them mercifully to sleep, until they could be repaired.

True, their bodies grew cold, the lungs stopped pumping, the heart stopped throbbing; true, no doctor could tell, on sight, whether a suspendee was "alive" or "dead." The life processes were not entirely halted, but they were slowed enormously—

enough so that chemical diffusion in the jellylike blood carried all the oxygen the body needed. But there was a difference: The dead were dead, whereas the suspendees could be brought back to life at any moment the Company chose.

But I couldn't make her see that. I couldn't even console her by reminding her that the old man was a mere Class E. For so was she.

I urged reasonably: "Rena, you think something is going on under the surface. Tell me about it. Why do you think your father was put in suspension?"

"To keep him out of the way. Because the Company is afraid of him."

I played a trump card: "Suppose I told you the *real* reason he's in the vaults."

She was hit by that, I could tell. She was staring at me with wonder in her eyes.

"You don't have to speculate about it, Rena. I looked up his record, you see."

"You—you—"

I nodded. "It's right there in black and white. They're trying to save his life. He has radiation poisoning. He was a war casualty. It's standard medical practice in cases like his to put them in suspension for a while, until the level of radioactivity dies down and they can safely be revived. Now what do you say?"

She merely stared at me.

I pressed on persuasively: "Rena, I don't mean to call your beliefs superstitions or anything like that. Please understand me. You have your own cultural heritage and—well, I know that it looks as though he is some kind of 'undead,' or however you put it, in your folk stories. I know there are legends of vampires and zombies and so on, but—"

She was actually laughing. "You're thinking of Central Europe, Tom, not Naples. And anyway..." She was laughing only with her eyes now, "...I do not believe that the legends say that vampires are produced by intravenous injections of chlorpromazine and pethidine in a lytic solution—which is, I believe, the current technique at the clinics."

I flared peevishly: "Damn it, don't you want him saved?"

The laughter was gone. She gently touched my hand. "I'm sorry. I don't mean to be a shrew and that remark wasn't kind. Must we discuss it?"

"Yes!"

"Very well." She faced me, chin out and fierce. "My father does not have radiation poisoning, Tom."

"He does."

"He does not! He is a prisoner, not a patient. He loved Naples. That's why he was put to sleep—for fifty years, or a hundred, until everything he knew and loved grows away from him and nobody cares what he has to say any more. They won't kill him—they don't have to! They just want him out of the way, because he sees the Company for what it is."

"And what is that?"

"Tyranny, Tom," she said quietly.

I burst out, "Rena, that's silly! The Company is the hope of the world. If you talk like that, you'll be in trouble. That's dangerous thinking, young lady. It attacks the foundations of our whole society!"

"Good! I was hoping it would!"

We were shouting at each other like children. I took time to remember one of the priceless rules out of the Adjusters' Handbook: *Never lose your temper; think before you speak.* We glared at each other in furious silence for a moment before I forced myself to simmer down.

Only then did I remember that I needed to know something she might be able to tell me. Organization, Defoe had said—an organization that opposed the Company, that was behind Hammond's death and the riot at the clinic and more, much more.

"Rena, why did your friends kill Hammond?"

Her poise was shaken. "Who?" she asked.

"Hammond. In Caserta. By a gang of anti-Company hoodlums."

Her eyes flashed, but she only said: "I know nothing of any killings."

"Yet you admit you belong to a subversive group?"

"I admit nothing," she said shortly.

"But you do. I know you do. You said as much to me, when you were prevented from reviving your father."

She shrugged.

I went on: "Why did you call me at the office, Rena? Was it to get me to help you work against the Company?"

She looked at me for a long moment. Then she said: "It was. And would you like to know why I picked you?"

"Well, I suppose—"

"Don't suppose, Tom." Her nostrils were white. She said coldly: "You seemed like a very good bet, as far as we could tell. I will tell you something you don't know. There is a memorandum regarding you in the office of the Chief of Expediters in Naples. I do not choose to tell you how I know of it, but even your Mr. Gogarty doesn't know it exists. It is private and secret, and it says of you, 'Loyalty doubtful. Believed in contact with underground movement. Keep under close but secret surveillance'."

That one rocked me, I admit. "But that's all wrong!" I finally burst out. "I admit I went through a bad time after Marianna died, but—"

She was smiling, though still angry. "Are you apologizing to *me*?"

"No, but—" I stopped. That was a matter to be taken up with Defoe, I told myself, and I was beginning to feel a little angry, too.

"All right," I said. "There's been a mistake; I'll see that it's straightened out. But even if it was true, did you think I was the kind of man to join a bunch of murderers?"

"We are not murderers!"

"Hammond's body says different."

"We had nothing to do with that, Tom!"

"Your friend Slovetski did." It was a shot in the dark. It missed by a mile.

She said loftily: "If he is such a killer, how did you escape? When I had my interview with you, and it became apparent that the expediters were less than accurate, the information came a little late. You could easily have given us trouble—Slovetski was in the next room. Why didn't he shoot you dead?"

"Maybe he didn't want to be bothered with my body."

"And maybe you are all wrong about us!"

"No! If you're against the Company, I *can't* be wrong. The Company is the greatest blessing the world has ever known—it's made the world a paradise!"

"It has?" She made a snorting sound. "How?"

"By bringing countless blessings to all of us. *Countless!*"

She was shaking with the effort of controlling her temper. "Name one!"

I swore in exasperation. "All right," I said. "It ended war."

She nodded—not a nod of agreement, but because she had expected that answer. "Right out of the textbooks and propaganda pieces, Tom. Tell me, why is my father in the vaults?"

"Because he has radiation poisoning!"

"And how did he get this radiation poisoning?"

"How?" I blinked at her. "You know how, Rena. In the war between Naples and—the war—"

Rena said remorselessly, "That's right, Tom, the war. The war that couldn't have existed, because the Company ended war—everybody knows that. Ah, Tom! For God, tell me, why is the world blind? Everyone believes, no one questions. The Company ended war—it says so itself. And the blind world never sees the little wars that rage, all the time, one upon the heels of another. The Company has ended disease. But how many deaths are there? The Company has abolished poverty. But am I living in riches, Tom? Was the old man who ran into the vaults?"

I stammered, "But—but, Rena, the statistical charts show very clearly—"

"No, Tom," she said, gentle again. "The statistical charts show *less* war, not no war. They show *less* disease."

She rubbed her eyes wearily—and even then I thought: Marianna wouldn't have dared; it would have smeared her mascara.

"The trouble with you, Tom, is that you're an American. You don't know how it is in the world, only in America. You don't know what it was like after the Short War, when America won and the flying squads of Senators came over and the governments that were left agreed to defederate. You're used to a big and united country, not little city-states. You don't have thousands of years of intrigue and tyranny and plot behind you, so you close your eyes and plunge ahead, and if the charts show things are getting a *little* better, you think they are perfect."

She shook her head. "But not us, Tom. We can't afford that. We walk with eyes that dart about, seeking danger. Sometimes we see ghosts, but sometimes we see real menace. You look at the charts and you see that there are fewer wars than before. We—we look at the charts and we see our fathers and brothers dead in a little war that hardly makes a ripple on the graph. You don't even see them, Tom. You don't even see the disease cases that don't get cured—because the techniques are 'still experimental,' they say. You don't—Tom! What is it?"

I suppose I showed the pain of remembrance. I said with an effort, "Sorry, Rena. You made me think of something. Please go on."

"That's all of it, Tom. You in America can't be blamed. The big lie—the lie so preposterous that it cannot be questioned, the thing that proves itself because it is so unbelievable that no one would say it if it weren't true—is not an American invention. It is European, Tom. You aren't inoculated against it. We are."

I took a deep breath. "What about your father, Rena? Do you really think the Company is out to get him?"

She looked at me searchingly, then looked hopelessly away. "Not as you mean it, Tom," she said at last. "No, I am no paranoid. I think he is—inconvenient. I think the Company finds him less trouble in the deep-freeze than he would be walking around."

"But don't you agree that he needs treatment?"

"For what? For the radiation poisoning that he got from the atomic explosion he was nowhere near, Tom? Remember, he is my father! I was with him in the war—and he never stirred a kilometer from our home. You've been there, the big house where my aunt Luisa now lives. Did you see bomb craters there?"

"*That's a lie!*" I had to confess it to myself: Rena was beginning to mean something to me. But there were emotional buttons that even she couldn't push. If she had been a man, any man, I would have had my fist in her face before she had said that much; treason against the Company was more than I could take. "You can't convince me that the Company deliberately falsifies records. Don't forget, Rena, I'm an executive of the Company! Nothing like that could go on!"

Her eyes flared, but her lips were rebelliously silent.

I said furiously: "I'll hear no more of that. Theoretical discussions are all right; I'm as broad-minded as the next man. But when you accuse the Company of outright fraud, you—well, you're mistaken."

We glowered at each other for a long moment. My eyes fell first.

I said sourly, "I'm sorry if I called you a liar. I—I didn't mean to be offensive."

"Nor I, Tom," she hesitated. "Will you remember that I asked you not to make me discuss it?"

She stood up. "Thank you very much for a dinner. And for listening. And most of all, for giving me another chance to rescue my father."

I looked at my watch automatically—and incredulously. "It's late, Rena. Have you a place to stay?"

She shrugged. "N—yes, of course, Tom. Don't worry about me; I'll be all right."

"Are you sure?"

"Very sure."

Her manner was completely confident—so much so that I knew it for an act.

I said: "Please, Rena, you've been through a tough time and I don't want you wandering around. You can't get back to Naples tonight."

"I know."

"Well?"

"Well what, Tom?" she said. "I won't lie to you—I haven't a place to go to here. I would have had, this afternoon, if I had succeeded. But by now, everything has changed. They—that is, my friends will assume that I have been captured by the Company. They won't be where I could find them, Tom. Say they are silly if you wish. But they will fear that the Company might—request me to give their names."

I said crisply, "Stay here, Rena. No—listen to me. You stay here. I'll get another room."

"Thank you, Tom, but you can't. There isn't a room in Anzio; there are families of suspendees sleeping in the grass tonight."

"I can sleep in the grass if I have to."

She shook her head. "Thank you," she repeated.

I stood between her and the door. "Then we'll both stay here. I'll sleep on the couch. You can have the bed." I hesitated, then added, "You can trust me, Rena."

She looked at me gravely for a moment. Then she smiled. "I'm sure I can, Tom. I appreciate your offer. I accept."

I am built too long for a hotel-room couch, particularly a room in a Mediterranean coastal fleabag. I lay staring into the white Italian night; the Moon brightened the clouds outside the window, and the room was clearly enough illuminated to show me the bed and the slight, motionless form in it. Rena was not a restless sleeper, I thought. Nor did she snore.

Rena was a most self-possessed girl, in fact. She had overruled me when I tried to keep the bellboy from clearing away the dinner service. "Do you think no other Company man ever had a girl in his room?" she innocently asked. She borrowed a pair of the new pajamas Defoe's thoughtful expediters had bought and put in the bureau. But I hadn't expected that, while the bellboy was clearing away, she would be softly singing to herself in the bath.

He had seemed not even to hear.

He had also leaped to conclusions—not that it was much of a leap, I suppose. But he had conspicuously not removed the bottle of champagne and its silver bucket of melting ice.

It felt good, being in the same room with Rena.

I shifted again, hunching up my torso to give my legs a chance to stretch out. I looked anxiously to see if the movement had disturbed her.

There is a story about an animal experimenter who left a chimpanzee in an empty room. He closed the door on the ape and bent to look through the key-hole, to see what the animal would do. But all he saw was an eye—because the chimp was just as curious about the experimenter.

In the half-light, I saw a sparkle of moonlight in Rena's eye; she was watching me. She half-giggled, a smothered sound.

"You ought to be asleep," I accused.

"And you, Tom."

I obediently closed my eyes, but I didn't stop seeing her.

If only she weren't a fanatic.

And if she had to be a fanatic, why did she have to be the one kind that was my natural enemy, a member of the group of irresponsible troublemakers that Defoe had ordered me to "handle"?

What, I wondered, did he mean by "handle"? Did it include chlorpromazine in a lytic solution and a plastic cocoon?

I put that thought out of my mind; there was no chance whatever that her crazy belief, that the Company was using suspension as a retaliatory measure, was correct. But thinking of Defoe made me think of my work. After all, I told myself, Rena was more than a person. She was a key that could unlock the whole riddle. She had the answers—if there was a movement of any size, she would know its structure.

I thought for a moment and withdrew the "if." She had admitted the riot of that afternoon was planned. It *had* to be a tightly organized group.

And she had to have the key.

At last, I had been getting slightly drowsy, but suddenly I was wide awake.

There were two possibilities. I faced the first of them shakily—*she might be right.* Everything within me revolted against the notion, but I accepted it as a theoretical possibility. If so, I would, of course, have to revise some basic notions.

On the other hand, she might be wrong. I was certain she *was* wrong. But I was equally certain she was no raddled malcontent and if she was wrong, and I could prove it to her, she herself might make some revisions.

Propped on one elbow, I peered at her. "Rena?" I whispered questioningly.

She stirred. "Yes, Tom?"

"If you're not asleep, can we take a couple more minutes to talk?"

"Of course." I sat up and reached for the light switch, but she said, "Must we have the lights? The Moon is very bright."

"Sure." I sat on the edge of the couch and reached for a cigarette. "Can I offer you a deal, Rena?"

"What sort of deal?"

"A horsetrade. You think the Company is corrupt and your father is not a casualty, right?"

"Correct, Tom."

"And I think the Company is not corrupt and your father has radiation poisoning. One of us has to be wrong, right?"

"Correct, Tom."

"Let's find out. There are ways of testing for radiation-sickness. I'll go into the clinic in the morning and get the answer."

She also lifted up on one elbow, peering at me, her long hair braided down her back. "Will you?"

"Sure. And we'll make bets on it, Rena. If you are wrong—if your father has radiation poisoning—I want you to tell me everything there is to tell about the riot today and the people behind it. If I'm wrong..." I swallowed, "...if I'm wrong, I'll get your father out of there for you. Somehow. I promise it, Rena."

There was absolute silence for a long time. Then she swung out of the bed and hurried over to me, her hands on mine. She looked at me and again I saw tears. "Will you do that, Tom?" she asked, hardly audible.

"Why, sure," I said awkwardly. "But you have to promise—"

"I promise!"

She was staring at me, at arm's length. And then something happened. She wasn't staring and she wasn't at arm's length.

Kissing her was like tasting candied violets; and the Moon made her lovelier than anything human; and the bellboy had not been so presumptuous, after all, when he left us the champagne.

CHAPTER NINE

Dr. Lawton was "away from his desk" the next morning. That was all to the good. I was not a hardened enough conspirator to seek out chances to make mistakes, and although I had a perfectly good excuse for wanting to go down into the vaults again, I wasn't anxious to have to use it.

The expediter-officer in charge, though, didn't even ask for reasons. He furnished me with what I wanted—a map of the vaults and a radiation-counter—and turned me loose.

Looking at the map, I was astonished at the size of this subterranean pyramid. Lawton had said we had eighty-odd thousand sleepers filed away and that had surprised me, but by the chart I held in my hand, there was space for perhaps ten times that many. It was beyond belief that so much space was really needed, I thought—unless there was some truth to Rena's belief that the Company used the clinics for prisons...

I applied myself to the map.

And, naturally, I read it wrong. It was very simple; I merely went to the wrong level, that was all.

It looked wrong as soon as I stepped out of the elevator. An elderly, officious civilian with a British accent barred my way. "You aren't one of us, are you?"

I said, "I doubt it."

"Then would you mind?" he asked politely, and indicated a spot on the side of the hall. Perhaps I was suggestible, but I obeyed his request without question. It was just as well, because a sort of procession rounded a bend and came down the corridor. There was a wheeled stretcher, with three elderly civilians puttering around it, and a bored medic following with a jar of something held aloft, feeding through a thin plastic tube into the arm of the man on the stretcher, as well as half a dozen others of more nondescript types.

The man who had stopped me nearly ran to meet the stretcher. He stared into the waxy face and whispered, "It's he! Oh, absolutely, it is he!"

I looked and the face was oddly familiar. It reminded me of my childhood; it had a link with school days and the excitement of turning twelve. By the way the four old men were carrying on, however, it meant more than that to them. It meant, if not the Second Coming, at least something close to it.

By then I had figured out that this was that rare event in the day of a clinic—a revival. I had never seen one. I suppose I could have got out of the way and gone about my conspiratorial business, and it is no credit to me as a conspirator that I did not. But I was fascinated.

Too fascinated to wonder why revivals were so rare...

The medic looked at his watch and, with careless efficiency, plucked the tube out of the waxy man's arm.

"Two minutes," he said to one of the civilians. "Then he'll be as good as he ever was. You've got his clothes and release papers?"

"Oh, definitely," said the civilian, beaming.

"Okay. And you understand that the Company takes no responsibility beyond the policy covering? After all, he was one of the first men suspended. We think we can give him another year or so—which is a year more than he would have had, at that—but he's not what you'd call a Grade A risk."

"Certainly," agreed the civilian. "Can we talk to him now?"

"As soon as he opens his eyes."

The civilian bent over the man, who no longer looked waxy. His face was now a mottled gray and his eyelids were flickering. He had begun to breathe heavily and irregularly, and he was mumbling something I couldn't understand. The civilian whispered in his ear and the revived man opened his eyes and looked at him.

It was like seeing the dead come to life. It was exactly that, in fact; twenty minutes before, no chemical test, no stethoscope or probing thumb in the eye socket could have detected the faint living glow in the almost-dead cells. And yet—now he looked, he breathed, he spoke.

"I made it," were his first understandable words.

"Indeed you did!" crowed the civilian in charge, while all of the others murmured happily to each other. "Sir, it is my pleasure to welcome you back to us. You are in Anzio, Italy. And I am Thomas Welbourne, at your service."

The faint eyes sparkled. Dead, near-dead or merely decrepit, this was a man who wanted to enjoy life. Minutes out of the tomb, he said: "No! Not young Tommy Welbourne!"

"His grandson, sir," said the civilian.

I had it just then—that face had watched me through a whole year of school. It had been in a frame at the front of the room, with half a dozen other faces. It had a name under it, which, try as I might, I couldn't recall; but the face was there all the same. It was an easy one to keep in mind—strong though sunken, ancient but very much alive.

He was saying, in a voice as confident as any youth's, "Ah, Tommy, I've lived to see it! Tell me, have you been to Mars? What is on the other side of the Moon? And the Russians—what are the Russians up to these days?"

The civilian coughed and tried to interrupt, but the figure on the stretcher went on heedlessly: "All those years gone—what wonders must we have. A tunnel under the Atlantic, I'll wager! And ships that fly a hundred times the speed of sound. Tell me, Tommy Welbourne! Don't keep an old man waiting!"

The civilian said reluctantly, but patiently, "Perhaps it will take a little explaining, sir. You see, there have been changes—"

"I know it, boy! That's what I'm asking you!"

"Well, not that sort of changes, sir. We've learned new virtues since your time—patience and stability, things of that sort. You see—"

The interesting part was over and the glances of the others in the party reminded me that I didn't belong here. I stole off, but not before the man on the stretcher noticed me and made a sort of clumsy two-fingered salute of hail and farewell as I left. It was exactly like the gesture in his picture on that schoolroom wall, up next to the presidents and the greatest of kings.

I found a staircase and climbed to another level of the boxlike clinic.

The local peasants called the vaults "coolers" or "ice cubes." I suppose the reason had something to do with the fact that they were cool and rectangular, on the whole—perhaps because, like icebergs, the great bulk of the vaults was below the surface. But whatever you called them, they were huge. And the clinic at Anzio was only one out of hundreds scattered all over the world.

It was all a matter of viewpoint. To me, the clinics were emblems of the Company's concern for the world. In any imaginable disaster—even if some fantastic plague struck the entire race at once—the affected population could be neatly and effectively preserved until medicine could catch up with their cures.

To Rena, they were prisons big enough to hold the human race.

It was time to find out which of us was right. I hurried through the corridors, between the tiers of sleepers, almost touching them on both sides. I saw the faint purplish gleam where Rena had spilled the fluid, and knelt beside the cocoon that held her father.

The UV sterilizers overhead made everything look ghastly violet, but in any light, the waxy face under the plastic would have looked dead as death itself. I couldn't blame Rena for weeping.

I took out the little radiation counter and looked at it awkwardly. There was nothing complicated about the device—fortunately, because I had had little experience with them. It was a cylinder with a flaring snout at one end, a calibrated gauge at the side, marked in micro-roentgens. The little needle flickered in the green area of the dial. I held it to myself and the reading didn't change. I pointed it up and pointed it down; it didn't change.

I held it to the radiation-seared body of Benedetto dell'Angela.

And it didn't change.

Radiation-seared? Not unless the instrument lied! If dell'Angela had ever in his life been within the disaster radius of an atomic explosion, it had been so long before that every trace of radioactive byproduct was gone!

Rena was right!

I worked like a machine, hardly thinking. I stood up and hurriedly touched the ion-tasting snout of the counter to the body on the shelf above Benedetto, the one above that, a dozen chosen at random up and down the aisle.

Two of them sent the needle surging clear off the scale; three were as untainted by radioactivity as Benedetto himself. A few others gave readings from "mild" to "lethal"—but all in the danger area.

Most were as untainted by radiation as Benedetto himself.

It was possible, I told myself frantically, that there were mysteries here I did not understand. Perhaps after a few months or a year, the radiation level would drop, so that the victim was still in deadly danger while the emitted radiation of his body was too slight to affect the counter. I didn't see how, but it was worth a thought. Anything was worth a thought that promised another explanation to this than the one Rena had given!

There had been, I remembered, a score or more of new suspendees in the main receiving vault at the juncture of the

167

corridors. I hurried back to it. Here were fresh cases, bound to show on the gauge.

I leaned over the nearest one, first checking to make sure its identification tag was the cross-hatched red one that marked "radiation." I brought the counter close to the shriveled face—

But I didn't read the dial, not at first. I didn't have to. For I recognized that face. I had seen it, contorted in terror, mumbling frantic pleas for mercy, weeping and howling, on the old Class E uninsurable the expediters had found hiding in the vaults.

He had no radiation poisoning...unless a bomb had exploded in these very vaults in the past twelve hours.

It wasn't pleasant to stand there and stare around the vaults that were designed for the single purpose of saving human life—and to wonder how many of the eighty thousand souls it held were also prisoners.

And it wasn't even tolerable to think the thought that followed. If the Company was corrupt, and I had worked to do the Company's business, how much of this guilt was mine?

The Company, I had said and thought and tried to force others to agree, was the hope of humanity—the force that had permanently ended war (almost), driven out disease (nearly), destroyed the threat to any human of hunger or homelessness (in spite of the starving old man who slept in the shadow of the crypt, and others like him).

But I had to face the facts that controverted the Big Lie. If war was ended, what about Naples and Sicily, and Prague and Vienna, and all the squabbles in the Far East? *If there was no danger from disease, why had Marianna died?*

Rena had said that if there was no danger of disaster, no one would have paid their premiums. Obviously the Company could not have wanted that, but why had I never seen it before? Sample wars, sample deaths—the Company needed them. And no one, least of all me, fretted about how the samples felt about it.

Well, that was behind me. I'd made a bet with Rena, and I'd lost, and I had to pay off.

I opened the cased hypodermic kit Rena had given me and examined it uncomfortably. I had never used the old-fashioned sort of needle hypodermic; I knew a little something about the high-pressure spray type that forced its contents into the skin without leaving a mark, but I was very far from sure that I could manage this one without doing something wrong. Besides, there wasn't much of the fluid left, only the few drops left in the bottom of the bottle after Rena had loaded the needle that had been smashed.

I hurried back along the corridor toward Benedetto dell'Angela. I neared again the red-labeled door marked Bay 100, glanced at it in passing—and stopped.

This was the door that only a handful of people could open. It was labeled in five languages: "Entrance Strictly Prohibited. Experimental Section."

Why was it standing ajar?

And I heard a faint whisper of a moan: "*Aiutemi, aiutemi.*"

Someone inside was calling for help!

If I had been a hardened conspirator, I would never have stopped to investigate. But, of course, I wasn't. I pushed the door aside, against resistance, and peered in.

And that was my third major shock in the past quarter of an hour, because, writhing feebly just inside the door, staring up at me with an expression of pain and anger, was Luigi Zorchi.

He propped himself up on his hands, the rags of his plastic cocoon dangling from his shoulders.

"Oho," he said faintly. "The apprentice assassin again."

I found water for him at a bubble-fountain by the ramp; he drank at least a quart before I made him stop. Then he lay back, panting, staring at me. Except for the shreds of plastic and the bandages around the stumps of his legs, he was nude, like all the other suspendees inside their sacks. The luxuriant hair had already begun to grow back.

He licked his lips. More vigorous now, he snarled: "The plan fails, does it not? You think you have Zorchi out of the way, but he will not stay there."

I said, "Zorchi, I'm sorry about all this I—I know more now than I did yesterday."

He gaped. "Yesterday? Only *yesterday*?" He shook his head. "I would have thought a month, at the least. I have been crawling, assassin. Crawling for days, I thought." He tried to shrug—not

169

easy, because he was leaning on his elbows. "Very well, Weels. You may take me back to finish the job now. Sticking me with a needle and putting me on ice will not work. Perhaps you should kill me outright."

"Listen, Zorchi, I *said* I was sorry. Let's let it go at that for a moment. I—I admit you shouldn't be here. The question is, how do you come to be awake?"

"How not? I am Zorchi, Weels. Cut me and I heal; poison me and I cure myself." He spat furiously. "Starve me, however, and I no doubt will die, and it is true that you have come very near to starving me down here." He glowered at the shelves of cocooned bodies in the locked bay. "A pity, with all this pork and beef on the rack, waiting for me, but I find I am not a monster, Weels. It is a weakness; I do not suppose it would stop any Company man for a moment."

"Look, Zorchi," I begged, "take my word for it—I want to help you. You might as well believe me, you know. You can't be any worse off than you are."

He stared at me sullenly for a moment. Then, "True enough," he admitted. "What then, Weels?"

I said hesitantly, "Well, I'd like to get you out of here…"

"Oh, yes. I would like that, too. How shall we do it?"

I rubbed the back of my neck thoughtfully, staring at him. I had had a sort of half-baked, partly worked out plan for rescuing Benedetto. Wake him up with the needle; find a medical orderly's whites somewhere; dress him; and walk him out.

It wasn't the best of all possible plans, but I had rank enough, particularly with Defoe off in Rome, to take a few liberties or stop questions if it became necessary. And besides, I hadn't really thought I'd have to do it. I had fully expected—as recently as half an hour ago!—that I would find Benedetto raddled with gamma rays, a certainty for death if revived before the half-life period of the radioelements in his body had brought the level down to safety.

That plan might work for Benedetto. But Zorchi, to mention only one possible obstacle, couldn't walk. And Benedetto, once I took off his beard with the razor Rena had insisted I bring for that purpose, would not be likely to be recognized by anyone.

Zorchi, on the other hand, was very nearly unforgettable.

I said honestly, "I don't know."

He nodded. "Nor do I, Weels. Take me then to your Defoe." His face wrinkled in an expression of fury and fear. "Die I can, if I must, but I do not wish to starve. It is good to be able to grow a leg, but do you understand that the leg must come from somewhere? I cannot make it out of air, Weels—I must eat. When I am in my home at Naples, I eat five, six, eight times a day; it is the way my body must have it. So if Defoe wishes to kill me, we will let him, but I must leave here *now*."

I shook my head. "Please understand me, Zorchi—I can't even do that for you. I can't have anybody asking me what I was doing down in this level." I hesitated only briefly; then, realizing that I was already in so deeply that secrecy no longer mattered, I told him about Benedetto dell'Angela, and the riot that failed, and my promise.

His reaction was incredulity. "You did not know, Weels? The arms and legs of the Company do not know what thoughts pass through its brain? Truly, the Company is a wonderful thing! Even the peasants know this much—the Company will do anything it must."

"I admit I never guessed. Now what?"

"That is up to you, Weels. If you try to take the two of us out, it endangers you. It is for you to decide."

So, of course, I could decide only one way.

I hid the hypodermic behind one of the bodies in Bay 100; it was no longer useful to me. I persuaded Zorchi to lie quietly in one of the tiers near Benedetto, slammed the heavy door to Bay 100, and heard the locks snap. That was the crossing of the Rubicon. You could open that door easily enough from inside— that was to protect any personnel who might be caught in there. But only Defoe and a couple of others could open it from without, and the hypodermic was now as far out of reach as the Moon.

I opened Benedetto dell'Angela's face mask and shaved him, then sealed it again. I found another suspendee of about the same build, made sure the man was not radioactive, and transferred them. I switched tags: Benedetto dell'Angela was now Elio Barletteria. Then I walked unsteadily to the ramp, picked up the intercom and ordered the medical officer in charge to come down.

171

It was not Dr. Lawton who came, fortunately, but one of his helpers who had seen me before. I pointed to the pseudo-Barletteria. "I want this man revived."

He sputtered, "You—you can't just take a suspendee out of his trance, Mr. Wills. It's a violation of medical ethics! These men are *sick*. They—"

"They'll be sicker still if we don't get some information from this one," I said grimly. "Are you going to obey Mr. Defoe's orders or not?"

He sputtered some more, but he gave in. His orderlies took Benedetto to the receiving station at the foot of the vault; one of them stood by while the doctor worriedly went through his routine. I sat and smoked, watching the procedure.

It was simple enough. One injection, a little chafing of the hands and feet by the bored orderly while the doctor glowered and I stonily refused to answer his questions, and a lot of waiting. And then the "casualty" stirred and moaned.

All the stand-by apparatus was there—the oxygen tent and the pulmotor and the heart stimulator and so on. But none of it was needed.

I said: "Fine, Doctor. Now send the orderly to have an ambulance standing by at the main entrance, and make out an exit pass for this casualty."

"No!" the doctor shouted. "This is against every rule, Mr. Wills. I insist on calling Dr. Lawton—"

"By all means," I said. "But there isn't much time. Make out the pass and get the ambulance, and we'll clear it with Dr. Lawton on the way out." He was all ready to say no again when I added: "This is by direct order of Mr. Defoe. Are you questioning his orders?"

He wasn't—not as long as I was going to clear it with Dr. Lawton. He did as I asked. One of the advantages of the Company's rigid regulations was that it was hard to enforce strict security on its personnel. If you didn't tell the staff that they were working for something needing covering up, you couldn't expect them to be constantly on guard.

When the orderly was gone and the doctor had scrawled out the pass, I said cordially, "Thank you, Doctor. Now would you like to know what all the fuss was about?"

"I certainly would," he snapped. "If you think—"

"I'm sorry," I apologized. "Come over here and take a look at this man."

I juggled the radiation counter in my hand as he stalked over. "Take a look at his eyes," I invited.

"Are you trying to tell me that this is a dangerously radioactive case? I warn you, Mr. Wills—"

"No, no," I said. "See for yourself. Look at the right eye, just beside the nose."

He bent over the awakening body, searchingly.

I clonked him with the radiation counter on the back of the head. They must have retired that particular counter from service after that; it wasn't likely to be very accurate any more.

The orderly found me bending over the doctor's body and calling for help. He bent, too, and he got the same treatment. Benedetto by then was awake; he listened to me and didn't ask questions. The blessings of dealing with conspirators—it was not necessary to explain things more than once.

And so, with a correctly uniformed orderly, who happened to be Benedetto dell'Angela, pushing the stretcher, and with myself displaying a properly made out pass to the expediter at the door, we rolled the sham-unconscious body of Luigi Zorchi out to a waiting ambulance.

I felt my pulse hammering as we passed the expediter at the door. I had thrown my coat over the place where legs should have been on "Barletteria," and Benedetto's old plastic cocoon, into which we had squeezed Zorchi, concealed most of him.

I needn't have worried. The expediter not only wasn't suspicious, he wasn't even interested.

Benedetto and I lifted Zorchi into the ambulance. Benedetto climbed in after him and closed the doors, and I went to the front. "You're dismissed," I told the driver. "I'll drive."

As soon as we were out of sight of the clinic, I found a phone, got Rena at the hotel, told her to meet me under the marquee. In five minutes, she was beside me and we were heading for the roads to the north.

"You win," I told her. "Your father's in back—along with somebody else. Now what? Do we just try to get lost in the hills somewhere?"

"No, Tom," she said breathlessly. "I—I have made arrangements." She giggled. "I walked around the square and around, until someone came up to me. You do not know how many gentlemen came before that! But then one of my—friends showed up, to see if I was all right, and I arranged it. We go up the Rome highway two miles and there will be a truck."

"Fine," I said, stepping on the gas. "Now do you want to climb back and tell your father—"

I stopped in the middle of the word. Rena peered at me. "Tom," she asked anxiously, "is something wrong?"

I swallowed, staring after a disappearing limousine in the rear-view mirror. "I—hope not," I said. "But your friends had better be there, because we don't have much time. I saw Defoe in the back of that limousine."

CHAPTER TEN

Rena craned her neck around the door and peered into the nave of the church. "He's kissing the Book," she reported. "It will be perhaps twenty minutes yet."

Her father said mildly, "I am in no hurry. It is good to rest here. Though truthfully, Mr. Wills, I thought I had been rested sufficiently by your Company."

I think we were all grateful for the rest. It had been a hectic drive up from Anzio. Even though Rena's "friends" were thoughtful people, they had not anticipated that we would have a legless man with us.

They had passports for Rena and myself and Benedetto; for Zorchi they had none. It had been necessary for him to hide under a dirty tarpaulin in the trunk of the ancient charcoal-burning car, while Rena charmed the Swiss Guards at the border. And it was risky. But the Guards charmed easily, and we got through.

Zorchi did not much appreciate it. He swore a ragged blue streak when we stopped in the shade of an olive grove and lugged him to the front seat again, and he didn't stop swearing until we hit the Appian Way. When the old gas-generator limped up a hill, he swore at its slowness; when it whizzed along the downgrades and level stretches, he swore at the way he was being bounced around.

I didn't regret rescuing Zorchi from the clinic—it was a matter of simple justice since I had helped trick him into it. But I did wish that it had been some more companionable personality that I had been obligated to.

Benedetto, on the other hand, shook my hand and said: "For God, I thank you," and I felt well repaid. But he was in the back seat being brought up to date by his daughter; I had the honor of Zorchi's company next to me...

There was a long Latin period from the church, a response from the altar boy, and then the final *Ite, missa est*. We heard the worshippers moving out of the church.

The priest came through the room we were waiting in, his robes swirling. He didn't look around, or give any sign that he knew we were there, though he almost stepped on Zorchi, sitting propped against a wall.

A moment later, another man in vaguely clerical robes entered and nodded to us. "Now we go below," he ordered.

Benedetto and I flanked Zorchi and carried him, an arm around each of our necks. We followed the sexton, or whatever he was, back into the church, before the altar—Benedetto automatically genuflected with the others, nearly making me spill Zorchi onto the floor—to a tapestry-hung door. He pushed aside the tapestry, and a cool, musty draft came up from darkness.

The sexton lit a taper with a pocket cigarette lighter and led us down winding, rickety steps. There was no one left in the church to notice us; if anyone had walked in, we were tourists, doing as countless millions of tourists had done before us over the centuries.

We were visiting the Catacombs.

Around us were the bones of the Christians of a very different Rome. Rena had told me about them: How they rambled under the modern city, the only entrances where churches had been built over them. How they had been nearly untouched for two thousand years. I even felt a little as though I really were a tourist as we descended, she had made me that curious to see them.

But I was disappointed. We lugged the muttering Zorchi through the narrow, musty corridors, with the bones of martyrs at our elbows, in the flickering light of the taper, and I had the curious feeling that I had been there before.

As, in a way, I had: I had been in the vaults of the Company's clinic at Anzio, in some ways very closely resembling these Catacombs—

Even to the bones of the martyrs.

I was almost expecting to see plastic sacks.

We picked our way through the warrens for several minutes, turning this way and that. I was lost in the first minute. Then the sexton stopped before a flat stone that had a crude, faded sketch of a fish on it; he leaned on it, and the stone discovered itself to be a door. We followed him through it into a metal-walled, high-ceilinged tunnel, utterly unlike the meandering Catacombs. I began to hear sounds; we went through another door, and light struck at our eyes.

I blinked and focused on a long room, half a dozen yards wide, almost as tall, at least fifty yards long. It appeared to be a section of an enormous tunnel; it appeared to be, and it was. Benedetto and I set Zorchi—still cursing—down on the floor and stared around.

There were people in the tunnel, dozens of them. There were desks and tables and file cabinets; it looked almost like any branch of the Company, with whirring mimeographs and clattering typewriters.

The sexton pinched out the taper and dropped it on the floor, as people came toward us.

"So now you are in our headquarters in Rome," said the man dressed as a sexton. "It is good to see you again, Benedetto."

"And it is much better to see you, Slovetski," the old man answered warmly.

This man Slovetski—I do not think I can say what he looked like.

He was, I found, the very leader of the "friends," the monarch of this underground headquarters. But he was a far cry from the image I had formed of a bearded agitator. There was a hint of something bright and fearful in his eyes, but his voice was warm and deep, his manner was reassuring, his face was friendly. Still— there was that cat-spark in his eyes.

Slovetski, that first day, gave me an hour of his time. He answered some of my questions—not all. The ones he smiled at, and shook his head, were about numbers and people. The ones he answered were about principles and things.

He would tell me, for instance, what he thought of the Company—endlessly. But he wouldn't say how many persons in the world were his followers. He wouldn't name any of the persons who were all around us. But he gladly told me about the place itself.

"History, Mr. Wills," he said politely. "History tells a man everything he needs to know. You look in the books, and you will learn of Mussolini, when this peninsula was all one state; he lived in Rome, and he started a subway. The archives even have maps. It is almost all abandoned now. Most of it was never finished. But the shafts are here, and the wiring that lights us still comes from the electric mains."

"And the only entrance is through the Catacombs?"

The spark gleamed bright in his eye for a second. Then he shrugged. "Why shouldn't I tell you? No. There are several others, but they are not all convenient." He chuckled. "For instance, one goes through a station on the part of the subway that is still in operation. But it would not have done for you, you see; Rena could not have used it. It goes through the gentlemen's washroom."

We chuckled, Slovetski and I. I liked him. He looked like what he once had been: a history teacher in a Company school, somewhere in Europe. We talked about History, and Civilization, and Mankind, and all the other capitalized subjects. He was very didactic and positive in what he said, just like a history teacher. But he was understanding. He made allowances for my background; he did not call me a fool. He was a patient monk instructing a novice in the mysteries of the order, and I was at ease with him.

But there was still that spark in his eye.

Rena disappeared almost as soon as we were safely in the tunnels. Benedetto was around, but he was as busy as Slovetski, and just as mysterious about what occupied him. So I had for company Zorchi.

We had lunch. "Food!" he said, and the word was an epithet. "They offer this to me for food! For pigs, Weels. Not for Zorchi!" He pushed the plate away from him and stared morosely at the table.

We were given a room to share, and one of Slovetski's men fixed up a rope-and-pulley affair so Zorchi could climb into his bed unaided. He was used to the help of a valet; the first time he tried it, he slipped and fell on the stumps of his legs. It must have hurt.

He shrieked, "Assassins! All of them! They put me in a kennel with the apprentice assassin, and the other assassins make a guillotine for me to kill myself on!"

We had a long talk with Slovetski, on the ideals and principles of his movement. Zorchi stared mutinously at the wall. I found the whole thing very interesting—shocking, but interesting. But Zorchi was immune to shock: "Perhaps it is news to you, Weels, that the Company is a big beast?" And he was interested in nothing in all the world but Zorchi.

By the end of the second day I stopped talking to him entirely. It wasn't kind. He disliked me, but he hated everyone else in the tunnel, so he had no one to talk to. But it was either that or hit him in the face, and—although many of my mores had changed overnight—I still did not think I could strike a man without legs.

And besides, the less I saw of Zorchi, the more time I had to think about Rena.

She returned on the third day, without a word of explanation to me of where she had been or what she had done. She greeted me and disappeared again, this time only for hours. Then she came back and said, "Now I am through, for a time. How have you liked our little hideaway?"

I said, "It gets lonesome."

"Lonesome?" Her brown eyes were wide and perfectly serious. "I had thought it would be otherwise, Tom. So many of us in this little space, how could you be lonesome?"

I took her hand. "I'm not lonesome now," I told her. We found a place to sit in a corner of the communal dining hall. Around us the life of the underground movement buzzed and swirled. It was much like a branch of the Company, as I have said; the work of this secret section seemed to be mostly a record-keeping depot for the activities that took place on the surface. But no one paid much attention to Rena and me.

What did we talk about? What couples have always talked about: Each other, and everything, and nothing. The only thing we did *not* talk about was my basic beliefs in regard to the Company. For I was too troubled in my mind to talk about them, and Rena sensitive enough not to bring them up.

For I had, with all honor, sworn an oath of allegiance to the Company; and I had not kept it.

I could not, even then, see any possibility of a world where the Company did not exist. For what the Company said of itself was true: Before the Company existed, men lived like beasts. There was always the instant danger of war and disease. No plan could be made, no hope could be held, that could not be wiped out by blind accident.

And yet, were men better off today? I could not doubt the truths I had been told. The Company permitted wars—I had seen it. The Company permitted disease—my own wife had died.

Somewhere there was an answer, but I couldn't find it. It was not, I was sure, in Slovetski's burning hatred of everything the Company stood for. But it could not be, either, in the unquestioning belief that I had once given.

But my views, it turned out, hardly mattered any more; the die was cast. Benedetto appeared in the entrance to the dining hall, peering about. He saw us and came over, his face grave.

"I am sorry, Mr. Wills," he said. "I have been listening to Radio Napoli. It has just come over the air: A description of you, and an order for your arrest. The charge is—murder!"

I gaped at him, hardly believing. "Murder! But that's not true; I certainly never—"

Benedetto laid a hand on my shoulder. "Of course not, Mr. Wills. It is a fiction of the Company's, beyond doubt. But it is a fiction that may cause your death if you are discovered, do not doubt that."

I swallowed. "Who—whom did I murder?"

Benedetto shrugged. "I do not know who he is. The name they gave was Elio Barletteria."

That was the suspendee whose place Zorchi had usurped. I sat back, bewildered. It was true, at least, that I had had some connection with the man. But—kill him? Was it possible, I asked myself, that the mere act of taking him out of his plastic sack endangered his life? I doubted it, but still—

I asked Benedetto. He frowned. "It is—possible," he admitted at last. "We do not know much about the suspendees, Mr. Wills. The Company has seen to that. It is my opinion—only an opinion, I am afraid—that if this man Barletteria is dead, it had nothing to do with anything you did. Still..." He shrugged, "...what difference does it make? If the Company calls you a murderer, you must be one, for the Company is always right. Is that not so?"

We left it at that, but I was far from easy in my mind. The dining hall filled, and we ate our evening meal, but I hardly noticed what I ate and I took no part in the conversation. Rena and her father considerately left me alone; Zorchi was, it seemed, sulking in our room, for he did not appear. But I was not concerned with him, for I had troubles of my own. I should have been...

After dinner was over, I excused myself and went to the tiny cubicle that had been assigned to Zorchi and myself. He wasn't there. Then I began to think: Would Zorchi miss a meal?

The answer was unquestionably no. With his metabolism, he needed many times the food of an ordinary person; his performance at table, in fact, was spectacular.

Something was wrong. I was shaken out of my self-absorption; I hurried to find Benedetto dell'Angela, and told him that Zorchi was gone.

It didn't take long for us to find the answer. The underground hideout was not large; it had only so many exits. It was only a matter of moments before one of the men Benedetto had ordered to search returned with an alarmed expression.

The exit that led through the subway station was ajar. Somehow Zorchi had hitched himself, on his stumps, down the long corridor and out the exit. It had to be while we were eating; he could never have made it except when everyone was in one room.

How he had done it did not matter. The fact remained that Zorchi was gone and, with him, the secrecy of our hiding place.

CHAPTER ELEVEN

We had to move. There was no way out of it.

"Zorchi hates the Company," I protested. "I don't think he'll go to them and—"

"No, Wills." Slovetski patiently shook his head. "We can't take a chance. If we had been able to recapture him, then we could stay here. But he got clean away." There was admiration in his eyes. "What a conspirator he would have made! Such strength and determination! Think of it, Wills, a legless man in the city of Rome. He cannot avoid attracting attention. He can barely move by himself. And yet, our men track him into the subway station, to a telephone...and that is all. Someone picks him up. Who? A friend, one supposes—certainly not the Company, or they would have been here before this. But to act so quickly, Wills!"

Benedetto dell'Angela coughed. "Perhaps more to the point, Slovetski, is how quickly we ourselves shall now act."

Slovetski grinned. "All is ready," he promised. "See, evacuation already has begun!"

Groups of men were quickly placing file folders into cartons and carrying them off. They were not going far, I found later, only to a deserted section of the ancient Roman Catacombs, from which they could be retrieved and transported, little by little, at a later date.

By sundown, Rena and I were standing outside the little church which contained the entrance to the Catacombs. The two of us went together; only two. It would look quite normal, it was agreed, for a young man and a girl to travel together, particularly after my complexion had been suitably stained and my Company clothes discarded and replaced with a set of Rome's best ready-to-wears.

It did not occur to me at the time, but Rena must have known that her own safety was made precarious by being with me. Rena alone had nothing to fear, even if she had been caught and questioned by an agent of the Company. They would suspect her, because of her father, but suspicion would do her no harm. But Rena in the company of a wanted "murderer"—and one traveling in disguise—was far less safe...

We found an ancient piston-driven cab and threaded through almost all of Rome. We spun around the ancient stone hulk of the Colosseum, passed the balcony where a sign stated the dictator, Mussolini, used to harangue the crowds, and climbed a winding, expensive-looking street to the Borghese Gardens.

Rena consulted her watch. "We're early," she said. We had *gelati* in an open-air pavilion, listening to the wheezing of a sweating band; then, in the twilight, we wandered hand in hand under trees for half an hour.

Then Rena said, "Now it is time." We walked to the far end of the Gardens where a small copter-field served the Class-A residential area of Rome. A dozen copters were lined up at the end of the take-off hardstand. Rena led me to the nearest of them.

I looked at it casually, and stopped dead.

"Rena!" I whispered violently. "Watch out!" The copter was black and purple; it bore on its flank the marking of the Swiss Guard, the Roman police force.

She pressed my hand. "Poor Tom," she said. She walked boldly up to one of the officers lounging beside the copter and spoke briefly to him, too low for me to hear.

It was only when the big vanes overhead had sucked us a hundred yards into the air, and we were leveling off and heading south, that she said: "These are friends too, you see. Does it surprise you?"

I swallowed, staring at the hissing jets at the ends of the swirling vanes. "Well," I said, "I'm not exactly *surprised*, but I thought that your friends were, well, more likely to be—"

"To be rabble?" I started to protest, but she was not angry. She was looking at me with gentle amusement. "Still you believe, Tom. Deep inside you: An enemy of the Company must be, at the best, a silly zealot like my father and me—and at the worst, rabble." She laughed as I started to answer her. "No, Tom, if you are right, you should not deny it; and if you are wrong—you will see."

I sat back and stared, disgruntled, at the purple sunset over the Mediterranean. I never saw such a girl for taking the wind out of your sails.

Once across the border, the Guards had no status, and it was necessary for them to swing inland, threading through mountains and passes, remaining as inconspicuous as possible.

It was little more than an hour's flight until I found landmarks I could recognize. To our right was the bright bowl of Naples; far to our left, the eerie glow that, marked bombed-out New Caserta. And ahead, barely visible, the faint glowing plume that hung over Mount Vesuvius.

Neither Rena nor the Guards spoke, but I could feel in their tense attitudes that this was the danger-point. We were in the lair of the enemy. Undoubtedly we were being followed in a hundred radars, and the frequency-pattern would reveal our copter for what it was—a Roman police plane that had no business in that area. Even if the Company let us pass, there was always the chance that some Neapolitan radarman, more efficient, or more anxious for a promotion, than his peers would alert an interceptor and order us down. Certainly, in the old days, interception would have been inevitable; for Naples had just completed a war, and only short weeks back an unidentified aircraft would have been blasted out of the sky.

But we were ignored.

And that, I thought to myself, was another facet to the paradox. For when, in all the world's years before these days of the Company, was there such complacency, such deep-rooted security, that a nation just out of a war should have soothed its combat-jangled nerves overnight? Perhaps the Company had not ended wars. But the *fear* of wars was utterly gone.

We fluttered once around the volcano, and dipped in to a landing on a gentle hump of earth halfway up its slope, facing Naples and the Bay. We were a few hundred yards from a cluster of buildings—perhaps a dozen, in all.

I jumped out, stumbling and recovering myself. Rena stepped lightly into my arms. And without a word, the Guards fed fuel to the jets, the rotor whirled, and the copter lifted away from us and was gone.

Rena peered about us, getting her bearings. There was a sliver of a moon in the eastern sky, enough light to make it possible to get about. She pointed to a dark hulk of a building far up the slope. "The Observatory. Come, Tom."

The volcanic soil was rich, but not very useful to farmers. It was not only the question of an eruption of the cone, for that sort of hazard was no different in kind than the risk of hailstorm or drought. But the mountain sides did not till easily, its volcanic slopes being perhaps steeper than those of most mountains.

The ground under our feet had never been in cultivation. It was pitted and rough, and grown up in a tangle of unfamiliar weeds. And it was also, I discovered with considerable shock, warm to the touch.

I saw a plume of vapor, faintly silver in the weak light, hovering over a hummock. Mist, I thought. Then it occurred to me that there was too much wind for mist. It was steam! I touched the soil. Blood heat, at least.

I said, with some difficulty, "Rena, look!"

She laughed. "Oh, it is an eruption, Tom. Of course it is. But not a new one. It is lava, you see, from the little blast the Sicilians touched off. Do not worry about it…"

We clambered over the slippery cogs of a funicular railway and circled the ancient stone base of the building she had pointed to. There was no light visible; but Rena found a small door, rapped on it and presently it opened.

Out of the darkness came Slovetski's voice: "Welcome."

This building had been the Royal Vulcanological Observatory of the Kingdom of Italy. Now it was a museum on the surface, and underneath another of the hideouts of Rena's "friends."

But this was a hideout somewhat more important than the one in the Roman Catacombs, I found. Slovetski made no bones about it.

He said, "Wills, you shouldn't be here. We don't know you. We can't trust you." He held up a hand. "I know that you rescued dell'Angela. But that could all be an involved scheme of the Company. You could be a Company spy. You wouldn't be the first, Wills. And this particular installation is, shall I say, important. You may even find why, though I hope not. If we hadn't had to move so rapidly, you would never have been brought here. Now you're here, though, and we'll make the best of it." He looked at me carefully, then, and the glinting spark in the back of his eyes flared wickedly for a moment. "Don't try to leave. And don't go anywhere in this building where Rena or dell'Angela or I don't take you."

And that was that. I found myself assigned to the usual sort of sleeping accommodations I had come to expect in this group. Underground—cramped—and a bed harder than the Class-C Blue Heaven minimum.

The next morning, Rena breakfasted with me, just the two of us in a tower room looking down over the round slope of Vesuvius and the Bay beneath. She said: "The museum has been closed since the bomb landed near, so you can roam around the exhibits if you wish. There are a couple of caretakers, but they're with us. The rest of us will be in conference. I'll try to see you for lunch."

And she conducted me to an upper level of the Observatory and left me by myself. I had my orders—stay in the public area of the museum. I didn't like them. I wasn't used to being treated like a small boy, left by his mother in a Company day nursery while she busied herself with the important and incomprehensible affairs of adults.

Still, the museum was interesting enough, in a way. It had been taken over by the Company, it appeared, and although the legend frescoed around the main gallery indicated that it was supposed to be a historical museum of the Principality of Naples, it appeared by examination of the exhibits that the "history" involved was that of Naples vis-a-vis the Company.

Not, of course, that such an approach was entirely unfair. If it had not been for the intervention of the Company, after the Short War, it is more than possible that Naples as an independent state would never have existed.

It was the Company's insistence on the dismantling of power centers (as Millen Carmody himself had described it) that had created Naples and Sicily and Prague and Quebec and Baja California and all the others.

Only the United States had been left alone—and that, I think, only because nobody dared to operate on a wounded tiger. In the temper of the nation after the Short War, the Company would have survived less than a minute if it had proposed severing any of the fifty-one states...

The museum was interesting enough, for anyone with a taste for horrors. It showed the changes in Neapolitan life over the past century or so. There was a reconstruction of a typical Neapolitan home of the early Nineteen-forties: a squalid hovel, packed ten persons to the room, with an American G.I., precursor of the Company expediters, spraying DDT into the bedding. There was, by comparison, a typical Class-B Blue Heaven modern allotment—with a certain amount of poetic license; few Class-B homes really had polyscent showers and auto-cooks.

It was the section on warfare, however, that was most impressive. It was in the far back of the building, in a large chamber anchored to bedrock. It held a frightening display of weapons, from a Tiger Tank to a gas-gun. Bulking over everything else in the room, even the tank, was the thirty-foot height of a Hell-bomb in a four-story display. I looked at it a second time, vaguely disturbed by something I hadn't quite placed—an indigo gleam to the metal of the warhead, with a hint of evil under its lacquered sheen...

It was cobalt. I bent to read the legend: *This is the casing of the actual cobalt bomb that would have been used on Washington if the Short War had lasted one more day. It is calculated that, loaded with a Mark XII hydrogen-lithium bomb, sufficient radioactive Cobalt-60 would have been transmuted to end all life on Earth within thirty days.*

I looked at it again, shuddering.

Oh, it was safe enough now. Until the hydrogen reaction could turn the ordinary cobalt sheathing into the deadly isotope-60, it was just such stuff as was used to alloy magnets and make cobalt glass. It was even more valuable as a museum piece than as the highly purified metal.

Score one for the Company. They'd put a stop to that danger. Nobody would have a chance to arm it and send it off now. No small war would find it more useful than the bomb it would need—and no principality would risk the Company's wrath in using it. And while the conspiracy might have planes and helicopters, the fissionable material was too rigidly under Company control for them to have a chance. The Super Hell-bomb would never go off. And that was something that might mean more to the Company's credit than anything else.

Maybe it was possible that in this controversy *both* sides were right. And, of course, there was the obvious corollary.

I continued my wandering, looking at the exhibits, the rubble of the museum's previous history. The cast of the Pompeiian gladiator, caught by the cinder-fall in full flight, his straining body reproduced to every contorted line by the incandescent ashes that had encased him. The carefully chipped and labeled samples from the lava flows of the past two centuries. The awe-inspiring photographs of Vesuvius in eruption.

But something about the bomb casing kept bothering me. I wandered around a bit longer and then turned back to the main exhibit. The big casing stretched upward and downward, with narrow stairs leading down to the lower level at its base. It was on the staircase I'd noticed something before. Now I hesitated, trying to spot whatever it was. There was a hint of something down there. Finally, I shrugged and went down to inspect it more closely.

Lying at the base was a heavy radiation glove. A used, workman's glove, dirty with grease. And as my eyes darted up, I could see that the bolts on the lower servicing hatches were half-unscrewed.

Radiation gloves and tampering with the casing!

There were two doors to the pit for the bomb casing, but either one was better than risking the stairs again where someone might see me. Or so I figured. If they found I'd learned anything…

I grabbed for the nearer door, threw it open. I knew it was a mistake when the voice reached my ears.

"—after hitting the Home office with a Thousand-kiloton bomb. It's going to take fast work. Now the schedule I've figured out so far—God's damnation! How did you get in here, Wills?"

It was Slovetski, leaning across a table, staring at me. Around the table were Benedetto and four or five others I did not recognize. All of them looked at me as though I were the Antichrist, popped out of the marble at St. Peter's Basilica on Easter Sunday.

The spark was a raging flame in Slovetski's eyes. Benedetto dell'Angela said sharply, "Wait!" He strode over to me, half shielding me from Slovetski. "Explain this, Thomas," he demanded.

"I thought this was the hall door," I stammered, spilling the first words I could while I tried to find any excuse…

"Wills! I tell you, answer me!"

I said, "Look, did you expect me to carry a bell and cry unclean? I didn't mean to break in. I'll go at once…"

In a voice that shook, Slovetski said: "Wait one moment." He pressed a bell-button on the wall; we all stood there silent, the five of them staring at me, me wishing I was dead.

There was a patter of feet outside, and Rena peered in. She saw me and her hand went to her heart.

"Tom! But—"

Slovetski said commandingly, "Why did you permit him his liberty?"

Rena looked at him wide-eyed. "But, please, I asked you. You suggested letting him study the exhibits."

Benedetto nodded. "True, Slovetski," he said gravely. "You ordered her to attend until our—conference was over."

The flame surged wildly in Slovetski's eyes—not at me. But he got it under control. He said, "Take him away." He did not do me the courtesy of looking my way again. Rena took me by the hand and led me off, closing the door behind us.

As soon as we were outside, I heard a sharp babble of argument, but I could make out no words through the door. I didn't need to; I knew exactly what they were saying.

This was the proposition: *Resolved, that the easiest thing to do is put Wills out of the way permanently.* And with Slovetski's fiery eyes urging the positive, what eager debater would say him nay?

Rena said: "I can't tell you, Tom. *Please* don't ask me!"

I said, "This is no kid's game, Rena! They're talking about bombing the Home Office!"

She shook her head. "Tom, Tom. You must have misunderstood."

"I heard them!"

"Tom, *please* don't ask me any more questions."

I slammed my hand down on the table and swore. It didn't do any good. She didn't even look up from the remains of her dinner.

It had been like that all afternoon. The Great Ones brooded in secret. Rena and I waited in her room, until the museum's public visiting hours were over and we could go up into the freer atmosphere of the reception lounge. And then we waited there.

I said mulishly: "Ever since I met you, Rena, I've been doing nothing but wait. I'm not built that way!"

No answer.

I said, with all of my patience: "Rena, I heard them talking about bombing the Home Office. Do you think I am going to forget that?"

Leadenly: "No, Tom."

"So what does it matter if you tell me more? If I cannot be trusted, I already know too much. If I can be trusted, what does it matter if I know the rest?"

Again tears. "*Please* don't ask me!"

I yelled: "At least you can tell me what we're waiting for!"

She dabbed at her eyes. "Please, Tom, I don't know much more than you do. Slovetski, he is like this sometimes. He gets, I suppose you would say, thoughtful. He concentrates so very much on one thing, you see, that he forgets everything around him. It is possible that he has forgotten that we are waiting. I don't know."

I snarled, "I'm tired of this. Go in and remind him!"

"No, Tom!" There was fright in her voice; and I found that she had told me one of the things I wanted to know. If it was not wise to remind Slovetski that I was waiting his pleasure, the probability was that it would not be pleasant for me when he remembered.

I said, "But you must know something, Rena. Don't you see that it could do no harm to tell me?"

She said miserably, "Tom, I know very little. I did not—did not know as much as you found out." I stared at her. She nodded. "I had perhaps a suspicion, it is true. Yes, I suspected. But I did not *really* think, Tom, that there was a question of bombing. It is not how we were taught. It is not what Slovetski promised, when we began."

"You mean you didn't know Slovetski was planning violence?"

She shook her head. "And even now, I think, perhaps you heard wrong, perhaps there was a mistake."

I stood up and leaned over her. "Rena, listen to me. There was no mistake. They're working on that casing. Tell me what you know!"

She shook her head, weeping freely.

I raged: "This is asinine! What can there be that you will not tell? The Company supply base that Slovetski hopes to raid to get a bomb? The officers he plans to bribe, to divert some other nation's quota of plutonium?"

She took a deep breath. "Not that, Tom."

"Then what? You don't mean to say that he has a complete underground separator plant—that he is making his own plutonium!"

She was silent for a long time, looking at me. Then she sighed. "I will tell you, Tom. No, he does not have a plant. He doesn't need one, you see. He already has a bomb."

I straightened. "That's impossible."

She was shaking her head. I protested, "But the—the *quotas*, Rena. The Company tracks every milligram of fissionable material from the moment it leaves the reactor! The inspections! Expediters with Geiger counters cover every city in the world!"

"Not here, Tom. You remember that the Sicilians bombed Vesuvius? There is a high level of radioactivity all up and down the mountain. Not enough to be dangerous, but enough to mask a buried bomb." She closed her eyes. "And—well, you are right, Tom. I might as well tell you. In that same war, you see, there was a bomb that did not explode. You recall?"

"Yes, but—"

"But it couldn't explode, Tom. It was a dummy. Slovetski is a brilliant man. Before that bomb left the ground, he had diverted it. What went up was a hollow shell. What is left—the heart of the bomb—is buried forty feet beneath us."

I stared at her, the room reeling. I was clutching at straws. I whispered, "But that was only a fission bomb, Rena. Slovetski—I heard him—he said a Thousand-kiloton bomb. That means hydrogen, don't you see? Surely he hasn't tucked one of those away."

Rena's face was an agony of regret. "I do not understand all these things, so you must bear with me. I know this; there has been secret talk about the Milanese generators, and I know that the talk has to do with heavy water. And I am not stupid altogether, I know that from heavy water one can get what is used in a hydrogen bomb. And there is more, of course—lithium, perhaps? But he has that. You have seen it, I think. It is on a pedestal in this building."

I sat down hard. It was impossible. But it all fell into place. Given the fissionable core of the bomb—plus the deuterium, plus the lithium-bearing shell—it was no great feat to put the parts together and make a Hell-bomb.

The mind rejected it; it was too fantastic. It was frightful and terrifying, and worst of all was that something lurking at the threshold of memory, something about that bomb on display in the museum...

And, of course, I remembered.

"Rena!" I said, struggling for breath. I nearly could not go on, it was too dreadful to say. "Rena! Have you ever looked at that bomb? Have you read the placard on it? *That bomb is cobalt!*"

CHAPTER TWELVE

From the moment I had heard those piercing words from Slovetski's mouth, I had been obsessed with a vision. A Hell-bomb on the Home Office. America's eastern seaboard split open. New York a hole in the ocean, from Kingston to Sandy Hook; orange flames spreading across Connecticut and the Pennsylvania corner.

That was gone—and in its place was something worse.

Radiocobalt bombing wouldn't simply kill locally by a gout of flaring radiation. It would leave the atmosphere filled with colloidal particles of deadly, radioactive Cobalt-60. A little of that could be used to cure cancers and perform miracles. The amount released from the sheathing of cobalt—normal, "safe" cobalt—around a fissioning hydrogen bomb could kill a world. A single bomb of that kind could wipe out all life on Earth, as I remembered my schooling.

I'm no physicist; I didn't know what the quantities involved might mean, once the equations came off the drafting paper and settled like a ravening storm on the human race. But I had a glimpse of radioactive dust in every breeze, in every corner of every land. Perhaps a handful of persons in Cambodia or Vladivostok or Melbourne might live through it. But there was no question in my mind: If that bomb went off, it was the end of our civilization.

I saw it clearly.

And so, having betrayed the Company to Slovetski's gang, I came full circle.

Even Judas betrayed only One.

Getting away from the Observatory was simple enough, with Rena shocked and confused enough to look the other way. Finding a telephone near Mount Vesuvius was much harder.

I was two miles from the mountain before I found what I was looking for—a Blue Wing fully-automatic filling station. The electronic scanners clucked worriedly, as they searched for the car I should have been driving, and the policy-punching slot glowed red and receptive, waiting for my order. I ignored them.

What I wanted was inside the little unlocked building—A hushaphone-booth with vision attachment. The important thing was to talk direct to Defoe and only to Defoe. In the vision screen, impedance mismatch would make the picture waver if there was anyone uninvited listening in.

But I left the screen off while I put through my call. The office servo-operator (it was well after business hours) answered blandly, and I said: "Connect me with Defoe, crash priority."

It was set to handle priority matters on a priority basis; there was neither fuss nor argument, though a persistent buzzing in the innards of the phone showed that, even while the robot was locating Defoe for me, it was double-checking the connection to find out why there was no vision on the screen.

It said briskly, "Stand by, sir," and I was connected with Defoe's line—on a remote hookup with the hotel where he was staying, I guessed. I flicked the screen open.

But it wasn't Defoe on the other end of the line. It was Susan Manchester, with that uncharacteristic, oddly efficient look she had shown at the vaults.

She said crisply, and not at all surprised: "Tom Wills."

"That's right," I said, thinking quickly. Well, it didn't much matter. I should have realized that Defoe's secretary, howsoever temporary, would be taking his calls. I said rapidly: "Susan, I can't talk to you. It has to be Defoe. Take my word for it, it's important. Please put him on."

She gave me no more of an argument than the robot had.

In a second, Defoe was on the screen, and I put Susan out of my mind. She must have said something to him, because the big, handsome face was unsurprised, though the eyes were contracted. "Wills!" he snapped. "You fool! Where are you?"

I said, "Mr. Defoe, I have to talk to you. It's a very urgent matter."

"Come in and do it, Wills! Not over the telephone."

I shook my head. "No, sir. I can't. It's too, well, risky."

"Risky for you, you mean!" The words were icily disgusted. "Wills, you have betrayed me. No man ever got away with that. You're imposing on me, playing on my family loyalty to your dead wife, and I want to tell you that you won't get away with it. There's a murder charge against you, Wills! Come in and talk to me—or else the police will pick you up before noon."

I said with an effort, "I don't mean to impose on any loyalty, but, in common decency, you ought to hear—"

"Decency!" His face was cold. "You talk about decency! You and that dell'Angela traitor you joined. Decency! Wills, you're a disgrace to the memory of a decent and honest woman like Marianna. I can only say that I am glad—glad, do you hear me?— that she's dead and rid of you."

I said, "Wait a minute, Defoe! Leave Marianna out of this. I only—"

"Don't interrupt me! God, to think a man I trusted should turn out to be Judas himself! You animal, the Company has protected you from the day you were born, and you try to destroy it. Why, you pitiful idiot, you aren't fit to associate with the dogs in the kennel of a decent human being!"

There was more. Much, much more. It was a flow of abuse that paralyzed me, less because of what he said than because of who was saying it. Suave, competent Defoe, ranting at me like a wounded Gogarty! I couldn't have been more astonished if the portrait of Millen Carmody had whispered a bawdy joke from the frontispiece of the Handbook.

I stood there, too amazed to be furious, listening to the tirade from the midget image in the viewplate. It must have lasted for three or four minutes; then, almost in mid-breath, Defoe glanced at something outside my range of vision, and stopped his stream of abuse. I started to cut in while I could, but he held up one hand quickly.

He smiled gently. Very calmly, as though he had not been damning me a moment before, he said: "I shall be very interested to hear what you have to say."

That floored me. It took me a second to shake the cobwebs out of my brain before I said waspishly, "If you hadn't gone through all that jabber, you would have heard it long ago."

The midget in the scanner shrugged urbanely. "True," he conceded. "But then, Thomas, I wouldn't have had you."

And he reached forward and clicked off the phone. Tricked! Tricked and trapped! I cursed myself for stupidity. While he kept me on the line, the call was being traced—there was no other explanation. And I had fallen for it!

I slapped the door of the booth open and leaped out.

I got perhaps ten feet from the booth.

Then a rope dropped over my shoulders. Its noose yanked tight around my arms, and I was being dragged up, kicking futilely. I caught a glimpse of the broad Latin faces gaping at me from below, then two men on a rope ladder had me.

I was dragged in through the bottom hatch of a big helicopter with no markings. The hatch closed. Facing me was a lieutenant of expediters.

The two men tumbled in after me and reeled in the rope ladder, as the copter dipped and swerved away. I let myself go limp as the rope was loosened around me; when my hands were free I made my bid.

I leaped for the lieutenant; my fist caught him glancingly on the throat, sending him reeling and choking backward. I grabbed for the hard-pellet gun at his hip—he was pawing at it—and we tumbled across the floor.

It was, for one brief moment, a chance. I was no copter pilot, but the gun was all the pilot I'd need—if only I got it out.

But the expediters behind me were no amateurs. I ducked as the knotted end of the rope whipped savagely toward me. Then one of the other expediters was on my back; the gun came out, and flew free. And that was the end of that.

I had, I knew, been a fool to try it. But I wasn't sorry. They had too much rough-and-tumble training for me to handle. But that one blow had felt good.

It didn't seem as worth while a few moments later. I was fastened to a seat, while the wheezing lieutenant gave orders in a strangled voice. "Not too many marks on him," he was saying. "Try it over the kidneys again..."

I never even thought of maintaining a heroic silence. They had had plenty of experience with the padded club, too, and I started to black out twice before finally I went all the way down.

I came to with a light shining in my eyes.

There was a doctor putting his equipment away. "He'll be all right, Mr. Defoe," he said, and snapped his bag shut and left the circle of light.

I felt terrible, but my head was clearing.

I managed to focus my eyes. Defoe was there, and a couple of other men. I recognized Gogarty, looking sick and dejected, and another face I knew—it was out of my Home Office training—an officer whose name I didn't recall, wearing the uniform of a lieutenant-general of expediters. That meant at least an expediter corps in Naples!

I said weakly, "Hi."

Defoe stood over me. He said, "I'm very glad to see you, Thomas. Coffee?"

He steadied my hands as I gulped it. When I had managed a few swallows, he took the cup away.

"I did not think you would resist arrest, Thomas," he said in a parental tone.

I said, "Damn it, you didn't have to arrest me! I came down here of my own free will!"

"Down?" His eyebrows rose. "Down from where do you mean, Thomas?"

"Down from Mount—" I hesitated, then finished, "All right. Down from Mount Vesuvius. The museum, where I was hiding out with the ringleaders of the anti-Company movement. Is that what you want to know?"

Defoe crackled: "Manning!" The lieutenant-general saluted and left the room. Defoe said, "That was the first thing I wanted, yes. But now I want much more. Please begin talking, Thomas. I will listen."

I talked. There was nothing to stop me. Even with my body a mass of aches and pains from the tender care of the Company's expediters, I still had to side with the Company in this. For the Cobalt-bomb ended all loyalties.

I left nothing important out, not even Rena. I admitted that I had taken Benedetto from the clinic, how we had escaped to Rome, how we had fled to Vesuvius…and what I had learned. I made it short, skipping a few unimportant things like Zorchi.

And Defoe sat sipping his coffee, listening, his warm eyes twinkling.

I stopped. He pursed his lips, considering.

"Silly," he said at last.

"Silly? What's silly!"

He said, "Thomas, I don't care about your casual affairs. And I would have excused your—precipitousness—since you have brought back certain useful information. Quite useful. I don't deny it. But I don't like being lied to, Thomas."

"I haven't lied!"

He said sharply, "There is no way to get fissionable material except through the Company!"

"Oh, hell!" I shook my head. "How about a dud bomb, Defoe?"

For the first time he looked puzzled. "Dud bomb?"

Gogarty looked sick. "There's—there's a report on your desk, Mr. Defoe," he said worriedly. "We—well—figured the half-masses just got close enough to boil instead of to explode. We—"

"I see." Defoe looked at him for a long moment. Then, disregarding Gogarty, he turned back to me, shoved the coffee at me. "All right, Thomas. They've got the warhead. Hydrogen? Cobalt? What about fuel?"

I told him what I knew. Gogarty, listening, licked his lips. I didn't envy him. I could see the worry in him, the fear of Defoe's later wrath. For in Defoe, as in Slovetski, there was that deadly fire. It blazed only when it was allowed to; but what it touched withered and died. I had not seen Defoe as tightly concentrated, as drivingly intent, before. I was sorry for Gogarty when at last, having drained me dry, Defoe left. But I was glad for me.

He was gone less than an hour—just time for me to eat a Class-C meal a silent expediter brought.

He thrust the door open and stared at me with whitely glaring eyes. "If I thought you were lying, Thomas..." His voice was cracking with suppressed emotion.

"What happened?" I demanded.

"Don't you know?" He stood trembling, staring at me. "You told the truth—or part of the truth. There *was* a hideout on Vesuvius. But an hour ago they got away—while you were wasting time. Was it a stall, Thomas? Did you know they would run?"

I said, "Defoe, don't you see, that's all to the good? If they had to run, they couldn't possibly take the bomb with them. That means—"

He was shaking head. "Oh, but you're wrong, Thomas. According to the director of the albergo down the hill, three skyhook helicopters came over—big ones. They peeled the roof off, as easy as you please, and they lifted the bomb out and then flew away."

I said stupidly, "Where?" He nodded. There was no emotion in his voice, only his eyes. He might have been discussing the weather. "Where? That is a good question. I hope we will find it out, Thomas. We're checking the radar charts; they can't hide for long. But how did they get away at all? Why did you give them the time?"

He left me. Perversely, I was almost glad. It was part of the price of switching allegiance, I was learning, that shreds and tatters of loyalties cling to you and carry over. When I went against the Company to rescue Benedetto, I still carried with me my Adjusters' Handbook. And I confess that I never lost the habit of reading a page or two in it, even in the Catacombs, when things looked bad. And when I saw the murderous goal that Slovetski's men were marching toward, and I returned to Defoe, I still could feel glad that Benedetto, at least, had got away.

But not far.

It was only a few hours, but already broad daylight when Gogarty, looking shaken, came into the room. He said testily, "Damn it, Wills, I wish I'd never seen you! Come on! Defoe wants you with us."

"Come on where?" I got up as he gestured furiously for haste.

"Where do you think? Did you think your pals would be able to stay out of sight forever? We've got them pinpointed, bomb and all."

He was almost dragging me down the corridor, toward a courtyard. I limped out into the bright morning and blinked. The court was swarming with armed expediters, clambering into personnel-carrying copters marked with the vivid truce-team insignia of the Company. Gogarty hustled me into the nearest and the jets sizzled and we leaped into the air.

I shouted, over the screaming of the jets, "Where are we going?"

Gogarty spat and pointed down the long purple coastline. "To their hideout—Pompeii!"

CHAPTER THIRTEEN

No one discussed tactics with me, but it was clear that this operation was carefully planned. Our copter was second in a long string of at least a dozen that whirled down the coastline, past the foothills of Vesuvius, over the clusters of fishing villages and vineyards.

I had never seen Pompeii, but I caught a glimpse of something glittering and needle-nosed, up-thrust in the middle of a cluster of stone buildings that might have been the ruins.

Then the first ten of the copters spun down to a landing, while two or three more flew a covering mission overhead.

The expediters, hard-pellet guns at the ready, leaped out and formed in a skirmish line. Gogarty and a pair of expediters stayed close by me, behind the line of attack; we followed the troops as they dog-trotted through a field of some sort of grain, around fresh excavations, down a defile into the shallow pit that held the ruins of first-century Pompeii.

I had no time for archeology, but I remember tripping over wide, shallow gutters in the stone-paved streets, and cutting through a tiny villa of some sort whose plaster walls still were decorated with faded frescoes.

Then we heard the spatter of gunfire and Gogarty, clutching at me, skidded to a halt. "This is specialist work," he panted. "Best thing we can do is stay out of it."

I peered around a column and saw a wide open stretch. Beyond it was a Roman arch and the ruined marble front of what once had been a temple of some sort; in the open ground lay the three gigantic copters Defoe had mentioned.

The vanes of one of them were spinning slowly, and it lurched and quivered as someone tried to get it off the ground under fire. But the big thing was in the middle of the area: The bomb, enormous and terrifying as its venomous nose thrust up into the sky. By its side was a tank truck, the side of it painted with the undoubtedly untrue legend that it contained crude olive oil. Hydrazine, more likely!

Hoses connected it with the base of the guided-missile bomb; and a knot of men were feverishly in action around it, some clawing desperately at the fittings of the bomb, some returning the skirmish fire of the expediters.

We had the advantage of surprise, but not very much of that. From the top of the ancient temple a rapid-fire pellet gun sprayed into the flank of the skirmish line, which immediately broke up as the expediters leaped for cover.

One man fell screaming out of the big skyhook copter, but someone remained inside, for it lurched and dipped and roared crazily across the field in as ragged a take-off as I ever saw, until its pilot got it under control. It bobbed over the skirmish line under fire, but returning the fire as whatever few persons were inside it leaned out and strafed the expediters. Then the skyhook itself came under attack as the patrol copters swooped in.

The big ship staggered toward the nearest of them. It must have been intentional: We could see the faint flare of muzzle-blast as the two copters fired on each other; they closed, and there was a brutal rending noise as they collided. They were barely a hundred feet in the air; they crashed in a breath, and flames spread out from the wreckage.

And Slovetski's resources still had not run out. There was a roar and a screech of metal, and a one-man cobra tank slithered out of one of the buildings and came rapidly across the field toward the expediters.

Gogarty, beside me, was sobbing with fear; that little tank carried self-loading rockets. It blasted a tiny shrine into rubble, spun and came directly toward us.

We ran. I didn't even see the second expediter aircraft come whirling in and put the cobra tank out of action with its heavy weapons. I heard the firing, but it was swallowed up in a louder screaming roar.

Gogarty stared at me from the drainage trench we had flung ourselves into. We both leaped up and ran back toward the open field.

There was an explosion as we got there—the fake "olive-oil" truck, now twenty yards from the bomb, had gone up in a violent blast. But we hardly noticed. For at the base of the bomb itself red-purple fire was billowing out. It screamed and howled and changed color to a blinding blue as the ugly squat shape danced and jiggled. The roar screamed up from a bull-bass to a shrieking coloratura and beyond as the bomb lifted and gained speed and, in the blink of an eye, was gone.

I hardly noticed that the sound of gunfire died raggedly away. We were not the only ones staring unbelievingly at the sky where that deadly shape had disappeared. Of the scores of men on both sides in that area, not a single eye was anywhere else.

The bomb had been fueled; we were too late. Its servitors, perhaps at the cost of their own lives, had torched it off. It was on its way.

The cobalt bomb—the single weapon that could poison the world and wipe out the human race—was on its way.

CHAPTER FOURTEEN

What can you do after the end? What becomes of any plot or plan, when an indigo-gleaming missile sprays murder into the sky and puts a period to planning?

I do not think there ever was a battlefield as abruptly quiet as that square in old Pompeii. Once the bomb had gone, there was not a sound. The men who had been firing on each other were standing still, jaws hanging, eyes on the sky.

But it couldn't last. For one man was not surprised; one man knew what was happening and was ready for it.

A crouching figure at the top of the ruined temple gesticulated and shouted through a power-megaphone: "Give it up, Defoe! You've lost, you've lost!" It was Slovetski, and beside him a machine-gun crew sighted in on the nearest knot of expediters.

Pause, while the Universe waited. And then his answer came; it was a shot that screamed off a cracked capital, missing him by millimeters. He dropped from sight, and the battle was raging.

Human beings are odd. Now that the cause of the fight was meaningless, it doubled in violence. There were fewer than a hundred of Slovetski's men involved, and not much more than that many expediters. But for concentrated violence I think they must have overmatched anything in the Short War's ending.

I was a non-combatant; but the zinging of the hard-pellet fire swarmed all around me. Gogarty, in his storm sewer, was safe enough, but I was more exposed. While the rapid-fire weapons pattered all around me, I jumped up and zigzagged for the shelter of a low-roofed building.

The walls were little enough protection, but at least I had the illusion of safety. Most of all, I was out of sight.

I wormed my way through a gap in the wall to an inner chamber. It was as tiny a room as ever I have been in; less than six feet in its greatest dimension—length—and with most of its floor area taken up by what seemed to be a rude built-in bed. Claustrophobia hit me there; the wall on the other side was broken too, and I wriggled through.

The next room was larger; and it was occupied.

A man lay, panting heavily, in a corner. He pushed himself up on an elbow to look at me. In a ragged voice he said: "Thomas!" And he slumped back, exhausted by the effort, blood dripping from his shirt.

I leaped over to the side of Benedetto dell'Angela. The noise of the battle outside rose to a high pitch and dwindled raggedly away.

I suppose it was inertia that kept me going—certainly I could see with my mind's vision no reason to keep struggling. The world was at an end. There was no reason to try again to escape from the rubber hoses of the expediters—and, after I had seen the resistance end, and an expediter-officer appeared atop the temple where Slovetski had shouted his defiance, no possibility of rejoining the rebels.

Without Slovetski, they were lost.

But I kept on.

Benedetto helped. He knew every snake-hole entrance and exit of all the hideouts of Slovetski's group. They had not survived against the strength of the Company without acquiring skill in escape routes; and here, too, they had a way out. It required a risky dash across open ground but, even with Benedetto on my back, I made it.

And then we were in old Pompeii's drainage sewer, the arched stone tunnel that once had carried sewage from the Roman town to the sea. It was a hiding place, and then a tunnel to freedom, for the two of us.

We waited there all of that day, Benedetto mumbling almost inaudibly beside me. In lucid moments, he told me the name of the hotel where Rena had gone when the Observatory was abandoned, but there seemed few lucid moments. Toward evening, he began to recover.

We found our way to the seashore just as darkness fell. There was a lateen-rigged fishing vessel of some sort left untended. I do not suppose the owner was far away, but he did not return in time to stop us.

Benedetto was very weak. He was muttering to himself, words that I could hardly understand. "Wasted, wasted, wasted," was the burden of his complaint. I did not know what he thought was wasted—except, perhaps, the world.

We slipped in to one of the deserted wharves under cover of darkness, and I left Benedetto to find a phone. It was risky, but what risk mattered when the world was at an end?

Rena was waiting at the hotel. She answered at once. I did not think the call had been intercepted—or that it would mean anything to anyone if it had. I went back to the boat to wait with Benedetto for Rena to arrive, in a rented car. We didn't dare chance a cab.

Benedetto was sitting up, propped rigidly against the mast, staring off across the water. Perhaps I startled him as I came to the boat; he turned awkwardly and cried out weakly.

Then he saw that it was I. He said something I could not understand and pointed out toward the west, where the Sun had gone down long before.

But there was still light there—though certainly not sunset.

Far off over the horizon was a faint glow! I couldn't understand at first, since I was sure the bomb had been zeroed-in on the Home Offices in New York; but something must have happened. From that glow, still showing in the darkness so many hours after the explosion as the dust particles gleamed bluely, it must have gone off over the Atlantic.

There was no doubt in my mind any longer. The most deadly weapon the world had ever known had gone off!

CHAPTER FIFTEEN

The hotel was not safe, of course, but what place was when the world was at an end? Rena and I, between us, got her father, Benedetto, upstairs into her room without attracting too much attention. We put him on the bed and peeled back his jacket.

The bullet had gone into his shoulder, a few inches above the heart. The bone was splintered, but the bleeding was not too much. Rena did what she could and, for the first time in what seemed like years, we had a moment's breathing space.

I said, "I'll phone for a doctor."

Benedetto said faintly, "No, Thomas! The Company!"

I protested, "What's the difference? We're all dead, now. You've seen—" I hesitated and changed it. "Slovetski has seen to that. There was *cobalt* in that bomb."

He peered curiously at me. "Slovetski? Did you suppose it was Slovetski who planned it so?" He shook his head—and winced at the pain. He whispered, "Thomas, you do not understand. It was my project, not Slovetski's. That one, he proposed to destroy the Company's Home Office; it was his thought that killing them would bring an end to evil. I persuaded him there was no need to kill—only to gamble."

I stared at him. "You're delirious!"

"Oh, no." He shook his head and succeeded in a tiny smile. "Do you not see it, Thomas? The great explosion goes off, the world is showered with particles of death. And then—what then?"

"We die!"

"Die? No! Have you forgotten the vaults of the clinics?"

It staggered me. I'd been reciting all the pat phrases from early schooling about the bomb! If it had gone off in the Short War, of course, it would have ended the human race! But I'd been a fool.

The vaults had been built to handle the extreme emergencies that couldn't be foreseen—even one that knocked out nearly the whole race. They hadn't expected that a cobalt-cased bomb would ever be used. Only the conspirators would have tried, and how could they get fissionables? But they were ready for even that. I'd been expecting universal doom.

"The clinics," Benedetto repeated as I stared at him.

It was the answer. Even radio-poisons of cobalt do not live forever. Five years, and nearly half of them would be gone; eleven years, and more than three-quarters would be dissipated. In fifty years, the residual activity would be down to a fraction of one per cent—and the human race could come back to the surface.

"But why?" I demanded. "Suppose the Company can handle the population of the whole world? Granted, they've space enough and one year is the same as fifty when you're on ice. But what's the use?"

He smiled faintly. "Bankruptcy, Thomas," he whispered. "So you see, we do not wish to fall into the Company's hands right now. For there is a chance that we will live…and perhaps the very faintest of chances that we will win!"

It wasn't even a faint chance—I kept telling myself that.

But, if anything could hurt the Company, the area in which it was vulnerable was money. Benedetto had been intelligent in that. Bombing the Home Office would have been an inconvenience, no more. But to disrupt the world's work with a fifty-year hiatus, while the air purged itself of the radioactive cobalt from the bomb, would mean fifty years while the Company lay dormant; fifty years while the policies ran their course and became due.

For that was the wonder of Benedetto's scheme: *The Company insured against everything.* If a man were to be exposed to radiation and needed to be put away, he automatically went on "disability" benefits, while his policy paid its own premiums!

Multiply this single man by nearly four billion. The sum came out to a bankrupt Company.

It seemed a thin thread with which to strangle a monster. And yet, I thought of the picture of Millen Carmody in my Adjuster's Manual. There was the embodiment of honor. Where a Defoe might cut through the legalities and flout the letter of the agreements, Carmody would be bound by his given word. The question, then, was whether Defoe would dare to act against Carmody.

Everything else made sense. Even exploding the bomb high over the Atlantic: It would be days before the first fall-out came wind-borne to the land, and in those days there would be time for the beginnings of the mass migration to the vaults.

Wait and see, I told myself. Wait and see. It was flimsy, but it was hope, and I had thought all hope was dead.

We could not stay in the hotel, and there was only one place for us to go. Slovetski captured, the Company after our scalps, the whole world about to be plunged into confusion—we had to get out of sight.

It took time. Zorchi's hospital gave me a clue; I tracked it down and located the secretary.

The secretary spat at me over the phone and hung up, but the second time I called him he grudgingly consented to give me another number to call. The new number was Zorchi's lawyer. The lawyer was opaque and uncommunicative, but proposed that I call him back in a quarter of an hour. In a quarter of an hour, I was on the phone. He said guardedly: "What was left in Bay 100?"

"A hypodermic and a bottle of fluid," I said promptly.

"That checks," he confirmed, and gave me a number.

And on the other end of that number I reached Zorchi.

"The junior assassin," he sneered. "And calling for help? How is that possible, Weels? Did my *avocatto* lie?"

I said stiffly, "If you don't want to help me, say so."

"Oh—" he shrugged. "I have not said that. What do you want?"

"Food, a doctor, and a place for three of us to hide for a while."

He pursed his lips. "To hide, is it?" He frowned. "That is very grave, Weels. Why should I hide you from what is undoubtedly your just punishment?"

"Because," I said steadily, "I have a telephone number. Which can be traced. Defoe doesn't know you've escaped, but that can be fixed!"

He laughed angrily. "Oh-ho. The assassin turns to blackmail, is that it?"

I said furiously, "Damn you, Zorchi, you know I won't turn you in. I only point out that I can—and that I will not. Now, will you help us or not?"

He said mildly, "Oh, of course. I only wished you to say 'please'—but it is not a trick you Company men are good at. Signore, believe me, I perish with loneliness for you and your two friends, whoever they may be. Listen to me, now." He gave me an address and directions for finding it. And he hung up.

Zorchi's house was far outside the city, along the road to New Caserta. It lay at the bend of the main highway, and I suppose I could have passed it a hundred thousand times without looking inside, it was so clearly the white-stuccoed, large but crumbling home of a mildly prosperous peasant. It was large enough to have a central court partly concealed from the road.

The secretary, spectacles and all, met us at the door—and that was a shock. "You must have roller skates," I told him.

He shrugged. "My employer is too forgiving," he said, with ice on his voice. "I had hoped to reach him before he made an error. As you see, I was too late."

We lifted Benedetto off the seat; he was just barely conscious by now, and his face was ivory under the Mediterranean tan. I shook the secretary off and held Benedetto carefully in my arms as Rena held the door before me.

The secretary said, "A moment. I presume the car is stolen. You must dispose of it at once."

I snarled over my shoulder, "It isn't stolen, but the people that own it will be looking for it all right. *You* get rid of it."

He spluttered and squirmed, but I saw him climbing into the seat as I went inside. Zorchi was there waiting, in a fancy motorized wheelchair. He had legs! Apparently they were not fully developed as yet, but in the short few days since I had rescued him *something* had grown that looked like nearly normal limbs. He had also grown, in that short time, a heavy beard.

The sneer, however, was the same.

I made the error of saying, "Signore Zorchi, will you call a doctor for this man?"

The thick lips writhed under the beard. "*Signore* it is now, is it? No longer the freak Zorchi, the case Zorchi, the half-man? God works many miracles, Weels. See the greatest of them all—it has transmuted the dog into a *signore!*"

I grated, "For God's sake, Zorchi, call a doctor!"

He said coldly, "You mentioned this over the phone, did you not? If you would merely walk on instead of bickering, you would find the doctor already here."

Plasma and antibiotics: They flowed into Benedetto from half a dozen plastic tubes like oil into the hold of a tanker. And I could see, in the moments when I watched, the color come back into his face, and the sunken eyes seem to come back to life.

The doctor gave him a sedative that made him sleep, and explained to us that Benedetto was an old man for such goings-on. But if he could be kept still for three or four weeks, the doctor said, counting the lire Zorchi's secretary paid him, there was no great danger.

If he could be kept still for three or four weeks. In scarcely ten days, the atmosphere of the planet would be death to breathe! Many things might happen to Benedetto in that time, but remaining still was not one of them.

Zorchi retired to his own quarters, once the doctor was gone, and Rena and I left Benedetto to sleep.

We found a television set and turned it on, listening for word of the cobalt-bomb. We got recorded *canzoni* sung by a reedy tenor. We dialed, and found the Neapolitan equivalent of a soap opera, complete with the wise, fat old mother and the sobbing new daughter-in-law. It was like that on all the stations, while Rena and I stared at each other in disbelief.

Finally, at the regular hourly newscast, we got a flicker: "An unidentified explosion," the announcer was saying, "far out at sea, caused alarm to many persons last night. Although the origins are not known, it is thought that there is no danger. However, there has been temporary disturbance to all long-lines communications, and air travel is grounded while the explosion is being investigated."

We switched to the radio: it was true. Only the UHF television bands were on the air.

I said, "I can't figure that. If there's enough disturbance to ruin long-distance transmission, it ought to show up on the television."

Rena said doubtfully, "I do not remember for sure, Tom, but is there not something about television which limits its distance?"

209

"Well—I suppose so, yes. It's a line of sight transmission, on these frequencies at any rate. I don't suppose it has to be, except that all the television bands fall in VHF or UHF channels."

"Yes. And then, is it not possible that only the distance transmission is interrupted? On purpose, I mean?"

I slammed my hand on the arm of the chair. "On purpose! The Company—they are trying to keep this thing localized. But the idiots, don't they know that's impossible? Does Defoe think he can let the world burn up without doing anything to stop it—just by keeping the people from knowing what happened?"

She shrugged. "I don't know, Tom."

I didn't know either, but I suspected—and so did she. It was out of the question that the Company, with its infinite resources, its nerve-fibers running into every part of the world, should not know just what that bomb was, and what it would do. And what few days the world had—before the fall-out became dangerous—were none too many.

Already the word should have been spread, and the first groups alerted for movement into the vaults, to wait out the day when the air would be pure again. If it was being delayed, there could be no good reason for it.

The only reason was Defoe. But what, I asked myself miserably, was Millen Carmody doing all this while? Was he going to sit back and placidly permit Defoe to pervert every ideal of the Company?

I could not believe it. It was not possible that the man who had written the inspiring words in the Handbook could be guilty of genocide.

Rena excused herself to look in on her father. Almost ashamed of myself, I took the battered book from my pocket and opened it to check on Millen Carmody's own preface.

It was hard to reconcile the immensely reassuring words with what I had seen. And, as I read them, I no longer felt safe and comforted.

There seemed to be no immediate danger, and Rena needed to get out of that house. There was nothing for Benedetto to do but wait, and Zorchi's servants could help him when it was necessary.

I took her by the arm and we strolled out into the garden, breathing deeply. That was a mistake. I had forgotten, in the inconspicuous air conditioning of Zorchi's home, that we were in the center of the hemp fields that had nearly cost me my dinner, so long ago, with Hammond. I wondered if I ever would know just why Hammond was killed. Playing both ends against the middle, it seemed—he had undoubtedly been in with Slovetski's group. Rena had admitted as much, and I was privately certain that he had been killed by them.

But of more importance was the stench in our nostrils. "Perhaps," said Rena, "across the road, in the walnut grove, it will not be as bad."

I hesitated, but it felt safe in the warm Italian night, and so we tried it. The sharp scent of the walnut trees helped a little; what helped even more was that the turbinates of the nostril can stand just so much, and when their tolerance is exceeded they surrender. So that it wasn't too long before, though the stench was as strong as ever, we hardly noticed it.

We sat against the thick trunk of a tree, and Rena's head fitted naturally against my shoulder. She was silent for a time, and so was I—it seemed good to have silence, after violent struggle and death.

Then she said: "Strange man."

"Me?"

"No. Oh, yes, Tom, if it comes to that, you, too. But I was thinking just now of Zorchi. Is it true, what you told me of his growing legs and arms so freely?"

"I thought everyone in Naples knew that. I thought he was a national hero."

"Of course, but I have never really known that the stories were *true*. How does it happen, Tom?"

I shrugged. "Heaven knows, I don't. I doubt if even Zorchi knows. His parents might have been involved in some sort of atomic business and got radiated, and so they produced a mutation. It's perfectly possible, you know."

"I have heard so, Tom."

"Or else it just happened. Something in his diet, in the way his glands responded to a sickness, some sort of medicine. No one knows."

"Cannot scientists hope to tell?"

"Well…" It was beginning to sound like the seeds of one of our old arguments. "…well, I suppose so. Pure research isn't much encouraged, these days."

"But it should be, you think?"

"Of course it should. The only hope of the world—" I trailed off. Through the trees was a bright, distant glare, and I had just remembered what it was.

"Is what, Tom?"

"There isn't any," I said, but only to myself. She didn't press me; she merely burrowed into my arm.

Perhaps the wind shifted, and the smell of the hemp fields grew stronger; perhaps it was only the foul thought that the glaring sky had triggered that contaminated my mood. But where I had been happy and relaxed—the C-bomb completely out of my mind for the moment—now I was too fully aware of what was ahead for all of us.

"Let's go back, Rena," I said. She didn't ask why. Perhaps she, too, was feeling the weight of our death sentence.

We caught the evening newscast; its story varied little from the early ones.

Benedetto still slept, but Zorchi joined us as we watched it.

The announcer, face stamped with the careful blend of gravity and confidence that marks tele-casters all over the world, was saying: "Late word on the bomb exploded over the North Atlantic indicates that there is some danger that radioactive ash may be carried to this area. The danger zones are now being mapped and surveyed, and residents of all such sections will be evacuated or placed in deep sleep until the danger is over.

"Blue Bolt policies give you complete protection against all hazards from this explosion. I repeat, Blue Bolt policies give you complete protection against all hazards from this explosion. Check your policies and be sure of your status. There is absolutely no risk for any person carrying the basic Blue Bolt minimum coverage or better."

I clicked off the set. "I wonder what the people in Shanghai are hearing tonight," I said.

Zorchi had only listened without comment, when I told him about the bomb that afternoon; he listened without comment now.

Rena said: "Tom, I've been wondering. You know, I—I don't have any insurance. Neither has my father, since we were canceled. And we're not the only ones without it, either."

I patted her hand. "We'll straighten this out," I promised. "You'll get your coverage back."

She gave me a skeptical look, but shook her head. "I don't mean just about father and me. What about all of the uninsurables, all over the world? The bomb goes off, and everybody with a policy files down into the vaults, but what about the others?"

I explained, "There are provisions for them. Some of them can be cared for under the dependency-clauses in the policies of their next of kin. Others have various charitable arrangements—some localities, for instance, carry blanket floater policies for their paupers and prisoners and so on. And—well, I don't suppose it would ever come to that, but if someone turned up who had no coverage at all, he could be cared for out of the loss-pool that the Company carries for such contingencies. It wouldn't be luxurious, but he'd live.

"You see," I went on, warming to my subject, "the Company is set up so the actual premiums paid are meaningless. The whole objective of the Company is service; the premiums are only a way to that goal. The Company has no interest other than the good of the world, and—"

I stopped, feeling like a fool. Zorchi was laughing raucously.

I said resentfully, "I guess I asked for that, Zorchi. Well, perhaps what I said sounds funny. But, before God, Zorchi, that's the way the Company is set up. Here…" I picked the Handbook from the end-table beside me and tossed it to him. "Read what Millen Carmody says. I won't try to convince you. Just read it."

He caught it expertly and dropped it on the floor before him. "So much for your Chief Assassin," he remarked pleasantly. "The words are no doubt honied, Weels, but I am not at this moment interested to read them."

I shrugged. It was peculiar how even a reasonable man—I have always thought of myself as a reasonable man—could make a fool of himself. It was no sin that habit had betrayed me into exalting the Company; but it was, at the least, quite silly of me to take offense when my audience disagreed with me.

I said, in what must have been a surly tone, "I don't suppose you are—why should you? You hate the Company from the word go."

He shook his head mildly. "I? No, Weels. Believe me, I am the Company's most devoted friend. Without it, how would I feed my five-times-a-day appetite?"

I sneered at him. "If you're a friend to the Company, then my best buddy is a tapeworm."

"Meaning that Zorchi is a parasite?" His eyes were furious. "Weels, you impose on me too far! Be careful! Is it the act of a tapeworm that I bleed and die, over and over? Is it something I chose, did I pray to the saints, before my mother spawned me, that I should be born a monster? No, Weels! We are alike, you gentlemen of the Company and I—we live on blood money, it is true. But the blood I live on, man—it is my own!"

I said mollifyingly, "Zorchi, I've had a hard day. I didn't mean to be nasty. I apologize."

"Hah!"

"No, really."

He shrugged, abruptly quiet. "It is of no importance," he said. "If I wished to bear you a grudge, Weels, I would have more than that to give me cause." He sighed. "It all looked quite simple twenty-four hours ago, Weels. True, I had worked my little profession in this area as far as it might go—with your help, of course. But the world was before me—I had arranged to fly next week to the Parisian Anarch, to change my name and, perhaps within a month, with a new policy, suffer a severe accident that would provide me with francs for my hobbies. Why is it that you bring bad news always?"

I said, "Wasn't I of some little assistance to you at one time?"

"In helping me from the deep-freeze? Oh, yes, perhaps. But didn't you help me into it in the first place, as well? And surely you have already had sufficient credit for aiding my escape—I observe the young lady looking at you with the eyes of one who sees a hero."

I said in irritation, "You're infuriating, Zorchi. I suppose you know that. I never claimed any credit for helping you out of the clinic. As a matter of fact, I don't think I ever mentioned it. Everyone assumed that I had just happened to bring you along—no one questioned it."

He flared, "You let them *assume*, Weels? You let them assume that Zorchi was as helpless a side of pork as those other dead ones—you let them guess that you stuck me with a needle, so that it would seem how brave you were? Is it not true that I had revived by myself, Weels?"

I felt myself growing angry. "Of course! But I just didn't see any reason to—"

"To divide the credit, is that it, Weels? No, say no more; I have closed the subject. However, I point out that there is a difference between the rescue of a helpless hulk and the mere casual assistance one may be invited to give to a Zorchi."

I let it go at that. There was no point in arguing with that man, ever.

So I left the room—ostensibly to look in on Benedetto, actually to cool off a little. Benedetto seemed fine—that is, the dressings were still in place, he had not moved, his breath and pulse were slow and regular. I took my time before I went back to the room where Zorchi still sat waiting.

He had taken advantage of the time to improve his mind. The man's curiosity was insatiable; the more he denied it, the more it stuck out all over him. He had thrown the Handbook on the floor when I gave it to him, but as soon as I was out of sight he was leafing through it. He had it open on his lap, face down, as he faced me.

"Weels." There was, for once, no sardonic rasp to his voice. And his face, I saw, was bone-white. "Weels, permit me to be sure I understand you. It is your belief that this intelligent plan of seeding the world with poison to make it well will succeed, because you believe that a Signore Carmody will evict Defoe from power?"

I said, "Well, not exactly—"

"But almost exactly? That is, you require this Millen Carmody for your plan?"

"It wasn't *my* plan. But you're right about the other."

"Very good." He extended the Handbook to me. "There is here a picture which calls itself Millen Carmody. Is that the man?"

I glanced at the familiar warm eyes on the frontispiece. "That's right. Have you seen him?"

"I have, indeed." The shaggy beard was twitching—I did not know whether with laughter or the coming of tears. "I saw him not long ago, Weels. It was in what they call Bay 100—you remember? He was in a little bag like the pasta one carries home from a store. He was quite sound asleep, Weels, in the shelf just below the one I woke up in."

CHAPTER SIXTEEN

So now at last I knew why Millen Carmody had permitted Defoe to turn the Company into a prison cell for the world. He couldn't forbid it, because the dead can forbid nothing, and Carmody was sleeping with the dead. No wonder Defoe was so concerned with the Naples sector!

How long? How long had Carmody been quietly out of the way, while Defoe made his plans and took his steps, and someone in a little room somewhere confected "statements" with Millen Carmody's signature on them and "interviews" that involved only one man?

It could not have been less than five or six years, I thought, counting back to the time when Defoe's name first began to register with me as an ordinary citizen, before I had married his cousin. Six years. That was the date of the Prague-Vienna war.

And the year following, Hanoi clashed with Cebu. And the year after that, Auckland and Adelaide.

What in God's name was Defoe's plan? Nothing as simple as putting Carmody out of the way so that he could loot the Company. No man could wish to be that rich! It was meaningless...

Defoe could be playing for only one thing—power.

But it didn't matter; all that mattered was that now I knew that Carmody was an enemy to Defoe. He was therefore an ally to Rena and to me, and we needed allies. But how might we get Carmody out of Bay 100?

There weren't any good answers, though Rena and I, with the help of grumbling comments from Zorchi, debated it until the morning light began to shine. Frontal assault on the clinic was ridiculous. Even a diversionary raid such as Rena had staged to try to rescue her father—only ten days before!—would hardly get us in through the triple-locked door of Bay 100. Even if Slovetski's movement had still been able to muster the strength to do it, which was not likely.

It was maddening. I had hidden the hypodermic Rena had brought in Bay 100 to get it out of the way. Undoubtedly it was there still—perhaps only a few yards from Millen Carmody. If fifty cubic centimeters of a watery purplish liquid could have been plucked from the little glass bottle and moved the mere inches to the veins of his arms, the problem would be solved—for he could open the door from inside as easily as Zorchi had, and certainly once he was that far we could manage to get him out.

But the thing was impossible, no matter how we looked at it.

I suppose I fell asleep sitting in that chair, because I woke up in it. It was in the middle of a crazy nightmare about an avenging angel with cobalt-blue eyes burning at me out of heaven; and I wanted to run from him, but I was frozen by a little man with a hypodermic of ice. I woke up, and I was facing the television set. Someone—Rena, I suppose—had covered me with a light spread. The set was blaring a strident tenor voice. Zorchi was hunched over, watching some opera; I might as well have been a thousand miles away.

217

I lay blearily watching the tiny figures flickering around the screen, not so much forgetting all the things that were on my mind as knowing what they were and that they existed, but lacking the strength to pick them up and look at them. The opera seemed to concern an Egyptian queen and a priest of some sort; I was not very interested in it, though it seemed odd that Zorchi should watch it so eagerly.

Perhaps, after all, there was something to his maudlin self-pity—perhaps I really did think of him as a monster or a dog, for I was as uneasy to see him watching an opera as I would have been to see an ape play the flute.

I heard trucks going by on the highway. By and by it began to penetrate through the haze that I was hearing a *lot* of trucks going by on the highway. I had no idea how heavily traveled the Naples-Caserta road might be, but from the sound, they seemed nearly bumper to bumper, whizzing along at seventy or eighty miles an hour.

I got up stiffly and walked over to the window.

I had not been far wrong. There was a steady stream of traffic in both directions—not only trucks but buses and private cars, everything from late-model gyromaxions to ancient piston-driven farm trucks.

Zorchi heard me move, and turned toward me with a hooded expression. I pointed to the window.

"What's up?" I asked.

He said levelly, "The end of the world. It is now official; it has been on the television. Oh, they do not say it in just so many words, but it is there."

I turned to the television set and flicked off the tape-relay switch—apparently the opera had been recorded. Zorchi glared, but didn't try to stop me as I hunted on the broadcast bands for a news announcer.

I didn't have far to hunt. Every channel was the same: The Company was issuing orders and instructions. Every man, woman and child was to be ready within ten days for commitment to the clinic...

I tried to imagine the scenes of panic and turmoil that would be going on in downtown Naples at that moment.

The newscaster was saying: "Remember, if your Basic Blue Bolt policy number begins with the letters A, B or C—if it begins with the letters A, B or C—you are to report to the local first aid or emergency post at six hundred hours tomorrow. There is no danger. I repeat, there is no danger. This is merely a precaution taken by the Company for your protection." He didn't really look as though there were no danger, however. He looked like a man confronted by a ghost.

I switched to another channel. An equally harried-looking announcer: "—reported by a team of four physicists from the Royal University to have produced a serious concentration of radioactive byproducts in the upper atmosphere. It is hoped that the cloud of dangerous gases will veer southward and pass harmlessly through the Eastern Mediterranean; however, strictly as a precautionary measure, it is essential that every person in this area be placed in a safety zone during the danger period, the peak of which is estimated to come within the next fourteen days. If there is any damage, it will be only local and confined to livestock—for which you will be reimbursed under your Blue Bolt coverage."

I switched to another channel. *Local* damage! Local to the face of the Earth!

I tried all the channels; they were all the same.

The Company had evidently decided to lie to the human race. Keep them in the dark—make each little section believe that only it was affected—persuade them that they would be under for, at most, a few weeks or months.

Was that, I wondered, Defoe's scheme? Was he planning to try somehow to convince four billion people that fifty years were only a few weeks? It would never work—the first astronomer to look at a star, the first seaman to discover impossible errors in his tide table, would spot the lie.

More likely he was simply proceeding along what must always have been his basic assumption: The truth is wasted on the people.

Zorchi said with heavy irony, "If my guest is quite finished with the instrument, perhaps he will be gracious enough to permit me to resume Aïda."

I woke Rena and told her about the evacuation. She said, yawning, "But of course, Tom. What else could they do?" And she began discussing breakfast.

I went with her, but not to eat; in the dining hall was a small television set, and on it I could listen to the same repeat broadcasts over and over to my heart's content. It was—in a way—a thrilling sight. It is always impressive to see a giant machine in operation, and there was no machine bigger than the Company.

The idea of suspending a whole world, even piecemeal, was staggering. But if there had been panic at first in the offices of the Company, none of it showed. The announcers were harried and there was bustle and strain, but order presided.

Those long lines of vehicles outside the window; they were going somewhere; they were each one, I could see by the medallion slung across each radiator front, on the payroll of the Company.

Perhaps the trick of pretending to each section that only it would be affected was wise—I don't know. It was working, and I suppose that is the touchstone of wisdom. Naples knew that something was going on in Rome, of course, but was doubtful about the Milanese Republic. The Romans were in no doubt at all about Milan, but weren't sure about the Duchy of Monaco, down the Riviera shore. And the man on the street, if he gave it a thought at all, must have been sure that such faraway places as America and China were escaping entirely.

I suppose it was clever—there was no apparent panic. The trick took away the psychological horror of world catastrophe and replaced it with only a local terror, no different in kind than an earthquake or a flood. And there was always the sack of gold at the end of every catastrophe: Blue Bolt would pay for damage, with a free and uncounting hand.

Except that this time, of course, Blue Bolt would not, could not, pay at all.

By noon, Benedetto was out of bed.

He shouldn't have been, but he was conscious and we could not make him stay put—short of chains.

He watched the television and then listened as Rena and I brought him up to date. Like me, he was shocked and then encouraged to find that Millen Carmody was in the vaults—encouraged because it was at least a handle for us to grasp the problem with; if we could get at Carmody, perhaps we could break Defoe's usurped power. Without him, Defoe would simply use the years while the world slept to forge a permanent dictatorship.

We got the old man to lie down, and left him. But not for long. Within the hour he came tottering to where we were sitting, staring at the television. He waved aside Rena's quick protest.

"There is no time for rest, my daughter," he said. "Do not scold me. I have a task."

Rena said worriedly, "Dear, you *must* stay in bed. The doctor said—"

"The doctor," Benedetto said formally, "is a fool. Shall I allow us to die here? Am I an ancient idiot, or am I Benedetto dell'Angela who with Slovetski led twenty thousand men?"

Rena said, "Please! You're sick!"

"Enough." Benedetto wavered, but stood erect. "I have telephoned. I have learned a great deal. The movement..." He leaned against the wall for support, "...was not planned by fools. We knew there might be bad days; we do not collapse because a few of us are put out of service by the Company. I have certain emergency numbers to call; I call them. And I find..." He paused dramatically, "...that there is news. Slovetski has escaped!"

I said, "That's impossible! Defoe wouldn't let him go!"

"Perhaps Slovetski did not consult him," Benedetto said with dignity. "At any rate, he is free and not far from here. And he is the answer we have sought, you understand."

"How?" I demanded. "What can he do that we can't?"

Benedetto smiled indulgently, though the smile was strained. His wound must have been giving him hell; it had had just enough time to stiffen up. He said, "Leave that to Slovetski, Thomas. It is his métier, not yours. I shall go to him now."

Well, I did what I could; but Benedetto was an iron-necked old man. I forbade him to leave and he laughed at me. I begged him to stay and he thanked me—and refused. Finally I abandoned him to Rena and Zorchi.

Zorchi gave up almost at once. "A majestic man!" he said admiringly, as he rolled into the room where I was waiting, on his little power cart. "One cannot reason with him."

And Rena, in time, gave up, too. But not easily. She was weeping when she rejoined me.

She had been unable even to get him to let her join him, or to consider taking someone else with him; he said it was his job alone. She didn't even know where he was going. He had said it was not permissible, in so critical a situation, for him to tell where Slovetski was.

Zorchi coughed. "As to that," he said, "I have already taken the liberty of instructing one of my associates to be ready. If the Signore has gone to meet Slovetski, my man is following him…"

So we waited, while the television announcers grew more and more grim-lipped and imperative.

I listened with only half my mind. Part of my thoughts were with Benedetto, who should have been in a hospital instead of wandering around on some dangerous mission. And partly I was still filled with the spectacle that was unfolding before us.

It was not merely a matter of preserving human lives. It was almost as important to provide the newly awakened men and women, fifty years from now, with food to eat and the homes and tools and other things that would be needed.

Factories and transportation gear—according to the telecasts— were being shut down and sealed to stand up under the time that would pass—"weeks," according to the telecast, but who needed to seal a tool in oil for a few weeks? Instructions were coming hourly over the air on what should be protected in each home, and how it was to be done. Probably even fifty years would not seriously damage most of the world's equipment—if the plans we heard on the air could be efficiently carried out.

But the farms were another matter. The preserving of seeds was routine, but I couldn't help wondering what these flat Italian fields would look like in fifty untended years. Would the radiocobalt sterilize even the weeds? I didn't think so, but I didn't know. If not, would the Italian peninsula once again find itself covered with the dense forests that Caesar had marched through, where Spartacus and his runaway slaves had lurked and struck out against the Senators?

And how many millions would die while the forests were being cleared off the face of the Earth again to make way for grain? Synthetic foods and food from the sea might solve that—the Company could find a way. But what about the mines—three, four and five thousand feet down—when the pumps were shut off and the underground water seeped in? What about the rails that the trains rode on? You could cosmoline the engines, perhaps, but how could you protect a million miles of track from the rains of fifty years?

So I sat there, watching the television and waiting. Rena was too nervous to stay in one place. Zorchi had mysterious occupations of his own. I sat and stared at the cathode screen.

Until the door opened behind me, and I turned to look.

Rena was standing there. Her face was an ivory mask. She clutched the door as her father had a few hours before; I think she looked weaker and sicker than he.

I said, for the first time, "Darling!" She stood silent, staring at me. I asked apprehensively, "What is it?"

The pale lips opened, but it was a moment before she could frame the words. Then her voice was hard to hear. "My father," she said. "He reached the place where he was meeting Slovetski, but the expediters were there before him. They shot him down in the street. And they are on their way here."

CHAPTER SEVENTEEN

It was quick and brutal. Somehow Benedetto had been betrayed; the expediters had known where he had come from. And that was the end of that.

They came swarming down on us in waves, at least a hundred of them, to capture a man, a girl and a cripple—Zorchi's servants had deserted us, melting into the hemp fields like roaches into a garbage dump. Zorchi had a little gun, a Beretta; he fired it once and wounded a man.

The rest was short and unpleasant.

They bound us and gagged us and flew us, trussed like game for the spit, to the clinic. I caught a glimpse of milling mobs outside the long, low walls as we came down. Then all I could see was the roof of the copter garage.

We were brought to a tiny room where Defoe sat at a desk. The Underwriter was smiling. "Hello, Thomas," he said, his eyes studying the bruise on my cheek. He turned toward Rena consideringly. "So this is your choice, eh, Thomas?" He studied Rena coolly. "Hardly my type. Still, by sticking with me, you could have had a harem."

Bound as I was, I started forward. Something hit me in the back at my first step, driving a hot rush of agony up from my kidneys. Defoe watched me catch my breath without a change of expression.

"My men are quite alert, Thomas. Please do not try that again. Once is amusing, but twice would annoy me." He sighed. "I seem to have been wrong about you, Thomas. Perhaps because I needed someone's help, I overestimated you. I thought long ago that beneath your conditioning you had brains. Manning is a machine, good for taking orders. Dr. Lawton is loyal, but not intelligent. And between loyalty and intelligence, I'll take brains. Loyalty I can provide for myself." He nodded gravely at the armed expediters.

Zorchi spat. "Kill us, butcher," he ordered. "It is enough I die without listening to your foolish babbling."

Defoe considered him. "You interest me, Signore. A surprise, finding you revived and with Wills. Before we're finished, you must tell me about that."

I saw Zorchi bristle and open his mouth, but a cold, suddenly calculating idea made me interrupt. "To get dell'Angela out as an attendant, I needed a patient for him to wheel. Zorchi had money, and I *expected* gratitude when I revived him later. It wasn't hard getting Lawton's assistant to stack his cocoon near Benedetto's."

"Lawton!" Defoe grimaced, but seemed to accept the story. He smiled at me suddenly. "I had hopes for you, then. That escape was well done—simple, direct. A little crude, but a good beginning. You could have been my number one assistant, Thomas. I thought of that when I heard of the things you were saying after Marianna died—I thought you might be awaking."

I licked my lips. "And when you picked me up after Marianna's death, and bailed me out of jail, you made sure the expediter corps had information that I was possibly not reliable. You made sure the information reached the underground, so they would approach me and I could spy for you. You wanted a patsy!"

The smile was gleaming this time. "Naturally, until you could prove yourself. And of course, I had you jailed for the things you said because I wanted it that way. A pity all my efforts were wasted on you, Thomas. I'm afraid you're not equipped to be a spy."

It took everything I had, but this time I managed to smile back. "On which side, Defoe? How many spies know you've got Millen Carmody down in Bay—"

That hit him. But I didn't have time to enjoy it. He made a sudden gesture, and the expediters moved. This time, when they dragged me down, it was very bad.

When I came to, I was in another room. Zorchi and Rena were with me, but not Defoe. It was a preparation chamber, racked with instruments, furnished with surgical benches.

A telescreen was flickering and blaring unheeded at one end of the room. I caught a glimpse of scenes of men, women and children standing in line, going in orderly queues through the medical inspections, filing into the clinic and its local branch stations for the sleep drug. The scenes were all in Naples; but they must have been, with local variations, on every telescreen on the globe.

Dr. Lawton appeared. He commanded coldly: "Take your clothes off."

I think that was the most humiliating moment of all.

It was, of course, only a medical formality. I knew that the suspendees had to be nude in their racks. But the very impersonality of the proceeding made it ugly. Reluctantly I began to undress, as did Rena, silent and withdrawn, and Zorchi, sputtering anger and threats. My whole body was a mass of redness; in a few hours the red would turn to purple and black, where the hoses of the expediters had caressed me.

Or did a suspendee bruise? Probably not. But it was small satisfaction.

Lawton was looking smug; no doubt he had insisted on the privilege of putting us under himself after I'd blamed him for Zorchi's escape. I couldn't blame him; I would have returned the favor with great joy.

Well, I had wanted to reach Millen Carmody, and Defoe was granting my wish. We might even lie on adjacent racks in Bay 100. After what I'd told Defoe, we should rate such reserved space!

Lawton approached with the hypospray, and a pair of expediters grabbed my arms. He said: "I want to leave one thought with you, Wills. Maybe it will give you some comfort." His smirk told me that it certainly would not. "Only Defoe and I can open Bay 100," he reminded me. "I don't think either of us will; and I expect you will stay there a long, long time."

He experimentally squirted a faint mist from the tip of the hypospray and nodded satisfaction. He went on: "The suspension is effective for a long time—several hundred years, perhaps. But not forever. In time the enzymes of the body begin to digest the body itself." He pursed his lips thoughtfully. "I don't know if the sleeping brain knows it is pain or not. If it does, you'll know what it feels like to dissolve in your own gutwash…"

He smiled. "Good night," he crooned, and bent over my arm.

The spray from the end of the hypo felt chilly, but not at all painful. It was as though I had been touched with ice; the cold clung, and spread.

I was vaguely conscious of being dumped on one of the surgical tables, even more vaguely aware of seeing Rena slumping across another.

The light in the room yellowed, flickered and went out.

I thought I heard Rena's voice...

Then I heard nothing. And I saw nothing. And I felt nothing, except the penetrating cold, and then even the cold was gone.

CHAPTER EIGHTEEN

My nerves throbbed with the prickling of an infinity of needles. I was cold—colder than I had ever been. And over everything else came the insistent, blurred voice of Luigi Zorchi.

"Weels! Weels!"

At first it was an annoyance. Then, abruptly, full consciousness came rushing back, bringing some measure of triumph with it. It had worked! My needling of Defoe and my concealing of Zorchi's ability to revive himself had succeeded in getting us all put into Bay 100, where the precious hypodermic and fluid were hidden. After being pushed from pillar to post and back, even that much success was enough to shock me into awareness.

My heart was thumping like a rusty cargo steamer in a high sea. My lungs ached for air and burned when they got it. But I managed to open my eyes to see Zorchi bending over me. Beyond him, I saw the blue-lighted sterilizing lamps, the door that opened from inside, and the racked suspendees of Bay 100.

"It is time! But now finally you awake, you move!" Zorchi grumbled. "The body of Zorchi does not surrender to poisons; it throws them off. But then because of these small weak legs, I must wait for you! Come, Weels, no more dallying! We have still work to do to escape this abomination!"

I sat up clumsily, but the drugs seemed to have been neutralized. I was on the bottom tier, and I managed to locate the floor with my legs and stand up. "Thanks, Zorchi," I told him, trying to avoid looking at his ugly, naked body and the things that were almost his legs.

"Thanks are due," he admitted. "I am a modest man who expects no praise, but I have done much. I cannot deny it. It took greatness to crawl through this bay to find you. On my hands and these baby knees, Weels, I crawled. Almost. I am overcome with wonder at so heroic—But I digress. Weels, waste no more time in talking. We must revive the others who are above my reach. Then let us, for God, go and find food."

Somehow, though I was still weak, I managed to follow Zorchi and drag down the sacks containing Rena and Carmody. And while waiting for them to revive, I began to realize how little chance we would have to escape this time, naked and uncertain of what state affairs were in. I also realized what might happen if Lawton or Defoe decided to check up on Bay 100 now!

For the few minutes while Rena revived and recognized me, and while I explained how I'd figured it out, it was worth any risk. Then finally, Carmody stirred and sat up. Maybe we looked enough like devils in a blue hell to justify his first expression.

He wasn't much like my mental image of the great Millen Carmody. His face was like his picture, but it was an older face and haggard under the ugly light. Age was heavy on him, and he couldn't have been a noble figure at any time. Now he was a pot-bellied little man with scrawny legs and a faint tremble to his hands.

But there was no fat in his mind as he tried to absorb our explanations while he answered our questions in turn. He'd come to Naples, bringing his personal physician, Dr. Lawton. His last memory was of Lawton giving him a shot to relieve his indigestion.

It must have been rough to wake up here after that and find what a mess had been made of the world. But he took it, and his questions became sharper as he groped for the truth. Finally he sat back, nodding sickly. "Defoe!" he said bitterly. "Well, what do we do now, Mr. Wills?"

It shook me. I'd unconsciously expected him to take over at once. But the eyes of Rena and Zorchi also turned to me. Well, there wasn't much choice. We couldn't stay here and risk discovery. Nor could we hide anywhere in the clinic; when Defoe found us gone, no place would be safe.

"We pray," I decided. "And if prayers help, maybe we'll find some way out."

"I can help," Carmody offered. He grimaced. "I know this place and the combination to the private doors. Would it help if we reached the garage?"

I didn't know, but the garage was half a mile beyond the main entrance. If we could steal a car, we might make it. We had to try.

There were sounds of activity when we opened the door, but the section we were in seemed to be filled, and the storing of suspendees had moved elsewhere.

We shut and relocked the door and followed Carmody through the seemingly endless corridors, with Zorchi hobbling along, leaning on Rena and me and sweating in agony. We offered to carry him, but he would have none of that. We moved further and further back, while the sight of Carmody's round, bare bottom ahead ripped my feeling of awe for him into smaller and smaller shreds.

He stopped at a door I had almost missed and his fingers tapped out something on what looked like an ornamental pattern. The door opened to reveal stairs that led down two flights, winding around a small elevator shaft. At the bottom was a long corridor that must be the one leading underground to the garage. Opposite the elevator was another door, and Carmody worked its combination to reveal a storeroom, loaded with supplies the expediters might need.

He ripped a suit of the heavy gray coveralls off the wall and began donning them. "Radiation suits," he explained. They were ugly things, but better than nothing. Anyone seeing us in them might think we were on official business. Zorchi shook off our help and somehow got into a pair. Then he grunted and began pulling hard-pellet rifles and bandoliers of ammunition off the wall.

"Now, Weels, we are prepared. Let them come against us. Zorchi is ready!"

"Ready to kill yourself!" I said roughly. "Those things take practice!"

"And again I am the freak—the case who can do nothing that humans can do, eh, Weels?" He swore thickly, and there was something in his voice that abruptly roughened it. "Never Zorchi the man! There are Sicilians who would tell you different, could they open dead mouths to speak of their downed planes!"

"He was the best jet pilot Naples had," Rena said quietly.

It was my turn to curse. He was right; I hadn't thought of him as a man, or considered that he could do anything but regrow damaged tissues. "I'm sorry, Luigi!"

"No matter." He sighed, and then shrugged. "Come, take arms and ammunition and let us be out of this place. Even the nose of Zorchi can stand only so much of the smell of assassins!"

We moved down the passage, staggering along for what seemed to be hours, expecting every second to run into some official or expediter force. But apparently the passage wasn't being used much during the emergency. We finally reached stairs at the other end and headed up, afraid to attract attention by taking the waiting elevator.

At the top, Carmody frowned as he studied the side passages and doors. "Here, I guess," he decided. "This may still be a less used part of the garage." He reached for the door.

I stopped him. "Wait a minute. Is there any way back in, once we leave?"

"The combination will work—the master combination used by the Company heads. Otherwise, these doors are practically bomb-proof!" He pressed the combination and opened the door a crack.

Outside, I could see what seemed to be a small section of the Company car pool. There were sounds of trucks, but none were moving nearby. I saw a few men working on trucks a distance from us. Maybe luck was on our side.

I pointed to the nearest expediter patrol wagon—a small truck, really, enclosed except for the driver's seat. "That one, if there's fuel. We'll have to act as if we had a right to it, and hope for the best. Zorchi, can you manage it that far?"

"I shall walk like a born assassin," he assured me, but sweat began popping onto his forehead at what he was offering. Yet there was no sign of the agony he must have felt as he followed and managed to climb into the back with Rena and Carmody.

The fuel gauge was at the half mark and, as yet, there was no cry of alarm. I gunned the motor into life, watching the nearest workmen. They looked up casually, and then went back to their business. Ahead, I could see a clear lane toward the exit, with a few other trucks moving in and out. I headed for it, my hair prickling at the back of my neck.

We reached the entrance, passed through it, and were soon blending into the stream of cars that were passing the clinic on their way out for more suspension cases.

The glass doors of the entrance were gone now, and workmen were putting up huge steel ones in their place, even while a steady stream of cases were hobbling or being carried into the clinic. Most of them were old or shabby, I noticed. The class-D type. The last ones to be admitted. We must have spent more time in the vault than I'd thought, and zero hour was drawing near.

Beyond the clinic, the whole of Anzio was a mass of abandoned cars that seemed to stretch for miles, and the few buildings not boarded up were obviously class-D dwellings, too poor to worry about. I cursed my way through a jam-up of trucks, and managed to find one of the side roads.

Then I pressed down on the throttle as far as I dared without attracting attention, until I could find a safe place to turn off with no other cars near to see me.

"Where to?" I asked. We couldn't go back to Zorchi's, since any expediter investigation would start there. Maybe we'd never be missed, but I couldn't risk it. If we had to, we could use some abandoned villa and hide out, but I was hoping for a better suggestion.

Zorchi looked blank, and Rena shrugged. "If we could only find Nikolas—" she suggested doubtfully.

I shook my head. I'd had a chance to think about that a little while the expediters took us to see Defoe, and I didn't like it. The leader of the revolution had apparently been captured by Defoe. According to Benedetto dell'Angela, he'd escaped. Yet Defoe hadn't tried to pump us about him. And when Benedetto set out to meet him, the expediters had descended at once.

It made an ugly picture. I had no wish to go looking for the man.

"There's my place," Carmody said finally. "I had places all over the world, kept ready for me and stocked. If Defoe let it be thought that I had retired, he must have kept them all up as I'd have done. Wait, let me orient myself. Up that road."

Places all over the world, with food that was wasted, and with servants who might never see their master! And I'd been brought up believing that the Underwriters were men of quiet, simple tastes! Carmody's clay feet were beginning to crumble up to the navel!

The villa was surrounded by trees, on a low hill that overlooked an artificial lake. It had been sealed off, but the combination lock yielded to Carmody's touch. There were beds made up and waiting, freezers stocked with food that sent Zorchi into ecstasy, and even a complete file of back issues of the Company paper. Carmody headed for those, with the look of a man hunting his lost past. He had a lot of catching up to do.

But it was the television set that interested me. It was still working, with taped material being broadcast. The appeal had been stepped up, asking for order and cooperation; I recognized the language as being pitched toward the lower classes now, though. And the clicking of a radiation-counter sounded as a constant background, with occasional shots of its meter, the needle well into the danger area.

Zorchi joined me and Rena, dribbling crumbs of meat down his beard. He snorted as he caught sight of the counter. "There is a real one in the other room, and it registers higher," he said. "It is interesting. For me, of no import. Doctors whom I trust have said Defoe is wrong; my body can resist damage from radiation—and perhaps even from old age. But for you and the young lady..."

He shut up at my expression, but the tape cut off and a live announcer came on before I could say anything. "A bulletin just in," he said, "shows that the government of Naples has unanimously passed a moritorium on all contracts, obligations and indebtedness for the duration of the emergency. The Company has just followed this with a declaration that it will extend the moritorium to include all crimes against the Company. During the emergency, the clinics will be available to all without prejudice, Director Defoe said today."

"A trap," Rena guessed. "We wouldn't have a chance, anyhow. But, Tom, does the other mean that—"

"It means your father was wrong," I answered. "As of right now—and probably in every government at the same time—the Company has been freed from any responsibility."

It didn't make any difference, of course. Benedetto had expected that everyone must secretly hate the Company as he did; he hadn't realized that men who have just been saved from the horrible danger of radiation death aren't going to turn against the agency that saved them. And damn it, the Company *was* saving them, after its opponents had risked annihilation of the race. Defoe would probably make sure the suspendees were awakened at a rate where he could keep absolute power, but not from any danger of bankruptcy.

Carmody had come out and listened, attracted by the broadcast radiation clicking, apparently. Now he asked enough questions to discover Benedetto's idea, and shook his head.

"It wouldn't work," he agreed with me. "Even if I still had control, I couldn't permit such a thing. What good would it do? Could money payments make food for a revived world, Miss dell'Angela? Would bankrupting the only agency capable of rebuilding the Earth be a thing of honor? Besides, even with what I've read, I can see no hope. There's nothing we can do."

"But if you can arouse the other Underwriters against Defoe," she insisted, "at least you can prevent *his* type of world!"

He shook his head. "How? All communications are in his hands. Even if I could fly to the Home Office, most of the ones I could trust—and there apparently are a few Defoe hasn't been able to retire—would be scattered, out of my reach. A week ago, there might have been a chance. Now, it's impossible. Impossible."

He shook his head sadly and wandered back toward the library. I could see that in his secret thoughts, he was wishing we'd left him safely in the vault. Maybe it would have been just as well.

"Cheer up," I told Rena. "Carmody's an old man—too old to think in terms of direct action, even when it's necessary. Defoe doesn't own the world yet!"

But later, when I located the books I wanted in the library and went out into the vine-covered bower in the formal garden, I wasn't as confident as I'd pretended.

Thinking wasn't a pleasant job, after all the years when I'd let others do my thinking for me. But now I had to do it for myself. Otherwise, the only alternative was to plan some means of quick death for us all before the radiation got too intense. And I couldn't accept that.

Rena had managed something Marianna couldn't have conceived—she'd quietly relinquished her fate into my hands, gambling on me with everything she had. Whether I wanted to or not, I'd taken the responsibility. Carmody was an old man; one who hadn't been able to keep Defoe from taking over in the first place. And Zorchi—well, he was Zorchi.

That night, the radiation detector suddenly took a sharp lift, its needle crossing over into the red. It was probably only a local rise. But it didn't make my thinking any more comfortable.

It was at breakfast that next morning when I finally took it up with Carmody. "Just what will the situation be at the clinic after they close down? How many will be kept awake? And what about their defenses?"

He frowned, trying to see my idea. Then he shrugged. "Too many, Tom. We had plotted out a course for such things as this a number of times in Planning. And our mob psychologists warned that there'd inevitably be a few who for one reason or another wouldn't come in in time, but who would then grow desperate and try to break in. Outlaws, looters, procrastinators, fanatics. That sort. So for some time, there should be at least twenty guards kept alert. And that's enough to defend a clinic. Atomic cannon at every entrance, of course, and the clinics are bomb-proof."

"Twenty, eh? And how about Defoe and Lawton? Will they sleep?" It seemed logical that they couldn't stay out of suspension for the whole fifty years or so. There'd be no profit to gaining a world after they were too old to use it.

"Not at first. There's a great deal of final administrative work to be done. There's a chamber equipped to keep a hundred or so men awake with radiation washed from the air, and containing adequate supplies, in cable contact with other clinics. They'll be there. Later, they'll take shifts, with only a couple of men awake at a time, I suppose. They may age a little that way, but not much."

He frowned again, and then slowly nodded. "It could be done, if we had some way to wait safely for six months. Getting back in is no problem for me."

"It's going to be done," I told him. "And a lot sooner. Are you willing to take the chance?"

"Have I any choice?" He shrugged again. "Do you think I haven't been sick at the idea of a man like Defoe in command of the Company for as long as he lives? Tom, my family started the Company. I've got an obligation to restore it to its right course. If there's any chance of keeping Defoe from being emperor of the world, I've got to take it. If you can put me in a position where I can get the honest Underwriters together again, where we can set up the Company as it was—"

"Why? So this will happen all over again?"

He looked shocked at Rena's question. "I don't blame you for being bitter, Miss dell'Angela. But with Defoe gone—"

"The Company made Defoe possible. In fact, it made him and Slovetski inevitable," I told him flatly. "That's its one great crime. Whenever you take power completely out of the hands of the many, it winds up in fewer and fewer hands. Those histories I was reading last night prove that. Carmody, what do you know about your own Company? Or the world? Leave the consolidation of power in Company hands out of it, and what has happened to progress?"

He frowned. "Well, we've leveled off a bit. We had to. We couldn't risk—"

"Exactly. You couldn't risk research that would lead to increased longevity—too many pensioners. You couldn't risk going to Mars—unpredictable dangers. You had to make the world fit actuarial charts. I remember seeing one of the first suspendees awakened. He expected things we could have done fifty years ago—and never will do. How many men today work their way out of their class? And why have classes so rigidly stratified? I've been reading your own speeches of nearly fifty years ago. I've got them here, together with some tables. Like to see them?"

He took the papers silently and began going through them, his shock giving way to a grudging realization. Maybe without the jolt of his awakening, he'd have laughed them off, but nothing was easy to dismiss with the hell brewing outside. At last he looked up.

"Tom, I'll admit the many times when I've been worried. I've considered starting research again countless times. I've been aware that dependence was growing too heavy on the Company. But we can't just toss it aside. It did bring an end to major war, when such a war would have ruined the Earth completely. It showed that nobody had to starve—that hardly anyone had to lack for any necessity, or die for lack of care. You can't throw that away."

"You can throw away its unrelated power." I knew I didn't have the answers. All this had been growing slowly in my mind since I'd first found Benedetto a political prisoner, but a lifetime wasn't enough to think it out, even with the books I'd found.

But I had to try. "In the middle ages, they had morality and politics tied into one bundle, Carmody. The church ruled. It wasn't good and they finally had to divorce church and state. Maybe the same applies to administrative politics and economics. The Company has shown what can be done economically. The church has survived as a great moral force outside material power. Now let's see if we can't put things in perspective.

"There's a precedent. The United States—the old government—was set up on the idea of balance of power: an elected Congress for the people to handle legislative tasks, a selected President to handle executive affairs, and a Judiciary mostly independent. On a world scale, as it can be done today—since the Company has really made it one world—the same can be done, with something like the Company to insure economics."

"I suppose every man who had any idealism has thought the same," Carmody said slowly. He sighed softly. "I remember trying to preach it to my father when I was just out of college. You're right. But can you set up such a perfect government? Can I? Tell me how, Tom, and I'll give you your chance, if I can."

Zorchi laughed cynically, but that was what I'd hoped Carmody might say.

"All right," I told him. "We can't do it. No one man is fit to rule, ever, or to establish rule. Oh, I had wish-dreams, a few days ago, I suppose, about what I'd do, *if!* But men have set out to establish new systems before, and done good jobs of it. Read the

Constitution—a system put together artificially by expert political thinkers, and good for two hundred years, at least! And they didn't have our opportunities. For the first time, the world has to wait. Get the best minds you can, Carmody. Give them twenty-five years to work it out. They can come up with an answer. And then, when the world is awakened, you can start with it, fresh, without upsetting any old order. Is that your answer?"

"Most of it." There was a sudden light in his old eyes. "Yes, the sleep does make the chance possible. But how are you going to get the experts and assemble them?"

I pointed to Zorchi. "Hermes, the messenger of the gods. He's a jet pilot who can get all over the world. And he can move outside, without needing to worry about radiation."

"So?" Zorchi snorted again. "So, I am now your messenger, Weels! Do you think I would trouble myself so much for all of you, Weels?"

I grinned at him. "You defiantly speak of being a man. That makes you part of the human race. I'm simply taking you at your word."

"So?" he repeated, his face wooden. "Such a messenger would have much power, Weels. Suppose I choose to be Zorchi the ruler?"

"Not while Zorchi the man is also Zorchi the freak," I said with deliberate cruelty. "Go look at yourself."

And suddenly he smiled, his lips drawing back from his teeth. "Weels, for the first time you are honest. And for that as well as that I *am* a man, I will be Zorchi the messenger. But first, should we not decide on a plan of action? Or do we first rule and then conquer?"

"We wait first," I told him.

On the wall, the radiation indicator clicked steadily, its needle moving further into the red.

CHAPTER NINETEEN

The second day, the television went off the air with the final curt announcement that anyone not inside the clinics at noon would be left outside permanently. Then the set went dead, leaving only the clucking and beeping of our own radiation indicator. I'd thrown it out twice and brought it back both times.

Civilization had ended on the third day, though all the conveniences in the villa went on smoothly, except for the meter reading that told us nothing could be smooth. It was higher than the predictions I had heard, though I still hoped that was only a sporadic local phenomenon that would level out later. In the face of that, it was hard to believe that even a few men would remain outside the clinics, though I was counting on it.

We waited another twenty-four hours, forcing ourselves to sit in the villa, discussing plans, when our nerves were yelling for action. We had only an estimate to go on. If we got there too soon, there would be more awake than we could handle. Too late and we'd be radiation cases, good for nothing but the vaults.

It was a relief to leave at last, taking our weapons in the truck. We were wearing the radiation suits, hoping they'd protect us, and Zorchi spent the last two days devising pads and straps to cushion and strengthen his developing legs.

The world was dead. Cars had been abandoned in the middle of the road, making driving difficult.

The towns and villas were deserted, boarded up or simply abandoned. We might have been the last men on Earth, and we felt that we were as we headed for Anzio. This wasn't just a road, or Naples—or all of Italy. It was the world.

Then Rena pointed. Ahead, a boy was walking beside a dog, the animal's left rear leg bound and split as if it had been broken. I started to slow, then forced myself to drive on. As we passed, I saw that the boy was about fourteen, and his face was dirty and tear-streaked. He shook one fist at us, and came trudging on.

"If we win, we'll have the door open when he gets there," Rena said. "For him and his dog! If not, it won't matter how long it takes him. You couldn't stop, Tom."

It didn't make me feel any better. But now dusk was falling, and we slowed, waiting until it was dark to park quietly near the garage. In front of the entrance, I could see a small ring of fires, and by their light a few figures moving about. They were madmen, of course—and yet, probably less mad than others who must be prowling through the towns, looting for things they could never use.

It seemed incredible that any one could be outside, but the psychologists had apparently been right. These were determined men, willing to wait for the forlorn chance that some miracle might give them a futile, even more forlorn chance to try battering down the great doors. Maybe somewhere in the world, such a group might succeed. But not here. As I watched, there was a crackle of automatic gunfire from the entrance. The guards were awake, all right, and not taking chances on any poor devil getting too close.

There were no guards in the vault garage. We were prepared in case someone might be stationed inside the private entrance, as much prepared as we could be; since Carmody had been listed as still living, an ordinary guard who recognized him would probably let us in first and then try to report—giving us time to handle him. But we were lucky. The door opened to Carmody's top-secret combination.

"We designed such combinations into a few doors in case of internal revolution locally while no Underwriters were around. We never considered having an Underwriter lead a revolution from outside," he whispered to us.

The underground passage was deserted, and this time Carmody led through another corridor, to a stairs that seemed to wind up forever. Zorchi groaned, then caught himself.

"It leads to the main reception room," Carmody said.

With the men outside, most of the guards who still remained awake might be there. But we had to chance it. We stopped when we reached the top, catching our breath while Zorchi sank to the floor, writhing silently.

Then Rena threw back the door, Zorchi's rifle poked through, and I was leaping for the main door controls, hoping the memory I had was accurate. I was nearly to them when the two guards standing beside them turned.

They yelled, just as my rifle spat. At that range, I couldn't miss. And behind, I heard Zorchi's gun spit. The second guard slumped sickly to the floor, holding his stomach. I grabbed for the controls, while other yells sounded, and feet began pounding toward me.

There was no time to look back. The doors were slowly moving apart and Carmody was beside me, smashing a maul from the storeroom onto the electronic controls of the atomic cannon. I twisted between the opening doors.

"We've seized the vaults," I shouted. "We need help. Any man who joins us will be saved!"

I couldn't wait to watch, but I heard a hoarse, answering shout, and the sound of feet.

Carmody's maul had ruined the door controls. But the other guards were nearly on us. I saw two more sprawled on the floor. Zorchi hadn't missed. Then Carmody's fingers had found another of the private doors that looked like simple panels here. Rena and Carmody were through, and I yanked Zorchi after me, just as a bullet whined over his head. Behind us, I heard uncontrolled yelling as men from outside began pouring in.

It was our only hope. They had to take care of the guards, who were still probably shocked at finding us *inside*. We headed for the private quarters where Defoe would be, praying that there would be only a few there.

This passage was useless to us, though. It led from office to office for the doctors who superintended here. We came out into an office, watching our chance for the hall we had to take. I could see the men who had been outside in action now. A few had guns of some kind, but the clubs in the hands of the others were just as deadly in such a desperation attack; men who had seen themselves already dead weren't afraid of chances. About a score of the expediter guards were trying to hold off at least twice their number.

Then the hall seemed clear and we leaped into it. Suddenly gongs began ringing everywhere. Some guard had finally reached or remembered the alarm system. Carmody cursed, and tried to move faster.

The small private vault for the executives lay through the administration quarters and down several levels, before it was entered through a short passageway. Carmody had mapped it for me often enough. But he knew it by physical memory, which was better than my training. He'd also taught me the combination, but I left the door to his practiced fingers when we came to it.

The elevator wasn't up. We couldn't wait. We raced down the stairs that circled it. Here Carmody's age told against him, and he fell behind. Rena and I were going down neck and neck with Zorchi throwing himself along with us. He had dropped his rifle and picked up a sub-machine gun from one of the fallen guards, and he clung to it now, using only one hand on the rail.

241

It was a reflection on a gun-barrel that saved us. The picked expediters were hidden in the dark mouth of the passageway, waiting for us to turn the stairs. But I caught a gleam of metal, and threw up my gun. Instantly, Zorchi was beside me, the submachine spitting as quickly as I could fire the first shot. "Aim for the wall. Ricochet!"

The ambushers had counted too much on surprise. They weren't ready to have the tables turned, nor for the trick Zorchi had suggested. Here we couldn't fire directly, but the bouncing shots worked almost as well. There were screams of men being hit, and the crazed pandemonium of others suddenly afraid.

Shots came toward us, but the wall that protected them—or was supposed to—ruined their shooting.

Zorchi abruptly dropped, landing with a thud on his side. I grunted sickly, thinking he was hit.

Then I saw the sub-machine gun point squarely into the passageway. It began spitting out death. By the time we could reach him, the expediters were dead or dying. There had been seven of them.

Zorchi staggered into the passage, through the bodies, crying something. I jumped after him, blinking my eyes to make out what he had seen. Then I caught sight of a door at the back being silently closed. It was a thick, massive slab, like the door to a bank vault.

Zorchi made a final leap that brought a sob of anguish as he landed on his weak legs, but his gun barrel slapped into the slit of opening. The door ground against it, strained and stopped. Zorchi pulled the trigger briefly.

For a second, then, there was silence. A second later, Defoe's voice came out through the thin slit. "You win. Dr. Lawton and I are alone and unarmed. We're coming out."

The door began opening again, somewhat jerkily this time. I watched it, expecting a trick, but there was none.

Inside the vault, the first room was obviously for guards and for the control of the equipment needed to wash all contamination out of the air and to provide the place with security for a century, even if all the rest of the Earth turned into a radioactive hell.

Lawton was slumped beside the controls, his head cradled in his arms. But at the sight of us, he stood up groggily, his mouth open, and shock on his face.

Defoe's eyes widened a trifle, but he stood quietly, and the bleak smile never faltered. "Congratulations, Thomas," he said. "My one fault again—I underrated the opposition. I wasn't expecting miracles. Hello, Millen. Fancy meeting you here."

"Search the place," I ordered.

Carmody went past the two without looking at them, with Rena close behind. A minute later, I heard a triumphant shout. They came back with a cringing man who seemed totally unlike the genial Sam Gogarty who had first introduced me to fine food and to Rena. His eyes were on Carmody, and his skin was gray white. He started to babble incoherently.

Carmody grinned at him. "You've got things twisted, Gogarty. Tom Wills is in charge of this affair." He turned toward one of the smaller offices. "As I remember it, there should be a transmitting setup in here. I want to make sure it works. If it does, some of the Underwriters are going to get a surprise, unless they're suspended."

Gogarty watched him go, and then sank slowly to a chair, shaking his head as he looked up at me. His lips twisted into bitter resignation. "You wouldn't understand, Tom. All my life, worked for things. Class-C, digging in a mine, eating Class-D, getting no fun, so I could buy Class-B employment. Then Class-A. Not many can do it, but I sweated it out. Thirty years living like a dog and killing myself with work and study. Not even a real woman until I met Susan, and she went to Defoe. But I wanted it easier for the young men. I wanted everybody to have a good life. No harm to anyone. Pull together, and forget the tough times. Then you had to come and blow the roof off..."

I felt sick. It was probably all true, and few men could make it. But if that's what it took to advance under the Company rules, it was justification enough for our fight. "You'll be all right, Sam," I told him. "You'll go to sleep with the others. And when you wake up, you may have to work like hell again, but it'll be to rebuild the Earth, not to ruin it. Maybe there'll even be a chance with Susan again."

Defoe laughed sardonically. "Very nice, Thomas. And I suppose you mean it. What's in the future for me?"

"Suspension until the new government gets organized and can decide your case. I'd like to vote now for permanent suspension."

His face lost some of his amusement. Then he shrugged. "All right, I suppose I knew that. But now will you satisfy my curiosity? Just how *did* you work the business with Bay 100?"

"What happened to Slovetski?" I asked. I couldn't be sure about some of my suspicions over Benedetto's death, but I couldn't take chances that the man might still be loose somewhere, or else hiding out here until we were off guard.

He shook his head. "I can answer, but I'm waiting for a better offer."

"Sam?" I asked.

Gogarty nodded slowly. "All right, Tom. I guess you're the boss now. And I think I'm even glad of it. I always liked you. I'll answer about Slovetski."

Defoe snarled and swung, then saw my rifle coming up, and straightened again. "You win once more, Thomas. Your great international rebel cooperated with us very nicely after we caught him. We arranged for him to receive all calls to his most secret hideout right here in this room. It netted us his fellow conspirators—including your father, Miss dell'Angela!"

She gasped faintly, but her head came up at once. "Nikolas was no traitor. You're lying!"

"Why should I lie?" he asked. "With the right use of certain drugs, any man can become a traitor. And Dr. Lawton is an expert on drugs."

"Where is he?" I asked.

He shrugged. "How should I know? He wanted a radioactive world, so I let him enjoy it. We put him outside just before we closed the doors permanently."

Gogarty nodded confirmation. I turned it over. He might even have been one of the men waiting outside. But it wouldn't matter. Without his organization and with a world where life outside was impossible, Slovetski's power was finished.

I turned to Zorchi. "The men who broke in will be going crazy soon," I told him. "While Rena finds the paging system and reassures them they'll all be treated in the reception room, how about getting Lawton to locate and revive a couple of the doctors you know and trust?"

Rena came back from the paging system, and Zorchi prodded Lawton with the gun, heading him toward the files that would show the location of the doctors. Gogarty stood up doubtfully, but I shook my head. Zorchi was able to handle a man of Lawton's type, even without full use of his legs, and I couldn't trust Gogarty yet.

"You can give me a hand with Defoe, Sam," I suggested. "We'd better strap him down first."

Gogarty nodded, and then suddenly let out a shocked cry, and was cringing back!

In the split second when both Rena and I had looked away, Defoe had whipped out an automatic and was now covering us, his teeth exposed in a taut smile. "Never underestimate an opponent, Thomas," he said. "And never believe what he says. You should have searched me, you know."

The gun was centered on Rena and he waited, as if expecting me to make some move. All I could do was stand there, cursing myself. I'd thought of everything—except the obvious!

Defoe backed toward the door and slipped around it, drawing its heavy weight slowly shut until only a crack showed. Then he laughed. "Give my love to Millen," he said, and laughed softly.

I jumped for the door, but his feet were already moving out of the passage. The door began opening again, but I knew it was too late. Then, it was open. And amazingly, Defoe stood not ten feet away.

At the other end of the passage, a ragged bloody figure was standing, swaying slowly from side to side, holding a rifle. I took a second look to recognize Nikolas Slovetski. He was moving slowly toward Defoe. And now Defoe jerked back and began frantically digging for the automatic he must have pocketed.

Slovetski leaped, tossing the gun aside in a way that indicated it must have been empty. A bullet from Defoe's automatic caught his shoulder in mid-leap, but it couldn't stop him. He crashed squarely on Defoe, swinging a knife as the other went down. It missed, ringing against the hard floor.

I'd come unfrozen by then. I kicked the knife aside and grabbed the gun from Defoe's hands. Slovetski lay limp on him, and I rolled the smaller man aside.

Defoe was out cold from the blow of his head hitting the floor. Gogarty had come out behind me and now began binding him up. He opened his eyes slowly, blinked, and tried to grin as he stared at the bonds. He swung his head to the figure on the floor beside him. "Shall we go quietly, Nikolas?" he asked, as Gogarty picked him up and carried him back to the private vault.

But his sarcasm was wasted on Slovetski. The man must have been dying as he stumbled and groped his way toward the place where he knew Defoe must be. And the bullet in the shoulder had finished him. Rena bent over him, a faint sob on her lips.

Surprisingly, he fought his way back to consciousness, staring up at her. "Rena," he said weakly. "Benedetto! I loved him. I—" Then his head rolled toward me. "At least, I lived to die in a revolution, Thomas. Dirty business, revolution. When in the course of human events, it becomes—"

He died before he could finish. I went looking for Lawton, to make sure Defoe was suspended at once. He'd be the last political suspendee, if I had anything to do with it, but there would be a certain pleasure in watching Lawton do the job.

CHAPTER TWENTY

The doors of the reception hall were closed again, but there was no lock now. One of the two doctors whom Zorchi had trusted was there now, waiting for the stragglers who came in slowly as a result of our broadcast. We couldn't reach them all, of course, but some could be saved. The men who had fought with us were treated and suspended. Even the boy and his dog had finally reached us and been put away.

In the main room of the executive vault, Carmody was waiting for Rena and me as we came in, haggard from lack of sleep, but somehow younger-looking than he had been since we had first revived him.

He stood up, managing a tired smile. "The first work's done, Tom," he said. "It wasn't too hard, once they learned Defoe was suspended; a lot of the others were afraid of him, I guess. So far, I've only contacted the ones I can trust, but it's a beginning. I've gotten tapes of their delegation of authority to you as acting assistant Chief Underwriter. I guess the factor that influenced them most was your willingness to give up all hopes of suspension for the emergency. And having Zorchi was a help, too—one man like him is worth an army now. I'll introduce you tomorrow."

He stumbled out, heading toward the sleeping quarters.

Well, I had the chance I'd wanted. And I had his promise to put off suspension until things were running properly. With time to develop a small staff, and with a chance to begin the work of locating the men to study the problems that had to be solved, I couldn't ask for much more.

Zorchi grinned at me. "Emperor Weels!" he mocked.

I grinned back. "If you ever say that seriously, Luigi, I want you to say it with a bullet through my brain. I've seen enough cases of power corrupting."

For a second, he studied me. "If that day should come, then there shall be the bullet. But now, even I must sleep," he said.

Then he glanced at Rena. "I have left orders that a priest should be wakened."

She colored faintly.

"You'll be best man, I suppose?" I asked.

This time, even his beard couldn't conceal his amusement. "Is Zorchi not always the best man?" he asked as he left us alone.

I stared at the vault that would be my home for the next twenty-five or fifty years—until I was an old man, and the rest of the world was ready to be awakened. "It's a lousy place to spend a honeymoon," I told Rena.

She leaned against me. "But perhaps a good place to bring up children," she said. "A place to teach them that their children will have a good world, Tom. That's all a woman ever wants, I guess."

I drew her to me. It was a good way to think of the future, whatever happened. And it *would* be a better world, where the virtues of the Company could be used.

Probably it wouldn't be perfect.

Even the best form of government all the experts could devise couldn't offer a permanent solution. But it could give men a chance to fight their way to a still better world.

THE END